SICK MICK

Writing on the Wall
Toxteth Library
Windsor Street, Liverpool
L8 1XF

Published by Writing on the Wall, 2024

© Remains with the author

Design and Layout by Jenny Dalton
Cover Design by Ged Doyle Plastic Design

978-1-916571-10-5

All rights reserved. No part of this publication may be reproduced, stored in a retrieval system, or transmitted, in any form or by any means, electronic, mechanical, photocopying, recording or otherwise, without the prior permission of the publishers.

0151 703 0020
info@writingonthewall.org.uk
www.writingonthewall.org.uk

This is a work of fiction. Unless otherwise indicated, all the names, characters, businesses, places, events and incidents in this book are either the product of the author's imagination or used in a fictitious manner. Any resemblance to actual persons, living or dead, or actual events is purely coincidental.

SICK MICK

BRIAN READE

WRITING ON THE WALL

SICK MICK

1

SATURDAY AFTERNOON

The BBC news studio in London's Broadcasting House was in a state of controlled panic. The incoming story had divided the small group of journalists working the weekend roster on how dramatically they should break it, but the corporation's meticulous planning had ensured that they were already primed to swing into action.

Veteran newsreader, Max Burch OBE, had been pulled from a Royal Television Society lunch at The Savoy and rushed through wardrobe and make-up. The lunch was in his honour; recognition of his lifetime devotion to the art of reading autocues with a peerless range of facial expressions. His fury at foregoing this orgasm-inducing ego massage vanished the second he learned the reason he would not be finishing his cedar salt and seaweed-crusted yellowfin tuna. The story was big and the world's most respected news organisation had decided its most revered broadcaster was the only man fit to enlighten the masses. The honour marked a personal triumph for Burch who, ten years earlier, had been toppled during an ageist putsch at the BBC and sentenced to the career gulag of narrating National Trust documentaries, fronting gold coin adverts and filling in for ex-boy band singers on *The One Show*.

But then his replacement, Rod Jacobs, was photographed by a tabloid newspaper blindfolded and handcuffed to a mediaeval rack in a Croydon sex dungeon and exiled to a life of anonymity, rearing sheep in his native West Wales. Although, sadly, he spent most of his time dodging the paparazzi who hid in trees, hoping to prove that rearing was not all that Rod was doing to his sheep.

With Britain split by warring cultural tribes, and the BBC accused of being a festering hotbed of metropolitan liberals, the Conservative Party-appointed Director-General was under pressure to restore balance, tradition and gravitas to the news bulletins. A gravitas this breaking story demanded. A gravitas Max Burch believed he was born to deliver.

He lowered himself slowly into the familiar seat and snuggled his backside into the brown padded leather. He stared at the sheet of A4 paper in his hands, brushed back the Ronald Reaganesque, midnight-black dyed hair, shot the cuffs of his charcoal grey, hand-made suit, tightened the knot on his maroon tie, chattered his teeth together three times, licked his lips twice, coughed, harrumphed, then stared hard down the barrel of the camera as a hand counted him in…three, two, one...

SICK MICK

'The BBC is interrupting its normal programming to bring you an important announcement,' he said, in his finest semi-funereal tone. 'A few moments ago, Buckingham Palace announced that The Duke of Dorset is gravely ill.'

He paused dramatically, or as the social media platform formerly known as Twitter would rightly accuse him seconds later, 'more theatrically than a ham shank playing Widow Twankie in a village hall,' to let the news sink in.

'The much-loved cousin of Queen Elizabeth II and mentor to King Charles, who is two weeks away from his 100th birthday, is in a coma in The National Hospital for Neurology and Neurosurgery, having been taken there after a pergola beam collapsed on him while visiting The Chelsea Flower Show this lunchtime.

'A statement from 10 Downing Street said the thoughts of the nation are with the royal family at this very difficult time as we all pray that The People's Duke pulls through.'

He allowed a three-beats-of-the-heart silence, narrowed his eyes and hardened his stare. 'I repeat: within the past few minutes Buckingham Palace has announced that The Duke of Dorset, universally regarded as The Nation's Great Grandfather, is gravely ill in The National Hospital for Neurology and

Neurosurgery in Central London. We will of course bring you any updates on His Grace as soon as we have them. In the meantime, BBC television will broadcast on all channels a special programme charting the near century-long life of the national treasure—known affectionately as Blinky—who symbolised the Blitz Spirit during World War II as a part-time air warden, and who became the public face of British stoicism during Covid-19, as he raised millions for the NHS by walking on a frame around a specially-constructed Anderson shelter on his Dorset estate.'

His voice became lower, slower and more emotional as it tapered off towards the end of the statement, turning into a virtual croak as he gave one last mournful stare into the camera; a stare that spoke directly to the soul of every viewer. A stare that said that he, Max Burch OBE, truly felt the pain he had just inflicted on them, because behind the fame that had elevated him to the dizzy heights of playing occasional games of bridge with Joan Collins, he was, like them, just a humble subject.

When the floor manager signalled that he was off air, Max swiftly turned his gaze, which had transformed from humble to demonic, to the left of the set where his producer nervously sign-acted applause.

As his eyes locked with hers, he ditched his

received pronunciation accent for his native, guttural Brummie. 'Why am I, Maximilian Burch, sitting here like Coco the Clown in a maroon tie,' he howled with the ferocity of a starving jackal, 'when it's common knowledge that one step down from black in the BBC's Royal Mourning Tie Scale is burgundy, you absolute fucking moron.'

Long live The Duke.

2

SATURDAY NIGHT

Mick tugged back the red velvet curtain ever so slightly and squinted through the thin shaft of light to weigh up his prey. Most of the punters were at the far end of the low-ceilinged cellar huddled around the bar, stocking up on drinks between acts. It was a decent enough crowd and the turns had mostly been on the money, but they hadn't lit the fuse. There was no buzz or crackle in the air. No blast of pulsating energy lifting the room. This left Mick perplexed.

'Why's it so flat?' he asked Anna, the comedy club promoter who had come to join him behind the curtain.

'Chill out big man,' she replied, in a thick, warm Lancashire brogue as she handed him a vodka and coke. 'Maybe they're in mass shock after hearing about this dying duke,' she replied sarcastically, hoping to lift Mick's mood.

'Oh yeah, sure. Less people care about the duke than they do about you, and I'm your only mate. And I don't care about you that much.'

'That's nice.'

'You know I love you, Hotpot Face,' Mick said before slugging the vodka down in one.

'Chokeslam 'em, Haystacks,' replied Anna, slapping his back, taking the glass and walking off stage.

Mick wasn't quite as big as legendary wrestler Giant Haystacks, but at 6'3", carrying 17 stone, a berserk head of black curly hair, a beard that looked like a busby hat had been soldered to his chin and a grimace that would terrify a smack-dealer's Pitbull at twenty paces, he had, shall we say, a brooding presence. Although, in truth, it was all an act. His stage armour. In real life he was more Hagrid than Haystacks.

As he scratched his beard and studied the audience more closely, he began to think Anna may have been on to something. Maybe they had been expecting near-the-knuckle material about old Blinky, and with the other acts limbo-dancing under the royal elephant in the room, they had become bored. He'd change that. Let's face it, he thought, if anyone here was overly-concerned about the duke's health they'd be sitting at home watching wall-to-wall TV tributes depicting him as a cross between Gandhi and God.

He surveyed the front rows for easy pickings. The Turkey-teethed fifty-something divorcé dressed twenty years younger than his age in the hope he'd look virile; the bored couple on their phones who had bought tickets to a comedy show because they had nothing left to say to each other and, slap bang in the middle of the front row a beaut: a loud, checked shirt-and-dungaree combination that not even a colour-blind lumberjack would choose, a dead red squirrel hanging from his head that he was passing off as a ponytail and the kind of creepy face you see in a paedophile identity parade.

This sad masochist had obviously taken his seat there so that he would be picked out, but Mick wasn't giving him the satisfaction. His acid wit could not be bought that cheaply.

Thankfully there were no stag parties in. Or rather, left in. A motley crew from Rochdale had been thrown out half-way through the opening act after one of their paralytic number yelled, 'You're about as funny as a suicide vest, ya Muslim bastard.'

To which Ranveer Bedi had purred back through his mic, 'And you're thicker than the metal plate in your head, because I'm a Sikh bastard.'

In The Laughter Bucket, racism, sexism, poverty-ism, disabled-ism, antisemitism, heterosexism, or any other ism that made the majority of the crowd feel the comedian had the hots for fascism was viewed in a dim light. That said, it wasn't what anti-woke warriors could call a hotbed of self-righteous snowflakes. You didn't have to take the knee on entry or refuse to urinate in a toilet set aside solely for your own gender to be accepted.

In this dank, sweaty, cheaply furnished, sticky-carpeted, rodent-smelling cellar, the biggest comedy crime was laziness. The punters expected you to be brave. Which is why Mick's gut was telling him to rip a new arse to this imposed period of national royal mourning. He couldn't ignore it, could he? Maybe best to kick off with it and move away if it bombed. Suck it and see, as the priest said to the blind altar boy. And yes, that's a gag Mick could get away with here because it was anti-establishment-coverupism. Plus, he'd been an altar boy, albeit without having been asked to swallow anything other than Holy Communion. And tonight, he was top of the bill. King of the hill.

As the audience was told the headline act would be on in two minutes and began to drift back to their seats, Mick went through his nerve-calming ritual. He had been doing stand-up for five years, shortlisted at the Edinburgh Festival for best newcomer, placed high up the bill at clubs across the country and was starting to inhale the precious oxygen of notoriety that comes with the occasional TV appearance. In fact, he was booked to play BBC's *Quays at One* show on Monday. Yet still his nerves made him feel sick before every gig. Which is why he had just smoked that settling spliff in the dressing room. But it didn't stop the feeling that he was about to take off his clothes and stand in the middle of a packed airport departures terminal in just a pair of too-tight boxers. It was a recurring dream he had most nights, alternating with him walking across a post-apocalyptic landscape in his grandad's oversized funeral suit. The one all the grandkids used to laugh at as it appeared to grow bigger as his ageing body stooped and shrank with every trip to the crematorium.

He reminded himself that, like playing football, making people laugh is all about the first touch. Fumble as you take the mic from the stand and it feels like you've got a bag of cement on each foot halting take-off. Snatch it clean and you will effortlessly soar like an eagle, swooping down at will to feast on the meat below.

'Laddies unt gendermensch,' bellowed Anna from the wings. 'Please give it up for Laughter Bucket's very own master of mirth, The Giant Haystacks of stand-up…Mister Miiiiiick O'Shea.'

As his theme tune, Bat Out Of Hell, boomed out (When Mick first went to the Edinburgh Fringe, minus a beard, one local journalist had labelled him Scouseloaf) on he strode ready to do battle.

'Liverpool, how are we?' he yelled, after lifting the mic from its stand with the dexterity of a veteran heart surgeon. His question answered with warm cheers and whistles. Good start.

'Well, you sound like you're all having a good time,' he said as he sought out the couple he'd spotted on their phones. 'Well, most of you. Look at these two here.' He pointed at them. 'I've seen couples looking happier when I've been carjacking them.'

Good belly laughs.

'Let me guess: you've been living together for six months, sex is a distant memory and when you go to bed now you realise not only do you not like each other's snoring, you hate each other's breathing?'

No attempt was made by the couple to gauge the other's reaction as their faces were coated in a permafrost of terror and locked on the stage. Mick did an impression of them, staring at the room like a petrified child on the Big Dipper, then told the pair to chill.

'What do you do for a living mate?' he asked the male member of the couple.

'I'm an erm, aud…auditor,' he nervously stuttered.

'An erm, aud…auditor? What, you get paid for walking round offices counting how many times people say 'erm'? Then do an erm, re…report?'

Mick walked along the front of the stage staring hard at the crowd, pretending to jot down notes on an imaginary clipboard.

'No, I'm a local government auditor,' said the

nerve-shattered punter.

'Jesus, no wonder she's bored shitless.' He puts on a woman's voice: 'Eh love, do you fancy a quickie on the couch before the erm, Domino's takeaway arrives?' He switches to a nerd's voice. 'I'm sorry dear, but Darlington council's pavement repair overspend is not going to calculate itself, is it?' He gets a huge laugh and stays in character as the nerd. 'And by the way, dear, I counted one erm in that request. That's seventeen today. Only three more allowed tonight. Shall I warm the plates?'

By now the room was rocking and Mick felt the way he always felt when he knew he had them eating out of his hand like puppies. It felt as though he was on a surfboard taking the waves of laughter with ease, letting them grow bigger, stronger, more powerful as he ducked and dived with expert precision through the swelling, crashing anarchy.

In his head there were five types of audience laughs. The road-digger: deep guttural ones that sound like a chorus of drills hitting Tarmac. The ejector seat, when the punchline takes the crowd from 0-10 as they're all thinking what you're thinking, but wouldn't dare to say it out loud. The extractor fan, when you push the boundaries of taste and there's a chorus of 'oohs' as they suck the air out of the room. The rip-snorter, when you're really hitting the mark and hands fly to faces as stuff is literally coming from their noses. And the Mount Everest, when you take their lungs to such an altitude they're struggling for breath. When, despite half of them not hearing or getting what you're saying, the laughter is so contagious it's like everyone in the room is choking on a humongous joint.

'You definitely need a new fella, love,' Mick said in his own voice to the woman. 'There must be one here.' He points at Lumberjack Man in the front row. 'What do you reckon? Not bad if you don't mind walking down the aisle to the tune of Duelling Banjos with the main rapist from *Deliverance*. That's if you can get his restraining order lifted.' It earned a road-digger.

'What about the guy behind you?' He pointed at Turkey Teeth and she turned to face him. 'He's single. Not that he had much say in that decision. And he's got all his own teeth. Sort of. And all his own clothes. Sort of.' Turkey Teeth looked around confidently, pleased with the attention.

'I've got to hand it to you, mate, you look very hip for a man who's a few years off his free bus pass. Any kids?'

'Yeah, one son,' he replied with a voice far too relaxed for what was coming next.

'And somewhere in a trendy city bar, right now, is that poor twenty-something lad, dressed like Prince

SICK MICK

Andrew telling his mates: 'Don't blame me, they were the only clothes left in the house. My dad's robbed all my gear again and gone on the pull down the Laughter Bucket.' It's a Grade A ejector-seat forcing Turkey Teeth's gnashers to glow even whiter as they clash with his scarlet face.

'Another great weekend for Andrew though, eh? Another family member close to death, another chance to get before the cameras and hide in plain sight. He's still eighth in line to the throne, you know. Meaning we're only seven accidents away from being ruled by King 'I Paid Twelve Million Quid To A Woman I've Never Met To Stop Her Suing Me For Sexual Abuse I Never Committed' The First.'

'By the way, who'd heard of a pergola before today? I thought it was a name for a baby penguin. You'll hear about them if the old fella snuffs it though. They'll be banned throughout the land. 'You can't put a duke-killer in your garden' they'll tell you on those smarmy home improvement shows.

'I can just imagine some of the conversations down our street tonight (puts on an even thicker Scouse accent) 'eh love, get down to Home Bargains tomorrow will ya, and see if they've got any of them, erm, pergolas left. I'm putting one up in the back yard and dropping it on my nut. Guaranteed compo claim. Royal seal of approval, like.' A road-digger.

'Okay, honest question here, folks: Hand on heart, who genuinely gave a shiny shit about this old duke before today?' Groans and cheers break out in equal measure. 'Come on, he's ninety-friggin-nine. That's one-and-a-half good innings. Admit it, if you hadn't copped him on his Zimmer during Covid or sitting in the free seats at the FA Cup Final you'd have thought he'd snuffed it years ago.

'The People's Duke, they're now calling him. The People's Duke? How do you fit those words together? That's like calling me The Obese Anorexic,' he turned side-on, pushed out his gut and rubbed it, to gales of laughter.

'And how did he become a national hero for pushing himself around that old shelter and raising a few quid for nurses? Instead of calling him a living saint why didn't someone shout 'sell your country estate, lad, and give £300 million to the NHS. Then we'll call you a national hero.' Cue much applause and whistling.

'Charles is on the telly telling us we're all willing dear old Blinky to make it to one hundred. No we're not. We're more worried that our dear old gran will have to wait until she's a hundred to get a new hip.' Cheers and clapping.

'I'm dreading Charles dying, though. Especially if my girlfriend is going through her time of the month and he comes back as a tampon and mistakes her entrance for Camilla's. That's our sex life shagged for good.' A full-on rip-snorter drowns out the few groans.

'Okay so some of you are thinking I'm pushing it here. Old Blinky's stopped blinking and here's me cracking gags about it. Well, you'll be desperate for jokes soon if he dies and we're launched into a week and a half of North Korean style mourning. Remember when the Queen went? Jesus, Mary, and Joseph. The country lost its mind. Teary-eyed people on the telly outside Balmoral saying–' He puts on a posh Scottish accent, '–I keep seeing rainbows. It's God telling us she is up there with him and all is well.

'No, it isn't, you brain-washed plank. It's nature reminding you that you live in a country where it permanently pisses down.' A road-digger.

'There were people demanding the Pope make the Queen a saint. And she's the head of the Church of England. That's like the Jews wanting to make the leader of Hamas a Chief Rabbi.

'I couldn't get on Porn Hub for a week. Every time I typed it in, I was redirected to Mourn Hub and videos of London queues. Rubberneckers with nothing better to do than gawp at a wooden box containing a dead pensioner, praying their crying gobs were caught on TV, before flogging their wristbands on eBay. So respectful.'

There were huge roars and whistles now as Mick turned to take a swig from a bottle of still water on the small stage table. Turning back, he noticed a man in his fifties in the third row, shaking his head at his wife who looked distracted as she nervously picked at her Swarovski necklace.

'Well, I was about to lay off Blinky but seeing as how it's offended a couple of you I'll carry on. You okay, folks?' he asked the dissenting couple, to which the man mouthed 'not funny' and gave Mick a downward thumb. Which was a bad move.

'Really? So were you hoping I'd turn into Michael McIntyre tonight and prance around saying,' he puts on high-pitched posh voice and bounces across the stage, 'don't worry folks, Mummy's a Chelsea Flower Show expert and she tells me our beloved duke will soon become compost mentis?' Mick stared down at him.

'You sad man,' the punter replied, taking his wife's hand and pushing past people to exit the row.

'I'm sad?' Mick yelled back. 'I'm not the one going home to weep about a rich old stranger who couldn't give a shit if your house burned down killing all your family. You're the definition of sad, mate.' As the punter slammed the door shut, Mick pointed at it.

'I don't hate the royals, you know. I get why they

are what they are. Who wouldn't live off the fat of the land if they could? It's sheep like him who keep them in clover. Loads of old people will snuff it through hypothermia today because they can't afford to pay their gas bill, but no-one will give a toss about them, will they?' Applause rings out. He was on a roll now. Lost in the moment.

'Why don't these forelock-tugging dickheads realise there's nothing magical about these inbreds they worship. They're not our superiors. They're just ordinary humans who came out of a certain fandango who came out of a certain cock and back and back centuries through other cocks and fandangos until they reach a really nasty cock who raped, pillaged and so horrifically battered the poorest people that they eventually gave up and went: Ok, lad, you can be the king.'

It's a nailed-on rip-snorter with bells and whistles. A good base camp to reach Mount Everest. 'Right. Now we've got that out of the way, moving on with what's left of my career...'

The cheers were so loud the ceiling vibrated and a few punters stood up to applaud. On the back row, staying very much seated, a smartly dressed man in his late twenties pulled a phone from his jacket pocket and watched it glow red, confirming the voice memo had indeed been running.

He smiled, then just as Mick said, 'but seriously folks,' he switched it off and headed for the door, missing the bit where Mick said, 'let's all hope the old fella pulls through, eh?'

3

SUNDAY MORNING

Pandora Fitzroy-Price, or Panda F-P to her friends, was on a multi-tasking high. Through her AirPods, apoplexy was being wrung from Tory MP Adrian Jenkins. Which was not exactly hard as the wildly ambitious, yet extremely dim backbencher, was so desperate for recognition you could ask him if he agreed with an Alabama senator's view that the way to cut crime among the inner-city black population was to introduce compulsory one-year shoe-shining courses for all juvenile offenders, and he'd say, 'This is compassionate Conservatism in action. Nobody wants to see chain-gangs being brought back just yet so this is the sensible first step to cutting crime among sections of society to whom law-breaking comes as naturally as dancing.'

And we know he'd say that because he once did.

On her laptop, Panda's typing hands were struggling to keep up with the furious pace of Jenkins' vitriol, not helped by obscenities so obscure she did not know how to spell some of them. And all the while a perspiring young TV intern kept flashing an ever-decreasing number of fingers at Panda to denote the minutes left before she would be on air, while using her other hand to point at the waiting make-up artist. But Panda was about to strike media exposure gold and nothing could distract her.

En route to the London Docklands *Brit Talk* TV studio from her Chelsea flat, an email had dropped from northern stringer Jason Garlick which induced her first hot flush in the back seat of a taxi since she was pinned down by the blond, charismatic leader of the Britain Out Of Brussels campaign group, who promised in between lunging kisses and sweaty groping that he intended not just to leave Europe but his wife. He eventually did. But for a younger version of Panda. Garlick was a libertarian activist from Runcorn who trawled around the North digging for dirt on all opponents of the Right. Any dirt he stumbled upon would be posted to his small band of geeky neo-con followers, which was how he came to Panda's attention. Her avaricious eyes, not to mention aversion to travelling within 200 miles of any hellhole where chips and gravy are deemed haute cuisine, saw the potential in having a spy up North. So she drowned him in flattery and reached an agreement that if he caught anything juicy she would promote it on her website, Pandora's Box, promising him a decent payday, a credit, and a word placed in the ears of her London media contacts. This translated to a truly insulting pittance he would be lucky to receive, an article credit only when Panda later discovered the story was an absolute turkey, and his name never mentioned to anyone of note as she wanted to keep the clog-wearing ferret-wrestler dangling on her string.

Garlick didn't mind though, as he enjoyed being courted by one of his alt-right heroines and, as a loyal soldier in the war against bleeding-heart liberals, he viewed providing hand grenades to Pandora's Box as an honour.

Have you guessed the logo on Pandora's Box by the way? Course you have. Yes, it's a drawing of a beautiful young woman staring into a gem-encrusted jewellery box from which a white cloud of light emerges. The beautiful young woman is Pandora and the light is the truth she unleashes. However, the similarity between the beautiful young woman and Panda was on a par with that of a newspaper columnist and the photo of themselves they were still trading under, which had been heavily touched-up two decades ago.

That is not to say the thirty-nine-year-old was unattractive. Indeed, to a certain type of man, albeit the type who decorates his garden shed in Third Reich memorabilia, she was perfect. Tall and stick-insect thin, her skin, due to excessive cosmetic work, smoother than an ironed condom, girlishly-long peroxide blonde hair, milk bottle veneers, jutting cheekbones and piercing, light-blue eyes that exuded dazzling charm...until you focussed on the dilated pupils and realised you were staring at a Great White shark who would eat your heart and sell your kidney for a Hermes scarf. Think every wild-eyed woman who has ever been paid to spout pro-Trump hatred on Fox News wearing the kind of flirtatiously-cut, cleavage-hinting, thigh-teasing dress that pleases that certain Third Reich type of man. Great Whites who all want to make their great country white again.

How did she get here? The same route taken by many of the people you see anchoring talk shows or in senior jobs in broadcasting and newspapers. Her rich parents (Charles Price, an Oxford Blue turned successful City investment banker, and Eleanor Fitzroy, a minor aristocrat) put her through Godolphin & Latymer School where, academically, she was profoundly mediocre. Despite failing to achieve the grades to study PPE at Oxford, her father called in a favour from an old friend, the senior admissions tutor, and she was granted a free pass. Or a Toby Young, as it is known.

She scraped a 2:2 but gained a First in networking and walked straight into a job on the *Daily Telegraph* diary, despite never having so much as a sentence of journalism published in her life. Indeed, the only creative piece of writing Pandora Price had done since leaving Oxford was to change her name by deed poll to Fitzroy-Price making her sound, she believed, a more cultured and beguiling woman, thus potentially having even more doors opened for her.

After a couple of uneventful years, during which she was paid to hang around society parties and West End clubs to search for famous people doing drugs or someone else's spouse, she was sacked for inventing a story about a left-wing MP having a love-child with an illegal Albanian refugee he had impregnated while doing a tour of an immigration centre in Kent.

Ironically, the lie was fed to her by a former MEP and ardent Eurosceptic who *had* actually impregnated an illegal immigrant. The foreigner-hating xenophobe who successfully portrayed himself as a man of the people — despite being an Eton-educated property magnate who wanted to get very rich at the workers' expense — had impregnated his Dutch researcher, who was working for him without papers, behind his Danish wife's back. Five mistresses and seven abortions later, it would be Panda's turn to be Lance Fleury's mistress. Four years down the line she was still hanging on to that promise to leave his wife for her. But being the maverick star of the UK's latest Fox-lite TV channel, *Brit Talk*, Lance Fleury was a hard man to walk away from.

Following her disgraced exit from Fleet Street,

Panda became a publishing PR, then a researcher for Tory MP Sir Mark Bridger, after his three previous female researchers had left through sexual harassment. 'Victim-wallowers,' the rotund knight of the realm labelled them as he patted Panda's shapely rear at the end of her interview. A viewpoint she told Sir Mark she shared, as she fluttered her long, fake eyelashes at him. She took to the Westminster bubble like a rat to a blocked sewer and became a lobbyist for the think-tank The Institute of Rightful Thinking, one of a dozen such organisations based in a large Georgian terrace in Westminster's Tufton Street. You know the ones: Free-market fanatics, climate-change deniers, NHS dismantlers, anti–trade union/ abortion/ welfare/ BBC/ immigration/ federalism forums. Or rather, you have definitely seen their swivel-eyed spokespersons on every TV panel and news review posing as independent experts while refusing to say where their funding comes from. Because it's from Big Pharma, American neo-con websites, far right European groups, wealthy conspiracy theorists and multi-national industrialists.

After a few deft TV appearances as a mouthpiece for The Institute of Rightful Thinking, she was offered her own show on Straight Talk Radio and set up Pandora's Box. She was now firmly focused on mega media stardom, pitching her persona somewhere

SICK MICK

between Marine Le Pen and Margaret Thatcher. A pitch so shrill and ghastly it deafened every dog in a three-mile radius of whatever studio couch she was wailing from.

'Okay, it's ready to go,' Panda barked down her phone at Giles, the talented but unpaid work experience graduate who ran the technical side of the website. 'Post it and copy-in Julia at *Mail Online*, telling her to wait an hour before running it.' She listened impatiently. 'Yes, of course they're crediting us. The deal is they call it a 'Pandora's Box Exclusive' in the second part. Get ready for a colossal response as I'm about to trail it live on *Brit Talk*. Must rush.'

She placed her phone and laptop into her Mulberry bag and waved away the make-up artist, asking if she was blind as well as incompetent because 'this face was in make-up before I left the house.' She demanded a bottle of Acqua Panna still water, then stood up, brushed down her black, lace-trimmed Maje mini-dress, applied lip gloss and swaggered towards studio one.

With it being Sunday morning there was a distinct absence of *Brit Talk*'s A-Listers in the building. Alphabetically-speaking, the talent was more towards X. Sitting behind a desk on a red, white and blue set was Keith 'The Griff' Griffin, a fifty-five-year-old, 5ft 7in, 16 stone hunk of joy. His day job, or rather night job, was as a 10pm to 1am shock jock on LBC radio. Telling it like it is, as they say. Putting the world to rights. For shift workers, insomniacs, and suicide-contemplators.

When The Griff wasn't writing to Ofcom demanding to know why there was a disproportionate amount of black faces in TV commercials, he penned a 'why, oh why' column in the *Sunday Express* addressing issues that pumped so much rage through his veins they made his face turn a darker shade of gammon: Personal pronouns, electric cars, refugees, veggie sausage rolls, rainbow laces, school sex lessons, burqas, the BBC, ex-footballers expressing political opinions, mental health sufferers, nose rings, gender-neutral toilets, civil servants working from home, breast-feeding in public and the EU flag (especially when waved at the sacred Last Night of The Proms).

He lamented how this 'once great country' was going to 'hell in a handcart,' worshipped his East Ender parents, part of 'the greatest generation' who faced down Hitler (even though they were both toddlers when the Fuhrer topped himself in his bunker) and told his ageing readership that if Britain could return to those days of conscription, imperial measures and a population almost entirely made up of the indigenous people (i.e. white), then all this 'once-great country's' problems would be solved.

SICK MICK

Obviously, we would first have to outlaw the Marxist Blob in charge of Whitehall, feckless welfare claimants and paedophiles. Oh, how he hated paedophiles, constantly telling his audience that God had yet to invent a suitable punishment for them.

Ironically, 'paedo' is a word that was applied to him regularly on social media, along with 'Gravy-swigging blurt, Jabba The Gut, Nazi Boy and a Bloated Virgin who only shags the flag because he'd couldn't lose his cherry at an orgy in a blind school.'

The Griff once tried to gain public sympathy by posting on X a list of the worst insults he'd received in the past twenty-four-hours. It earned 45 reposts and 122 likes. But, also, 898 replies suggesting those slurs did not quite cover what an abomination of a human being he was, with a few hundred new ones thrown in.

If there is one group The Griff hated more than paedos it was 'woke lefties' whom he believed were out to deny people like him their God-given right to free speech. Being a self-styled true defender of liberties he was opposed to any form of thought censorship. Especially when it was being foisted on 'a sleep-walking nation' by groups of people he would like to see rounded up and, a la the Chinese model, sent to 're-education camps.'

The Griff's no-nonsense tone struck a chord with

the *Brit Talk* producers who, three months previously, had offered him his own Sunday morning show, despite having a face so unsuited to TV one critic claimed it looked like it had been 'put together with offcuts from an abattoir floor.' His brief was to offer a feisty alternative to the cosy chats being done with leading politicians on Sky and BBC, by 'speaking the unspeakable.'

But his worryingly low ratings hinted he was speaking the unhearable. And on a morning when every TV channel was devoting its output to the ill duke, it seemed unlikely that today would be the day he grabbed a subject by the throat and soared into the public consciousness. But not that unlikely.

Pandora sat down on the couch, gave a flirty smile to The Griff which made his porcine face glow even pinker as he winked back, before weighing up her competitors—sorry, her fellow guests—whom she intended to chew up, spit out and leave crawling across the studio floor begging for mercy.

Already on the couch was Sue Nolan, a 66-year-old Fleet Street veteran columnist, who deposited hysterical reactionary turds all over a *Daily Mail* page every Saturday; and Adam Moore, a comedian who failed to break into the TV panel show circuit so developed an act about the leftie mafia running the mainstream media. He was consequently hailed 'a gale of fresh air in a liberal cesspit' by The Campaign for Real Comedy and became a mainstay of the Fox-lite TV circuit, despite being as funny as an attack of severe gout.

Everyone was dressed in black, in case the duke passed away while they were on air, and the backdrop showed a photo of Blinky pushing his Zimmer around his estate as his team of servants stood around clapping. Panda and Sue faked sadness at his condition and delight at seeing each other, joking about how hard it is for a girl to carry off black. The Griff cleared his throat as he was counted in, before telling his viewers, 'We are a nation united in hope that its Great Grandfather will pull through,' as shots of Union flags at half-mast on buildings across the country flashed up on-screen.

He introduced his 'all-star' panel, each wearing the kind of faux-sombre look a Health Minister feigns on Question Time when an audience member tells them her mother has waited two years for a piles operation, then spoke of the inspiration that is the Duke of Dorset and how his legacy will live on in the hearts of the nation whatever fate befalls him, before neatly segueing into the section at the top of every show called The Griff Riffs.

The Griff Riffs is a three-minute rant about 'today's hot topic,' which translates to whichever one of his pet hates is most boiling his urine. Today it was bleeding-heart liberals. Again.

'So, ladies and gentlemen, another traumatic time for our beloved royal family, another show of hate from the Left. 'Quelle surprise,' as the French border police say when a boatload of illegals heads to our shores to be greeted with open arms by an army of on-the-make lawyers.

'Do you know, I wondered this morning if it was too soon to show the bile produced by some of these nasty cretins but then I thought it's never too soon for them to spew their anti-patriotic poison, is it? So have a butcher's at some of these outpourings on social media from lefties, offended by everything but their own repulsive views.'

On screen viewers were shown the following tweets:

> Great news. Soon there will be one less parasitical mouth sucking off the taxpayer's t*ts [the asterisk inserted by *Brit Talk* producers as a sign of respect]

> So spending a couple of nights handing out gas-masks counts as a war hero now? What an insult to the real heroes.

SICK MICK

> Rich, old Etonian stranger nears death. Sorry, where's the story?

> Why is no-one mentioning how dodgy it is that the only charity he wanted to work with were the Boy Scouts?

> I'm just clearing my throat for 'Blinky's in the mud, in the mud, Blinky's in the mud.'

After staring at the camera for three seconds, shaking his jowls and saying nothing, The Griff produced a copy of that day's *Observer*, flicked through the first two pages, which carried commentary on the duke's condition, and called it a 'pitiful amount of space to devote to one of the biggest British stories since the Queen died.' By contrast he held up the *Mail on Sunday*, announced that it had devoted twenty-four pages of the main paper, plus a twelve-page pullout, to the life and times of The People's Duke, before turning the *Observer*'s page three to camera and saying:

'So, what story do these crackpot lefties believe, after the royal drama, will most interest the man on the Clapham Omnibus? You guessed it: the LGBT crowd feeling unsafe on the London Underground after a series of alleged homophobic attacks and demanding they be assigned their own carriages, or, wait for it, safe queer spaces.'

The camera panned to the panellists who were all shaking their heads. Seeing herself on camera, Sue Nolan spoke into it:

'Why do we give this minority such attention? It's like the trans lobby, or the selfish cockwobblers who want it both ways, as I called them in yesterday's column. And by the way, how come queers can call themselves queers but us non-queers are guilty of a criminal offence if we do?'

'Hang on, Sue, you can't call trans people selfish cockwobblers, or the human rights crowd will sue you for committing a hate crime,' said Adam Moore. 'But now that you've started, can I call cyclists 'lycra-clad Road Tax dodgers' and vegans 'anaemic lentil-botherers'?'

'Woh there, time out guys,' The Griff cut in. 'This is my solo riff. You'll get your chance later.

'As I was saying, this virtue-signalling garbage about safe queer spaces is an insult to us all on any day of the year, but banging on about it today of all days, as a senior royal lies in a coma? That insults every right-thinking person across the British Commonwealth.

'But you know what, I'm glad they ran it because it sums up how the Left despises this great country of ours and everything it stands for.

'This goes back decades, by the way. Before the Second World War the Left were Stalin apologists. During the war, one of their own, George Orwell, wrote that his socialist intellectual friends felt there was something disgraceful in being an Englishman and that it was their duty to snigger at every British institution.

'Since the war they have despised our greatest ally America, and Israel, even in their hour of need after the massacre by the hard left Hamas militants, preferring instead to suck up to the butchers in Iran, Moscow, and North Korea.

'Anyone who is against criminal gangs of illegal immigrants coming here to play the system is a racist. Anyone who wants the NHS to work properly through privatisation, so their dear old mum can have her varicose veins sorted, is a free-market fascist.

'They want to rip down every statue and historic symbol because they are ashamed that the Union Jack used to cover half the globe and want to burn that beautiful flag because they see it as a symbol of oppression and bigotry.

'That's why they delight in this great duke's demise and sneer at the monarchy. Because they know it is the bedrock of our great democracy. The flourishing bloodline to a glorious past.

'It was the same when Margaret Thatcher died. Remember them all singing 'ding dong the witch is dead.' Appalling. But you know why they hated her so much? Because they feared her. They knew she was right about everything. Every single thing.

'These people force the notion of tolerance down our throats when it comes to their own pathetic obsessions like trans rights, yet are the most intolerant bullies on Earth.

'Well, there is a simple solution for all of them who are today mocking the serious illness of the Nation's Great Grandfather because they hate this country so much: Sell your Islington home, give up your university lecturer's job, leave behind your £4,000 electric bike, your Arsenal executive box season ticket and your favourite Notting Hill vegan restaurants, cancel your Amnesty International direct debits and piss off to what's left of The Gaza Strip.'

To The Griff's left Pandora nodded her head, Adam Moore gave him a double thumbs up and Sue Nolan burst into applause, and almost into tears, as she shouted, 'bravo, bravo.'

'Well, that's my take on today's hot topic. I now want to hear what my all-star panel thinks. Sue, if your reaction was anything to go by, I think you're with me on this,' he said.

Nolan attempted a disgusted grimace, but her face

was an expression-free zone. After twenty years of Botox her skin was so tight that Ringo Starr could play a ten-minute drum solo on it, so she just turned her usual blank death mask to camera.

'Seriously Keith, you could not have put it better. My blood boils when I hear these disgusting people. Whatever your political views on the monarchy, His Grace is first and foremost a much-loved member of a family. He's a human being who is fighting for his life and his loved ones deserve to support him in peace.

'Sadly, it takes me back to when King Charles went through his own health ordeal, a man I had met and greatly admired, and the lefties attacked him for queue-jumping, which insulted the many decent and ordinary people of Britain. Once again, all this bile makes me wonder what has happened to the patriotic country we once were and confirms why we need laws to close down the worst offenders on social media.'

This was an interesting reply on many fronts from Sue. Firstly, the millionaire with three homes and six flats that she rented out across London was neither decent nor ordinary. Indeed, only last month Private Eye reported she had screamed, 'don't you know who I fucking am?' at a traffic warden about to give her a ticket in Knightsbridge after she'd been invited on a free trolley dash of Harrods beauty section in return for a puff piece in *OK!* Magazine. 'I know so many people in high places that you will be ending your career if that ticket touches my screen, you jobsworth low-life shit,' the People's Pundit added.

Second, the patriotic bit. Despite being an ardent Brexiteer she owned a villa in Gascony where she spent three months of the year.

As for silencing all of those tweeters, Sue had spent the past four years at the front of the *Daily Mail*'s Keep Our Speech Free campaign, viciously tearing into the cancel culture fanatics who want to silence every voice in Britain that doesn't agree with them.

Oh, and that stuff about greatly admiring the king? Back in the 1990s, when he was conducting an affair behind Princess Diana's back, she had attacked, 'this disloyal, cowardly, pathetic excuse for a man' and his 'manipulative whore with a face like a dog licking pee off a nettle' on a weekly basis, claiming if he took the throne with Camilla as his queen she would emigrate. She didn't.

'Great points as ever Sue, which will strike a chord with all of our patriotic viewers,' chirped The Griff. 'Adam, give us a comedian's take on this.'

Moore put his hands in the air, palms facing outwards, as though surrendering, and said, 'What can I tell you? It's one of those days that a comedian is as useful as an ash-tray on a motorbike. I have nothing funny to say.'

SICK MICK

Instead of The Griff being honest and answering, 'well no change there, pal,' he thanked him for his honesty, and then turned to camera with the kind of look that Al Jolson wore in the first ever talkie when he mouthed, 'you ain't heard nothin' yet,' and said, 'if only every comedian, or indeed so-called comedian, took Adam's view this would be a better country. Pandora, I believe you've got a world exclusive for us, and I have to warn viewers that what you are about to hear is beyond bad taste. It is horrendous. But we felt it was our public duty to bring it to your attention.'

The screen became divided in half, with The Griff's face on one side of it and a copy of the Pandora's Box exclusive on the other. The Griff began to read it out:

'A TV comedian cracked vile jokes about the Duke of Dorset and King Charles to a live audience only hours after news broke that our beloved Blinky was in a coma, Pandora's Box can exclusively reveal.

'Mick O'Shea, who has appeared on BBC shows, delivered an obscene tirade against the duke and the wider Royal Family in his home city of Liverpool last night, causing paying customers to storm out of the comedy club in disgust.

'But far from making leftie lout O'Shea realise his act was in bad taste, his depraved act only became darker. In a ten-minute rant at The Laughter Bucket club, O'Shea claimed His Grace was not a national hero and nobody gave a 'shit' about the fact that 'Blinky has stopped blinking' because if he had really cared about the country, he would have sold his country estate and given £300 million to the NHS.

'The snarling Scouser then moved onto King Charles, mocking his emotional statement about his uncle and claiming to be worried that if the monarch died he may come back as a tampon and enter his girlfriend.'

Griff paused to allow viewers to hear the gasps from the panel. Then continued.

'He called Royal grievers 'brain-washed planks' and 'forelock-tugging dickheads' who were getting their kicks on Mourn Hub.

'In his final salvo he called the Royal Family 'inbreds' who are worshipped for simply having the luck to be reproduced by certain genitalia and are only heads of state because they are descended from rapists and pillagers who subjugated the poor and stole their land.'

Another pause for gasps, and this time, jeers.

'Today there were calls to ban O'Shea from appearing on any British TV channels, with Conservative MP Adrian Jenkins telling Pandora's Box, 'This is the leftie hate mob showing themselves in their true light. They are traitors and degenerates who need to be silenced. At the very least this nasty piece of work, who threatens all of our freedoms and liberties, needs to be jailed. I, and I must stress this isn't official Conservative party policy, would happily birch him in public.'

The Griff broke off, saying he couldn't read any more, and fighting to keep back a smile that was attempting to burst through either side of his mouth announced, 'your texts are flying into us thick and fast. Keep them coming. And tell your friends to tune into Brit Talk as we have a lot more to come on this breaking scandal.'

He turned to Panda and thanked her for her 'exceptional public service journalism,' telling viewers she had secured a recording of O'Shea's act which they would be playing in full after the break. With subtitles for the hard of Scouse hearing.

'But before we briefly cut away I'd like to tell this sick, so-called comedian, that our lawyers have heard the recording and we are seriously considering suing you for breaching the obscenity laws. You need to be deplatformed. You see, you gobby leftie scumbag, you can't just go around in this country saying in public whatever your depraved mind thinks in private.'

All three anti-cancel culture warriors on the couch heartily applauded their liberty-loving host.

4

SUNDAY LUNCHTIME

Mick swung the black cab out of Prince Alfred Road onto Wavertree High Street feeling like an excited kid on the dodgems.

One of the reasons he helped out his mate Robbo on his Ticket to Ride Beatles taxi tours was to enjoy the thrill of turning the huge steering wheel that cut an acute angle with such effortless grace. If he ever made it big, he thought, he'd treat himself to a Hackney Cab so he could do that wicked turn in packed traffic, park wherever he wanted, keep the light on, grinning, when he went past stranded once-a-year Christmas drinkers and pick up old ladies with shopping bags at bus stops, taking them home for free just to see the smiles on their faces when he told them to keep their purses shut. Which reminded him of the three bags of groceries in the boot that he'd bought from Lidl yesterday that needed dropping off at The Florrie food bank.

His iPhone throbbed on the leather passenger seat next to him. There were six missed calls from his agent, Ayesha, and now Sadie, his girlfriend, was messaging him: RING AYESHA ASAP URGENT

The muted phone had been trying in vain to catch

his attention throughout the time he had been parked outside the small, terraced house that was George Harrison's first home at 12 Arnold Grove, explaining to Zak and Coco, who were sprawled across the back seat, how the young Beatle would freeze his undropped balls tip-toeing to the outside loo in winter. But the Twentysomethings merely stifled yawns and sifted through Instagram posts on their iPhones.

Robbo had told Mick that these were special guests booked by a London talent agency who could give Ticket to Ride some decent national publicity, so they needed to be handled with care. Zak and Coco were the reigning winners of the ITVx reality dating show set in southern Chile called Horny in Cape Horn (HICH) and had become influencers on the back of their TV fame. As a shared love of hip-hop had drawn them together, their management had decided to send them on a tour of British cities to bring the musical vibe to their two million followers across multiple social media platforms.

The couple were the peak of physical perfection. Tall and tanned with not a morsel of excess fat beneath the sponsored designer summer outfits they were monetising. Zak was blond, chisel-faced and ripped, his perfectly-honed muscles trying to escape from his uber-tight tee-shirt in ten different places. Think

SICK MICK

Aryan leading man in a Nazi propaganda film. Coco was dark and devastating with a meticulously-coiffured afro, deep, soulful eyes and lips so full and plump she wore a permanently seductive pout. In short, they had everything going for them. Apart from an ounce of humility, modesty, or self-awareness.

'Are you seriously expecting us to pay for this?' Zak had asked Mick at the start of the tour, informing him that the point of mega influencers was that their presence alone was more than adequate recompense.

After Mick lied that he had a family of six whose stomachs needed something more nutritious than influence, Coco leaned forward and said, 'Your voice is really sort of jarring so can we run this whole thing on?'

When they had reached Ringo's house at Admiral Grove and Mick asked if they wanted to get out and film, Zak had replied: 'What, that poky little gaff? I don't think so. Besides, wasn't Ringo the group's basic bitch?'

As the couple laughed in unison, Mick, struggling to contain his loathing, asked diplomatically. 'Do you actually like the Beatles?' to which Coco replied, 'well they're not exactly Lil Nas X are they?'

'So why are you doing the tour?'

'Look, this ain't it, chief,' said Zak. 'Just cut with the attitude, take us to a few Insta-worthy places, tell us why the fuck we're there and we'll go spread your pearls of Fab Four wisdom. Is that ok with you, Mal?'

'No problemo, amigo. Pearls of Fab Four wisdom coming up,' said Mick, warming to the prospect of the comedic possibilities that lay ahead.

Oh, yes. Mal. That was the name Mick assumed when he posed as a Ticket to Ride tour guide, in memory of Mal Evans, the group's tall, hairy roadie who played the hammer on Maxwell's Silver Hammer and was shot dead by police in his Los Angeles home after he had waved a rifle at them while high on Valium. Mick felt he had much to identify with in Mal. He also wanted anonymity from fans of his comedy, and more importantly, His Majesty's tax inspectors, which is why he wore clear-lensed John Lennon spectacles and tied his long hair up into a bun, stuffed inside a rasta hat.

He loved doing the tours when Robbo was short of a driver, even though he rarely stuck to the script, preferring to go with the first thing that landed in his head. Robbo had never actually ridden with him so never knew that he was making up most of the stories as he went along. But the feedback from the customers was mostly good, so he let his best mate carry on doing his own thing.

Having said that, when Mick thought his customers were full of bullshit, he dished up some of his own.

SICK MICK

There had been a review on Trip Advisor that said: this guy knows as much about the Beatles as a Japanese soldier who hid in the Burmese jungle during World War II and emerged in 1995 with Alzheimer's. And one Beatles aficionado, possessing a detailed knowledge of every aspect of Fab Four history, had written to Paul McCartney telling him his legacy was being destroyed by a 'fraud on the make.' But at the time Paul was extricating himself from his marriage to Heather Mills, his worst mistake since recording The Frog Chorus, which ended up costing him £25 million, so Mal the rip-off Beatles cabbie was understandably deemed small fry.

The part-time job paid almost as much as a comedy gig and meant he could keep the cab for the day. To Mick it was another performance. Another interface with the global public. And a never-ending source of rich material.

At the Picton Clock roundabout his route was meant to take him right, down Church Road towards John Lennon's childhood home in Newcastle Road, but instead he took a left onto Mill Lane and pulled the taxi over just past Harry's Continental chip shop and Curl Up and Dye hairdressers.

'Where are we?' asked Coco.

'Wavertree,' Mick replied.

'Wave-er-what?' asked Zak.

'Tree. Wave-a-tree. So-called because in olden times the baron who ran the place went insane with syphilis, believed the trees were gods and told all of the serfs they had to wave at them or they'd be burnt at the stake every full moon.'

'Yay, now you're getting it, hun. This is the content we're after,' said Coco.

'Good. The one thing about my tours is you're guaranteed to hear things that no other guide dares to tell you. See that?' he asked, pointing at a small, circular 18th century brick building which was standing in the shade of trees in a patch of grass next to Childwall Road.

'That's called the Wavertree lock-up. It was built to imprison people overnight who'd got so drunk in the many pubs around here that they were causing trouble.' This was true.

'Now what many people don't know is that John Lennon and Paul McCartney were both thrown in there as teenagers after a drunken brawl in the Coffee House pub, which you can see away to your left behind the clock tower.' This was not true.

'Oh my God, really?' gasped Coco as she put her phone into a gimbal, a hand-held, motorised gadget that kept it steady during filming, and climbed out of the taxi for a closer inspection. 'I had heard Lennon was problematic, violence-wise.'

SICK MICK

'What were they brawling about?' asked Zak.

'Erm, the lyrics to Twist and Shout,' Mick stuttered, letting the baloney flow as he followed the couple onto the pavement.

'But what *exactly*?' asked Zak. 'Our followers need all the juicy details.'

'Well,' Mick said, clearing his throat as he thought about what to say next. 'John wanted it to be a fighting song called Fist and Clout. Paul said he couldn't see how that would work, so John showed him by starting a punch-up. It was bad. Like really bad. Like Tarantino. Blood everywhere.'

'Oh my god, I'm actually going to die. That's perf,' said Coco. 'Hope you're getting all this, Zak.'

'Now look at that children's playground behind you,' said Mick, as the couple turned around. 'When George was six he fell off one of those swings and knocked himself unconscious. As he came to, laying on his back, what do you think were the first words that he said to his big brother Harry as he opened his eyes?'

There was silence as the influencers looked at each other with a puzzled expression, then back at Mick. 'How the fuck do we know?' said Zak.

'Go on, have a guess. It was a day like today,' Mick said, shading his eyes with a hand and blinking up at the cloudless sky. 'Think about it. George was lying on his back when his eyes opened, looking up at the sky. And he said…?'

'My head, like, really hurts?' chipped in Coco. Mick shook his head then replied triumphantly: 'Here comes the sun. Because he could make it out behind Harry's head. So now you'll know, whenever you hear the song, what it's all about.'

Zak and Coco looked at each, then at the playground, mostly populated with bored weekend fathers staring at their phones while young kids screamed, 'watch this Dad' from the swings and roundabouts, in a vain bid to grab their estranged parents' attention.

'We need to get this,' said Zak.

'Bet,' said Coco.

'Do you know which swing?' asked Zak.

'Erm, yeah,' said Mick, pointing to a row of three hanging from a metal frame. 'The one in the middle of those three. Although they're not actually the swings that were there when George used them. Mind you it has been said that if you look closely enough you can still see a trace of his blood on the concrete, a bit like one of those crying statues of the Virgin Mary in Venezuela.' The last piece of waffle made even less sense than the previous nonsense he'd been spouting, but by now the influencers were oblivious as they hurried towards the playground gates, iPhones in gimbals, ready to distribute Mal's pearls of wisdom to their millions of devoted followers.

Mick jumped back into his cab, slumped wearily into the driver's seat and gave off a loud yawn, rubbed his face, grabbed his phone and stared at the missed calls and messages. He knew they meant that he was in deep trouble. He had sensed it all morning. It was a familiar feeling: A queasiness in the guts, a low-pitched alarm humming in his brain. Anatomical red flags which signalled that he had screwed up and a reckoning was loitering around the corner. That consequence was wielding an ice pick, readying itself to respond to one of Mick's rash actions with a blow to his skull.

He had been conscious of an underlying nausea since walking off stage last night. Something wasn't right. When he had asked Anna the promoter how it had gone, she told him he'd smashed it, but the answer came too quickly and from a false place. Her voice was too high-pitched. Her eyes too big and too desperate to please.

His girlfriend Sadie, who was in the audience that night, had typically dispensed with the diplomacy, called him a 'stupid bollix,' told him he'd pushed his luck by tap-dancing all over the duke's yet-to-be-dug grave for five minutes too long and that she was amazed only two punters had walked out. Punters who, according to Jacqui on the front desk, demanded their money back with menaces and had been pulled aside by a smartly-dressed man with a notebook who asked them questions and wrote down their answers.

Bat out of Hell blared from his now unmuted phone, snapping him out of his thoughts. It was Ayesha. He sucked in a breath, put on the comic mask again, and steadied himself for consequence's ice-pick.

'Look, Fagin, if you're after 15 percent of my taxi job, it's a no-no. You don't take a cut of a hobby you money-grabbing old—'

'Glad you sound chipper,' said Ayesha, a thirty-eight-year-old no-nonsense ball-breaker who had been a high-achieving executive in London's top comedy talent agency, Grin, before moving back to Manchester to head up the northern office.

'Why wouldn't I be? It's a lovely day,' Mick replied.

'So you haven't looked on social media or turned the TV on?'

'Nah. Waste of time.'

'What were you on last night?' she cut in.

'Is this a drugs test?'

'Calling a national hero a fraud, announcing your fears over the king dying and disappearing up Sadie's vagina, describing a grieving family as a shower of murderers and pillagers who were lucky enough to spill out of certain cocks and fannies. Why didn't you

SICK MICK

go all the way and call the duke a royal kiddy-fiddler?'

'Because that job's already taken, maybe?' he asked.

'Mick, someone recorded your car crash of a show last night.'

'Car crash? They loved it. Apart from one old quilt and his missus.'

'And a journalist plant who rightly guessed you'd piss all over the comatose royal, who taped and leaked your rant to the media. And now you're all over the *Daily Mail* and a big talking point on every TV and radio channel.'

'Are you saying I should try this every week, then?'

'I'm saying they want your head.'

'You're joking. Have they seen it?'

'Yes. The journalist also took a picture of you in full Looney Tunes mode and it's plastered all over their websites, above your new nickname 'Sick Mick.' And if the messages left on my phone from reporters are anything to go by, every paper will be after your head by tomorrow morning.'

'I'd better wash my hair then.'

'Listen to me. You need a plan.'

'Hang on. What's that saying about there being no such thing as bad publicity?'

'This is way past bad publicity.'

'So you're saying I should stand on my step like an owl arse MP who's been caught shagging his secretary and read out a fake apology? 'Cos that's not happening. Jesus, hang on.' Mick heard a loud car horn plus the crunching of brakes from a speeding Audi Q7, and looked out of the window to see Zak and Coco walking backwards into the road as they yelled excitedly into their phones.

He started to tell Ayesha what that car incident was about but she cut him dead with, 'Mick, I really need you to get serious here.'

'Okay, I'm listening.'

'I, I mean we, have to turn this around.'

'Agreed.'

'Look, it's not the end of the world. The BBC still want you on *Quays at One* tomorrow.'

'Oh, I wonder why that is?'

'Sorry?'

'Will they put me in stocks and throw shit at me or go straight for the public hanging?'

'Leave all that to me. You just lie low until tomorrow, ok?'

'Don't worry, Fagin. Your meal ticket gets the picture. After I've taken Ken and Barbie back to their hotel I'm heading home. Sadie's up, so I was just going to chill with her. Watch a film. *The Fugitive*, maybe?'

'Hilarious.'

'That's me.'

'Just make sure you don't answer your phone or

your door.'

'You mean my dad's door? They're not going to bother him, are they?'

'Probably.'

'Well, I hope they get him before he's been to the pub. I've got to shoot.'

'What?'

'The show must go on.' He threw his phone down, jumped out of the cab and jogged to Zak and Coco who were about to cross the road and head to the Coffee House pub to tell the world the story of Fist and Clout.

'Ok guys let's cross over here because it's full of history,' he said, pointing to a zebra crossing. As they reached him he asked, 'So who's going to tell me why this is a massive part of the Beatles story?'

'Did one of them, like, I dunno, die here?' asked a bored Coco.

'No, but top marks for an educated guess,' said Mick. 'Ok, I'll give you a clue. That supermarket over there,' he pointed at a large art deco building on the corner, 'used to be a cinema called The Abbey.'

They stared at it blankly.

He pointed at the supermarket and said, 'Abbey.' Then at Childwall Road and said, 'Road.' Then at the zebra crossing.

'Oh my God,' spluttered Zak. 'This is where they

shot the cover of the Abbey Road album.' Mick nodded and applauded.

'A-may-zing,' said Coco, adding, 'why didn't you like, just show us this place when we pulled up?'

'Because I'm full of surprises. Now give me those ugly contraptions you've got your phones in and I'll get a picture of you two striding across the crossing like two of the Fab Four.'

'Why can't we film ourselves doing it?' Zak asked, pulling his gimbal away from Mick's outstretched hand.

'Why do you think?'

'I dunno. Because they're a bit too cool for old vanilla Mally?'

'No, because the Beatles weren't into selfies,' Mick replied, followed by the inaudible mutter: 'And I'm not into pretentious pricks.'

5

SUNDAY AFTERNOON

Sadie sighed, dragged herself up from the roll-arm settee she'd been stuck to for the past two hours and answered the front door for the third time that day.

'No,' she told the young female reporter who was affecting a sympathetic expression that belied her lethal motives. 'Mick isn't at home. I don't know when he'll be back. Do you want to leave me your card so I can put it in the bin with all the others?' she asked mock-politely, before slamming the uPVC door in the reporter's cursing face and heading back to the couch muttering, 'where's that feckin' big oaf got to?'

Vinny, Mick's dad, was in his armchair in the corner of the small terraced living room, bad leg up on a poof, staring silently at the sombre scenes on TV. His bad leg consisting of a prosthetic one, from below the knee, that he'd been lumbered with since a good one was smashed to pieces by an Iraqi landmine during the First Gulf War. Back then the tall, athletic, dark-haired soldier with a swarthy complexion passed down through ancestors from Ireland's West Coast was nicknamed Travis after his uncanny resemblance to Robert De Niro's character in *Taxi Driver*.

Now aged sixty-two, having put on a bit of timber,

he looked more like De Niro's portrayal of an ageing Jake Le Motta in *Raging Bull*. But Vinny O'Shea, with a thick mop of silver-grey hair, still had his moody good looks. He was still a man with a presence, his economy with words and emotions giving him a certain doleful aura.

'What's with the sudden interest in our Mick?' Vinny asked.

'Ach, it's just this story they've whipped up about whether we should be having live comedy shows when a royal is kicking the bucket,' she lied convincingly.

'Anything that brightens up this festival of misery has to be good,' he replied.

Operation Deep Sleep, the codename given to the designated procedures when a senior regal figure lies at death's door, had swung into action, with some of the junior royals doing walkabouts outside Windsor Castle, taking flowers from tourists who grinned inappropriately into their phones, capturing the giddy moment for posterity. Sadie and Vinny had just watched King Charles make an emotional address to the nation about his dear uncle, thanking him for his sterling service and asking God to see him over the century line where he had a personal telegram waiting for him. He also offered his best wishes to TV gardener Ian Hitchmough, who had been showing the

SICK MICK

duke around the pergola, and who only escaped being hit by the falling beam as he was on all fours at the time beseeching Blinky to feel his recycled bamboo decking. Sadly, the celebrity gardener suffered a heart attack when he saw the duke floored and he too was now in intensive care at a London hospital.

'By the way, why's he called Blinky?' asked Vinny.

'Something to do with him having a twitchy eye,' Sadie replied.

'I'll bet he had a twitchy arse when that beam was coming down on him,' said Vinny, chuckling.

Sadie didn't join in the laughter, though. In fact, she surprised herself at how annoyed she had been at Mick's act last night. The Belfast-born nurse, who moved to Liverpool ten years ago to study, counted herself a traditional royalist. Not in a putting on the sash and drinking a gallon of Buckfast every July 12th way. No, she was more imbued with a dutiful fondness for the Royal Family, having grown up in a loyalist, Presbyterian household.

Although her parents' fondness for her had been sorely stretched when, after graduating in sports science at John Moores University followed by a postgraduate course in nursing, she took a job in a private South Liverpool abortion clinic, with most of her clients being women from the same Northern Ireland streets as her, seeking a late, legal termination.

Her choice of career could not have upset them more if she'd opened a bakery shop at the end of their road specialising in gay wedding cakes.

After a few years toiling to keep the world's population down, she moved to Liverpool Broadgreen Hospital's urology clinic, where her objective was, theoretically at least, to keep life pouring into the world. She worked in the prostate cancer clinic, helping men through their biopsies, guiding those who had been diagnosed with cancer down the best treatment path and aiding those who encountered erectile dysfunction issues post-surgery to, well, rise again.

It was there that she met Mick, sitting in the recovery room with his dad who had just had a biopsy. Or, as Vinny put it very loudly when a nervous woman waiting for her husband to come out of surgery asked if the procedure had been painful, 'Painful? I've had the bottom half of my leg blown off love and that was worse. I don't know what was going on down there with all them needles and probes but it felt like a double-decker bus was reversing up my jacksie.'

Mick was supposed to be soothing Vinny's recovery with tea, digestives, and sympathy but all he could do was crack jokes about his dad's very sore nether regions. The moment Mick connected with this young,

SICK MICK

red-haired nurse with huge, dreamy eyes behind what he termed 'sexy secretary glasses' was when Vinny asked her, in a voice that was slurred due to the stinging pain from below, 'when will I get my test results back?'

'Sorry, I didn't quite catch that Mr O'Shea,' Sadie replied.

'He said when will I get my testicles back?' Mick boomed.

As Vinny punched Mick on the shoulder all three fell about laughing. Sadie told Mick he should be working here with her as a morale-raiser and he asked her out for a drink to discuss the offer. Three phone calls to the clinic later, each one funnier than the one before, she accepted. Almost two years later, this visually odd couple (she was petite, reserved, slim and freckled with a milky white complexion; Mick was huge, fat, dark and loud) were still together. Although now it was more of a weekend romance. Last year she had moved to London to work in a Harley Street penis rejuvenation clinic, which translated to twenty-minute sessions of holding the members of rich men who were struggling to get it up as she sent shockwaves through their flaccid phalluses. A genital therapist, Sadie termed herself. An electro-wanker, Mick called her. A Harley Street cosmetic clinician, her parents were told she was, as Sadie feared that to admit she'd gone from being an abortionist to a cock masseur would have resulted in ex-communication from their flock.

'Is everything okay with Mick?' Vinny asked, still staring at the telly where black-and-white Pathé News footage of a young Blinky guiding people into London Underground stations was being repeated for the fortieth time.

The experienced nurse always chose her words wisely with Vinny as she deemed his mental health to not be in a good place. She had decent grounds for concern. He had suffered for decades with PTSD after losing his leg and seeing comrades killed in the desert back in 1990. Throw in a broken heart due to his wife leaving him after one too many drunken rages (brought on by PTSD) when Mick was seven, then having to bring his son up single-handedly, and it was easy to see why Vinny lived permanently on the cusp of a deep depression. Sadie also feared he was showing all the signs of early onset dementia, a disease which had claimed his mother.

'Yeah, it's just a wee bit of an over-reaction to last night's show,' she replied.

'Wants to get himself a proper job, that lad.'

'Well you can't accuse him of being lazy. He's out working again this morning in the taxi, even though his supposed beloved has come all the way from

SICK MICK

London to spend a romantic weekend with him.'

Vinny left it for a bit, then asked: 'Everything good between you two?'

'Grand, aye. Why do you ask?'

'No reason. Just, you're good for each other. Well, you're good for Mick. And this house. It's a different place when you're here. It feels, I don't know, alive.'

'Sure it's not that deathly when I'm not here. Youse get on really well, considering.'

'Considering I'm a manic depressive with a gammy leg?'

'No. Considering you're two grown fellas set in your own ways.'

'I suppose what I'm saying is it would be nice to know there was someone for Mick when I've gone.'

'Where are you going? Don't tell me you've won the Lottery and are pissing off to get yourself a Thai bride?'

'I wish,' said Vinny laughing, then staring at the carpet lost in his thoughts.

'Shall we see if there's anything on the telly that's not going to send both of us to an early grave?' asked Sadie.

She picked up the controls that had fallen from the arm of Vinny's chair onto the carpet and surfed the channels. It was wall-to-wall grief, apart from a Jamie Oliver cookery show, but she didn't want Vinny throwing his prosthetic leg at the telly again. She found an old episode of Frasier on Paramount Comedy and left it on that, then walked to the window, lifted one of the Venetian blind slats and stared outside.

Moses Street, part of the Dingle's Holy Land area named after Biblical prophets, was similar to the street you used to see on the opening credits of the BBC sitcom, *Bread*. A long row of two-up, two-down terraces, sweeping steeply down towards the Mersey and its once bustling docks.

The late Spring sun was reflecting off the windscreens of parked cars, two of which, directly opposite the O'Shea household, had reporters sitting in the front seat typing into laptops. One worked for a local news agency; the other was a freelance who had been sent by the *Daily Mail*. Their photographers leaned up against the boot of one of the cars, cameras at the ready, throwing their heads back as they shared an anecdote.

Sadie turned away from the window, checked her watch, went to grab her phone from her fleece, thought better of it, then slumped onto the settee again.

'Can't stand that pale streak of piss,' Vinny said, pointing at Frasier's brother Niles. 'I think he's funny,' said Sadie, realising too late that he wasn't seeking her opinion just hinting that she should find something else to watch.

'Don't worry about me. I'm going to my room,' Vinny said.

'You're not going the pub?'

'No. Feel a bit knackered. Might do a bit of reading then have a doze.'

As he got up from his chair and walked out of the door to the stairs at the end of the small hallway, Sadie channel-hopped. After two travel shows, one Repair Shop, three quizzes and two foreign news channels showing footage of the crowds outside Windsor Castle, she landed on the familiar visage of Lance Fleury ranting to camera, which made her instinctively draw her mouth downwards the way she did whenever she clocked a jar of anchovies. When she saw the ticker tape banner running across the bottom of the screen she did her best not to faint. It read: 'Should Leftie Louts like Mick O'Shea be silenced?'

She switched the telly off in case Vinny returned to the room then took the stairs two at a time towards Mick's bedroom, fell on to his bed, grabbed the TV controls from the side table, turned on his 65" TV mounted on the wall and went in search of Fleury.

And there he was in full rent-a-gob-mode. The small of stature, perma-tanned opportunist who leapt onto every passing right-wing bandwagon and rode it all the way to the knackers' yard. The shifty-eyed bundle of smarm whose tongue had been so far up Donald Trump's back passage it could taste the tungsten-strength hairspray as it seeped through his scalp. The hate-inciting bigot who conned the older generation of working-class people — living in depressed towns who felt left behind by global capitalism — that he was on the same side as them, despite being a multi-millionaire property developer and country sports fanatic who had done more damage to the health of the country than the Black Death, Covid and Simon Cowell combined.

The fifty-seven-year-old agent provocateur had been invited onto *Brit Talk*'s early afternoon show and was being interviewed by its anchor, Sandra 'Newbs' Newbury, via Zoom from his back garden shed. The subject was Mick O'Shea.

'This twisted guy is not a lone voice. There are many thousands—possibly hundreds of thousands—of left-wing malcontents who despise British history because, well, it simply doesn't suit their agenda.

'They want us to rename streets dedicated to philanthropists who may, or may not, have been involved in the slave trade. A trade that, ironically, us British were the first to outlaw.

'They demand we offer profuse apologies and pay reparations to dictators who run benighted lands which used to be affluent in the days of Empire but have been dragged to their knees by corrupt kleptocracies. Despite the fact that you don't hear us British demanding reparations from the Vikings or the Romans.

'And you know, when we see fit young men from those countries coming here for economic reasons, the same virtue-signallers say we should let them in with open arms because they're fleeing persecution and poverty. Well they can't have it both ways, can they?'

'Yes, but specifically on this Mick O'Shea guy,' interrupted Newbs, who had been told in her ear to keep Fleury on the *Brit Talk* exclusive. 'Isn't the timing of his so-called humour appalling?'

'Well this man is clearly a despicable low-life. I mean how can you speak so heartlessly about our beloved royal family in their hour of pain? God knows what kind of family he comes from. One I'm guessing that has no respect for the monarchy and this country. His name would suggest that like those Premier League Irish footballers who refuse to wear a poppy, he's happy to take for granted all the wealth and liberty he enjoys over here because of past sacrifices made by the British people.

'And I hate to say this, and I will get a lot of stick on social media for it, but maybe in this guy's part of the world, where they boo their own national anthem and call themselves 'Scouse not English', they need to be reminded how much they take from the system they so despise.'

'A lot of our viewers are in agreement with you Lance,' said Newbs. 'We've been inundated with emails echoing your sentiments, and please keep them coming folks.

'This one from Peter in Wetherby reads: Whatever happened to charging traitors with treason. Punishable by hanging. No wait, that's too good for this scumbag.

'Jesus Christ, Mick, what have you gone and done?' shrieked Sadie, as she switched off the telly and pushed her face into the pillow running her brain through all the consequences that would be heading their way. She pulled her phone from her fleece pocket and rang him, but once again it went straight to answerphone. She began texting when the phone rang with Mick's name flashing up. She pressed the accept button and heard a comedy Chinese voice say; 'Harro, Shanghai Palace takeaway, what you want?'

'What the feck's going on Mick?' implored Sadie, switching the phone to speaker, throwing it on the bed and raking back her hair.

'The impression was that crap then?' he replied.

'They're throwing ten kinds of shite over you on the telly, there's a load of reporters outside the house, I think Vinny knows, and I'm supposed to be going back to London in a few hours.'

'I was taking around a couple of arseholes from that *Horny in the Horn* show so I couldn't ring you. And get on this—'

'Shut the feck up will ya, for God's sake. You're a feckin' joke.'

'Yeah, that's my job, love. Good spot.'

'You're in trouble here, you know? So, what are you planning to do about it?'

'Zilch. Ayesha's got it sussed. I'm heading over to Salford where she's booked me into a hotel. Robbo said I can have the cab, Ayesha's going to bring me some new clothes and I'll go and do that BBC gig tomorrow and smooth everything over.'

'Smooth everything over? You? Jesus. You do know you'll only screw things up worse than they already are, don't you? Aren't you worried?'

'Nah. I'm not worried. Ayesha's a lesbian so she'll have great taste in men's clothes.'

'About what everyone is saying about you?'

'It's not everyone though, is it? It's just a handful of easily offended pricks. You were there last night. You saw the show. I wasn't that bad.'

'You were. Even I was grimacing.'

'That's what I do. I'm a grimace-maker.'

'You're a big gobshite.'

'That as well.'

'And plenty more besides.'

'Look, these things blow over quickly. It'll all be forgotten in a few days.'

Raised voices from the street made Sadie walk to the window and pull back the curtains. Below she could see a photographer chasing away a hooded youth who had tried to steal a camera he had left on his car bonnet. Behind him, another hoodie rode his bike past doing a huge wheelie, yelling, 'Yes lad, go 'ed.'

'I hope for your sake those press people disappear soon because I don't know what Vinny's going to do once I'm gone if they keep knocking on the door,' said Sadie.

'My dad's sound. He knows the score.'

'Does he though? I'm worried about him. He's becoming more and more withdrawn. It's like he's in a world of his own. He was talking about dying before. And he forgets things. I'm going to say it, and don't get mad at me, but we should get him checked out.'

'Let me worry about my dad and you worry about yours, eh?'

'What do you mean?'

'Well he must be worried about the effect all this sad royal news will have on the king.'

'What are you going on about now?'

'If it sends Charles downhill, the prospect of another King William coming to the throne will have your old fella banging that big Orange drum of his so hard he'll have a massive heart attack.'

'That's a lovely thing to say about—'

'My future father-in-law?'

'Wise up. When he hears what you've been saying about the Royal Family I've more chance of marrying The Pope.'

SICK MICK

6

MONDAY MORNING

Lance Fleury loved nothing better than waking up in his suite in London's Waldorf Hotel and wallowing in its Edwardian opulence. The grand dame of Aldwych was, to him, just how a gentleman's lodgings should be—high-pillared ceilings, gold cornicing, art deco print carpet, discreet staff and only a stone's throw away from his Covent Garden club, The Garrick. It was an unashamed throwback to the days of Empire.

The Waldorf had been his unofficial London base since he set up the IFUK party (Independence for the United Kingdom) twenty years ago with the sole intention of making himself a household name as a populist agitator. Oh, and also removing the UK from the European Union whose parliament Fleury ended up being a member of for more than two decades, entitling him to an eye-popping pension despite only occasionally turning up in its Strasbourg parliament to scream abuse at the Belgians and French and, in his final appearance, show his backside sporting a freshly tattooed Union Jack to the EU president while playing Land of Hope and Glory on a kazoo.

He ditched IFUK in 2019 to set up the MUKGA party (Make the United Kingdom Great Again) partly because he felt the Westminster politicians were not fully implementing the extreme Brexit he had championed and also because he had fallen under the spell of the American MAGA movement and aspired to be Britain's Donald Trump. Even though whenever he had stood for election to Westminster he had failed miserably. Once, in Lincolnshire, he gained fewer votes than a comedian called Lord Biro of the Church of the Militant Elvis Party, whose manifesto pledges included turning all public schools into pound shops, installing euthanasia booths in all pubs that held karaoke nights and urging Richard Branson to start a chain of Virgin Brothels, offering a 20% discount to pensioners.

There had been persistent questioning over the years as to who was funding Fleury's lodgings at the Waldorf but the hotel management always passed it off as a 'personal arrangement.' Fingers had been pointed at China, the Kremlin, the America First movement and a hedge fund firm based in the Cayman Islands traceable back to a British billionaire whose father had edited Oswald Mosley's favourite fascist newspaper, *The Blackshirt*. But it remained a mystery.

Fleury liked to keep his presence there out of the spotlight. He never used it for photo-ops, preferring Wetherspoons' nearby Moon Under the Water Pub where he would arrange to be photographed chewing the fat with blue-collared men of toil on their lunch break over pints of lager.

He rather liked that political journalists referred to his unofficial London HQ as Waldorf Towers as he felt it gave him a Trumpian air. But he did worry about his visitors' movements being monitored as this was his shag pad. Any woman who entered his suite of rooms was always armed with a laptop bag, briefcase or files to show any curious photographer that she was there on business. And if work went on late into the night—and let's face it, as Fleury often remarked, bringing down the global elites is not a part-time job—then there was a spare room for her to sleep in. Not that his wife and mother of their three children, Freja, cared. Like the wider British public, she had seen through his affairs many years ago, and was past caring. As for Fleury's core support, they loved the fact that their hero was a bit of a Jack the Lad with plenty of lead left in his pencil.

Although, as he slowly awoke that morning something was nagging away at him, which he was sure may have been related to his pencil's lead levels. He had a vague memory of falling asleep, agitated and unfulfilled, as a soothing female voice told him not to worry, that 'it' happens and 'it' is probably down to him working too hard.

He could hear that voice now, rising from the couch at the end of the bed, begging him to listen to her as she read aloud from the morning papers which lay strewn at her slippered feet.

'Oh my God!' Panda screamed. 'The *Mail* have splashed on it.' She held up that morning's *Daily Mail* front page with the headline: THE SICK FACE OF LEFTIE BRITAIN next to a photo of Mick O'Shea. A photo had been carefully chosen by the *Mail* from the Laughter Bucket's website, as his face was twisted into a maniacal snarl making him look like a cross between Charles Manson and hunchbacked Scooby Doo villain, The Creeper. A perfect fit with the headline, to be fair.

She skipped through the story, the shameful tale of this vile 'so-called comedian' who had denigrated the comatose duke and his grieving family, then simpered with pleasure as she came across the line 'as exclusively revealed on the Pandora's Box website.'

'How good is that publicity?' she said, but all Lance could think of was how he had failed to give her a pleasurable simper last night.

Panda passed him *The Sun*. Fleury stared at the front page, which carried a photo of Meghan Markle crying as she hugged the mother of a boy killed in a recent Arizona mass school shooting, and muttered, 'what a bitch.'

The paper was splashing on an uncorroborated

rumour that Prince Harry would not be rushing back from California to join in the royal grieving as he planned to accompany Meghan on a world promotion tour for her latest Netflix series about how she felt more violated by unnecessary global media attention than the late Princess Diana.

It did, however, carry a blurb across the top of the front page trailing a 'hard-hitting' inside piece from 'no-nonsense' columnist Ron Riddell: 'This vile comic's sick jibes as a royal hero lies dying show how the BBC luvvie mafia are lower than a slug's a**e.' (Asterisks inserted by the editor to show she edits a wholesome family newspaper.)

The phrase 'BBC' made Fleury snap out of his depression. 'Why are they calling him part of the BBC mafia?' he asked Panda, who was shouting 'wanker' at the *Daily Mirror* where a columnist had written: 'Fair play to Mick O'Shea for cutting through the tsunami of confected sycophancy by speaking up for millions of Republicans forced again to sit in silence and swallow another heart-tugging advert for an unelected mediaeval farce.'

Lance, who had slipped on his fluffy Waldorf dressing gown and headed to the coffee machine to make an Americano (the cappuccinos, lattes and espressos being too European for his palate), shook his head in disgust and said, 'God I'd love to shut that rag down for good. But you didn't answer. What's this guy's link to the BBC?'

Panda told him that Mick had been booked to appear on that day's lunchtime show from the BBC's Salford base, *Quays at One*, and they were refusing to cancel his appearance.

'Result,' said Fleury. 'Just what the story needs. Of course, the BBC are refusing to cancel this guy because he's one of them—a repugnant joke. They only want to cancel people like me. Do you know I haven't had a Question Time invite since I left IFUK. And as for Have I Got News For You? Nothing for ten years. Cancelled. For not being Gary Lineker or Jo Brand or Stephen Fry or one of the countless other lib-tards they spunk licence money over.'

Panda was only half-listening to this rant, mainly because she had heard it before. Countless times. She had moved on to the *Daily Express* splash: FURY OVER CHARLES TAMPON GAGS, which more or less rehashed the fury vented by the *Mail*. Although it gave more of a shout-out to the couple in the audience who walked out of Mick's show labelling them 'the true voices of Middle England who speak for us all.' They had clearly never been to the Laughter Bucket in Liverpool's Baltic Triangle area, which is as far removed from Middle England as the favelas of Rio.

When she reached the fourteenth paragraph and the

sentence, 'once again Lance Fleury spoke for the nation on Brit Talk by calling O'Shea the scum of the earth—' Lance ceased ranting, sat down next to Panda on the couch, grabbed the paper, studied the article, and nodded his head.

'Ok, it's time to get serious. We need to own this story and I mean own it,' he said, outlining his plan of action for the day. A cab into *Brit Talk* after breakfast, the pair watching *Quays at One* together, then devoting the entire hour of his 7pm show to the story. Panda would be his main guest and his producer would line up someone like Rosie Parkinson, a former speechwriter for Ed Miliband turned token liberal stooge on Fox Lite talk shows, who willingly gets burnt at the alt-right stake for a £500 fee.

'I've got my Northern stringer to dig around for dirt on him,' said Panda. 'And Julia at *Mail Online* says they're going to be all over him at Salford—'

'Fuck Julia from *Mail Online*,' Lance interrupted. 'This must stay my story. Sorry, *our* story. We need to be a step ahead of it while everyone else gets on with the grieving for the duke schtick. We need to find O'Shea and get him to come on my show under the pretence that we'll give him space to plead his case. Then I will break the bastard.

'This is revenge time. For too long the BBC and the Twitterati have belittled me. We need to strike back.

This guy is the line in the sand. This is where we take a stand,' he said, punching his right fist hard into his left hand as Panda put her arm around him and kissed his cheek.

'I love it when you get angry,' she simpered, dragging his mind back to what it was that had so irked him when he awoke.

He feigned a laugh and replied: 'By the way, talking about taking a stand, I don't know what exactly happened last night.'

'It's ok, honestly. I think you were just tired.'

'You know it's not you, don't you?'

'Of course.'

'You know you're the one, and as soon as I—' Panda put her left index finger to his lips, placed her right hand inside his dressing gown and rubbed his hairy chest, saying, 'shush.'

He pulled her head towards his and kissed her hard on the lips, held it for five seconds then released her.

'Maybe we should take a break together somewhere when all of this blows over. Get a bit of sun on us, relax. Could be just what we need.'

'That would be so good. We've both been under a lot of stress lately. Me trying to take the website to the next level. You with the whole messaging mess.'

'Yes, well that's well behind me now, thank you very much.'

SICK MICK

The messaging mess concerned a lucrative sideline which involved Fleury recording personalised video messages for members of the public willing to pay him £100-a-pop.

Inevitably some of his many haters duped him with dynamite phrases he hadn't spotted or didn't understand.

Last Valentine's Day he was targeted by IRA sympathisers who conned him into saying what he thought were harmless Gaelic messages between loved-up couples (they even showed him how to phonetically pronounce the Gaelic).

Within minutes of delivering what Fleury thought were romantic phrases the videos had gone viral, the subtitles showing him saying, with a huge smile on his face, 'Brits out,' 'We're off to Dublin in the green, in the green, where the helmets glisten in the sun,' and 'I shit on Maggie's grave.'

He laughed it off, claiming he was conned by terrorist sympathisers, and pledged to fully scrutinise all future messages for hidden political meanings.

That lasted a couple of weeks until he got lazy again and knocked them out without giving a second thought to their veracity.

Last month, a couple of hoax scripts landed Fleury in serious trouble.

The first was paid for by someone who claimed she

wanted to celebrate the divorce of her friend from a controlling husband, a single mum whom she called by her surname.

It read: 'from river to sea, my pal Stein will be free.'

Substitute 'Palestine' for 'my pal Stein' and you can understand why the rage of anti-semitism groups went nuclear.

The Jewish Chronicle splashed on the story, accusing Fleury of 'incredible naivety' at best and 'knowing racism' at worst. Questions were asked in parliament and there was a huge demonstration by The Union of Jewish Students outside the Brit Talk studios, leading to Fleury giving a grovelling apology on-air for his 'indefensible gullibility' and a public vow to ditch his association with the celebrity video firm.

'You know this story could be the real making of you,' he told Panda. 'Or rather, a word from me in the right ear could just push the bosses over the edge into giving you your own show.'

'That's all I've ever wanted,' she replied, by now simpering for Britain.

'And you deserve it,' said Fleury, going in for another kiss but pulling away when he heard a rap on the door.

'That'll be breakfast. What better way to go into

battle for king and country than with a full English down you?'

7

MONDAY LUNCHTIME

Quays at One is what the TV industry likes to refer to as a daytime magazine show.

You've been unable to avoid a thousand of them: a smiley couple who feign a sizzling on-screen chemistry despite their relationship being as cold and practical as that between a U-bend and a toilet brush, sitting in a bright, cheap IKEA set, giggling at weak innuendos and churning out inane, formulaic dross to give students, pensioners, the jobless, baby-minders, sickie-throwers and the terminally ill something to gawp at without engaging their brains.

Quays, as it came to be known, was the product of a BBC focus group, which decided it wanted to see more fun chat and less depressing news plus regional programming and nostalgia, hence the hat being tipped to the dire and defunct *Pebble Mill at One* show.

Quays was an inconsequential, non-agenda setting, little-talked about, time-filling box-ticker in between the lunchtime news and afternoon game shows, which rarely troubled the ratings analysts. But today it had generated some heat following mainstream and social media trailing the appearance of the comedian one tabloid hailed as Britain's Most Hated Man.

And there he was, sitting in the corner of the green room, munching on a cardboard plate of quartered cheese-and-pickle sandwiches and a bowl of Cool Original Doritos, half-listening to his agent Ayesha Ritter who was in his face like a boxing trainer before the first round bell, briefing her man about the blows that would soon be raining down on him.

Ayesha had pugilistic steel in her blood. Her grandparents were Windrush generation migrants who came to England from Jamaica in the 1950s to rebuild postwar Britain and give their children a better life. They moved to Manchester's Moss Side and found work in the NHS but, thanks to their skin colour, not necessarily a better life.

Their daughter, Agnes, married a white electrician from Oldham, they moved to Withington, and had three children, the smartest of whom, Ayesha, gained an English degree at Edinburgh University.

During her four years in the Scottish capital, she worked behind the scenes at the annual comedy festival establishing valuable contacts and, on graduating, moved to London to work for the talent management firm, Grin. It was there one of her acts, fellow Mancunian Sarina McCall, fell instantly in love with Ayesha's cutting wit, don't-bullshit-me attitude, golden brown skin, high-cheekboned face and long, athletic legs. They eventually relocated north together.

SICK MICK

Her briefing to Mick today was carefully worded and short. Not unlike a West Wing staffer with Donald Trump. She knew there was little point in trying to provide him with a reasoned defence of Saturday's act, and absolutely no point in telling him to apologise because he was only going to say whatever came into his head. Especially after smoking that joint he was refusing to own up to, despite his eyes and his request for pickled onions and Minstrels arguing strongly for his guilt. She just had to impress on him the need to keep his answers brief and to the point, his line of defence consistent and not to get involved in arguments or go off on any wild flights of fancy. And definitely not to smile as though he was stoned.

She filled him in on the show hosts: Alan Staveley, a young-looking sixty-year-old with a dyed blond wedge haircut that refused to leave the 1980s, who, for more than two decades, had presented his own morning show with his wife Carol, but was forced to go solo when she had a breakdown.

The official line was that her health issues had been triggered by the menopause which impacted on her emotional ability to handle such a high pressure job. Showbiz journalists suggested Carol had become addicted to painkillers, but their readers put it down to something closer to home. A poll by the *Daily Star* showed that 90% of respondents believed her breakdown was almost certainly down to having to work with her husband—a conspiracy-theory loving pedant with a Christmas cracker sense of humour. As one reader put it, 'thirty minutes living with that smug **** would send me gaga, never mind thirty years.'

'He's so off-the-wall you never know what he's thinking,' Ayesha told Mick. 'But mostly he goes with his gut reaction. So act humble. If you come over at all macho he'll take you on to prove his alpha male credentials.'

His on-screen partner was Charlotte Channing, a fine-looking thirty-eight-year-old brunette, formerly a Sky News anchor, who took time off to have twins and never fully regained her place in the pecking order since two younger blondes grabbed the chance her maternity leave presented and ran with it.

'She's a professional yummy mummy who can't stop mentioning her two darling babies, so she'll keep bringing it back to how you've upset the royal family.'

'Have I?' asked Mick.

'You know what I mean. That's what they'll accuse you of. So just say you meant no harm to the family. The good news is she's far more savvy than Staveley and tends to side with the underdog. So make eye contact with her when you sit down. Get her to like you.'

'No chance of that,' said Mick.

SICK MICK

'You'll be fine. Just try not to say anything stupid.' They both grinned at each other knowing how low the chances were of that happening.

On set, Staveley and Channing were seated on a turquoise couch, with a matching rug separating them from a similarly-coloured guest settee. Joining Mick on that couch was right-wing rottweiler Audrey Woodington — a seventy-five-year-old former Tory Minister, ardent Catholic, staunch monarchist and professional virgin. She was such a font of compassion, such a profound proponent of the notion of live and let live, she had been sacked from the Cabinet after writing an anti-sodomy paper in which she proposed that any prisoner contracting a sexually transmitted disease in a British jail, including those who had been raped, should have an extra month added to their sentence. As proof of her empathetic nature in this time of national grieving she wore a long black dress. Joining Audrey on the guest couch was Eilish Murray, a thirty-six-year-old professor in Comedy Writing and Performance Studies at Salford University. The proud native of Inverness sported red pigtails and a tartan boiler suit, which befitted her chosen academic subject, but also a stern expression suggesting that even a young Lenny Bruce would have struggled to coax a smirk from her.

The hosts, both dressed in black, were in their spots

conversing with the producer through their ear-pieces Audrey and Eilish were seated at either end of the opposite sofa, scrolling through their phones, when Mick was walked on to the set by a runner and told to sit in between the women. He was wearing a dark blue polo shirt and jeans, having refused Ayesha's request to wear a black suit, arguing he might as well wear a bowler hat with the words PHONEY TOSSER written on it.

'Ta, love,' he said to the runner, and then, 'room for a big one?' as he planted his hefty frame between his fellow guests. 'Alright girls,' he said, before bursting into a chorus of 'clowns to the left of me jokers to the right, here I am, stuck in the middle with you.'

The response was colder than a polar vortex, causing Mick to mouth a silent 'oops' towards the show's hosts, with Channing returning a welcoming if wary smile, and Staveley completely ignoring him.

The show kicked-off with Channing announcing what was coming up: a look at the life of the Duke of Dorset through the eyes of a former butler who went from being accused of stealing personal effects from the royal household to a Reality TV sensation after publishing a best-selling biography, *What The Butler Saw But Never Touched*; a chat with the show's resident agony aunt about how to cope with the grief of seeing someone dying who you had never met but felt like you had known all of your life because you had seen them on the television a few times; and a celebrity chef giving tips on the tasty, and more importantly tasteful, snacks to rustle up if you are having people round to watch rolling news coverage of a royal coma.

'The first subject today, folks, is a serious one,' said Staveley, arching his eyebrows to let the audience know what he was about to say might shock them, but this was such a grave matter, Quays at One had a public duty to address it.

'You may have seen some of today's front pages which vent anger at comedian Mick O'Shea who, hours after news broke that His Grace was gravely ill, launched into a 'sick' routine—their words not mine— about the veteran royal, mocking not just him but the wider Windsor family. It's fair to say he has caused outrage across the land, and we have him with us today to explain why he thought The Nation's Great Grandfather's serious health condition was so funny.' The camera panned towards an expressionless Mick as Staveley continued.

'Now Mick, we had originally booked you on today's show to talk about the psyche of comedians following the tragic suicide of up-and-coming stand-up star, Tom Priest. But following what many are describing as a despicable rant against the hospitalised duke we've naturally changed the subject. Today's

Topic of the Day on Quays at One is: how low should comedians be allowed to go?

'I suppose the first question has to be why? Why did you do it?'

'Because I'm a comedian and I'm paid to make people laugh. Simple as,' Mick replied with a nonchalant shrug.

'But surely there are certain subjects at certain times that are plain out of bounds on taste grounds, and this was one of them?' retorted Staveley.

'Look, most of it was ad-libbed. I didn't sit down and write gags after hearing that a stray plank had bounced off old Blinko's bonce…'

'Old Blinko?' screeched Audrey so loudly it almost shattered the camera lens. 'A stray plank bounced off his bonce?' she shrieked even louder. 'Dear God, where is the respect!'

Staveley cut her dead: 'Please let him finish. You'll have plenty of time to have your say, Audrey.'

'Thanks,' Mick continued. 'I was saying that I hadn't prepared any gags about Blink, sorry the duke's accident, it was improv. I know my audience, they know me, and I guessed if I didn't give them my take on the story and all the enforced mourning we'll all be expected to take part in even if we aren't feeling sad, then I'd be, erm, copping out.'

It was Channing's turn. 'But didn't something

instinctively tell you, and I say this as a mother-of-two,' Staveley winced so hard it looked like he was having a mini-stroke. 'That a family is suffering here? An extended family, the British nation is suffering? Didn't you think to yourself, maybe I shouldn't add to the hurt?'

'The way this is coming out,' said Mick, starting a giddy, shoulder-shaking laugh, then checking himself and feigning a sombre expression, 'it looks like I'd interrupted News at Ten or something, to do a live broadcast to the nation because I wanted to slaughter the Royal Family. It wasn't like that. I was in my local comedy club. I knew the audience. They all knew me. It was like a gang sitting around their mate's house getting stone–' he checks himself, '–having a good time, and the big mouth, the class clown —me — just going off on one, playing for laughs.'

'So how come members of the audience were so affronted by what you were saying they walked out in disgust?' asked Staveley.

'Two did, a middle-aged couple, who were probably in the wrong place if I'm honest. That can happen during any show. They asked for a refund, and we gave them it.'

'But didn't that tell you that you had crossed a taste boundary and should leave it be?' said Channing.

'That's not how stand-up comedy works. If you're

getting laughs you carry on riffing on the subject until you run out of steam with it.'

'I'd like to bring former Conservative minister Audrey Woodington in here to get her take,' said Staveley. 'Audrey, what do you think about Mick's defence?'

'Incredible, appalling, treacherous. Do you need me to go on?' she trilled with the severest of frowns.

'Why not stick on a black cap and sentence me to death, love?' quipped Mick.

'In days gone by, young man, that is exactly what would have happened. And some might say that would be no bad thing,' said Audrey in her best headmistress tone. 'I had the unfortunate experience of hearing a recording of the act in its entirety yesterday and found it in staggeringly bad taste,' she added.

'Can I just say you didn't hear it in its entirety because whoever recorded it cut the bit when I said that I hoped the duke pulled through,' said Mick, coming over a tad smug.

'Bravo,' said Audrey, clapping. 'Was that before or after you joked about the king dying and coming back as your girlfriend's, erm, your girlfriend's…sorry I can't even bring myself to say it.'

'Tampon,' said Staveley with a David Brent-to-camera expression.

SICK MICK

'Anyway, my first thought was why was this comedy club open on the same night the nation had heard such terrible news?' Audrey continued. 'It should have been closed out of respect, not open to paying customers allowing the likes of him–' She stabbed a stubby index finger fiercely at Mick, '– to make money out of the duke's condition.'

'Your response, Mick?' asked Staveley.

'Yeah, I could ask her why she's sitting here slagging off my offensive act when she could be out laying flowers at Buckingham Palace or something. But I know the answer,' he rubs his thumb against his index and middle fingers. 'She'd rather sit here doing what she's just accused me of — making money.'

Audrey wailed, 'Well I never. The audacity,' and there was a deep groan in the green room, where Ayesha watched the PR disaster movie unfold on a monitor, through the middle and ring fingers of each hand.

'Let's hear from Eilish Murray, a professor in Comedy Writing and Performance Studies at Salford University,' said Channing. 'As an academic in this field, what are your thoughts on Mick's act and his defence of it?'

'Let me start by saying I've heard a recording of the segment in this routine that's being debated and the majority of it didn't make me laugh. Sorry,' she said to

Mick who stared at the camera with a deadpan expression and muttered, 'Harsh.'

'But in his defence, there should be no boundaries with live comedy in a club, unless the law is being broken. It's up to the audience to decide what is funny and what is offensive. And if a comedian's material offends then they should not buy into it,' said Eilish.

'But what *is* so funny about the prospect of a beloved senior royal possibly shuffling his mortal coil and heading off to his palace in the sky?' asked Staveley, creating a clip that would soon go viral thanks to the Accidental Partridge X account.

'Well, as Mark Twain noted, the source of humour is in sorrow. There is no joy in heaven,' replied Eilish. 'Laughing at violent misfortune actually goes back to the cavemen. The most successful form of comedy through the ages has been slapstick. Think Laurel and Hardy, The Three Stooges, Abbott and Costello. People falling through windows, pianos dropping on heads is what made early cinema so successful.'

'I've never heard such rubbish,' squawked Audrey. 'What has the gentle, family-friendly comedy of Laurel and Hardy got to do with mocking the sickness of an elderly duke and denigrating our king in the most personal and repulsive manner. The kindest thing I can say about this so-called comedian sitting next to me is he needs to see a psychiatrist.'

SICK MICK

'Nah, sod that,' said Mick. 'If I opened up to a shrink he'd nick my entire act and replace me within a week.'

'Come on, Mick, drop the macho act, and for once give a serious reply,' said Staveley.

'Ok, well first off, I don't think my act was repulsive,' Mick answered.

'That section where you talk about the reproductive genitalia of deceased kings and queens was worse than repulsive,' Audrey replied.

'It's only sex, love. Have you ever heard of it?' By now Ayesha had her head in her left hand, her right hand holding a Styrofoam glass of watery coffee she wished was a tumbler of neat Jameson's whisky.

Channing, conscious of the lunchtime hour, attempted to steer the conversation away from sex by saying, 'As a mother-of-two–' Staveley was now on the cusp of a full stroke. '–I'd like to ask you, Mick, if you were brought up in a family that disliked the Royals or did your family see itself as patriotic?'

Mick burst out laughing, then put his hand to his mouth and apologised.

'What is so funny about the notion of a family loving its country?' barked Audrey.

'Nothing,' said Mick. 'My dad turned into Long John Silver for his country. That's how much he loved it.'

'Sorry?' said Channing.

'You know, pieces of eight, pieces of eight,' Mick replied, the spliff really kicking in now.

'Pathetic,' said Audrey.

'No, he's more prosthetic than pathetic, actually,' said Mick, giving a military salute to the complete bemusement of everyone on the set.

'Where is this going?' asked Staveley.

'What's patriotism if it's not just liking the best things about your country?' said Mick. 'I happen to think our daft sense of humour is the best thing about Britain. A lot of people will be watching this asking why we've all of a sudden turned into Iran with the likes of the Ayatollah here–' He points at Audrey. '– telling us all what we can and can't laugh at.

'Anyone remember when some Islamic terrorists killed those French journalists for mocking Mohammed? We all defended their right to take the piss, sorry, 'pee' didn't we? We said these fanatics can't censor our humour. They can't tell us we can't make jokes about Allah. Didn't we? And Allah's a god, and a god beats a duke in the Top Trumps blasphemy set of cards.'

'He's making his point very strangely, Audrey, but he does have a point when he mentions the Charlie Hebdo killings,' Channing cut in. 'I'm sure you agreed with the sentiments behind the Je Suis Charlie t-shirts?'

'There is no comparison,' she shrieked back.

'Of course there is,' said Mick, 'Potato, po-tar-toe; tomato, to-mar-toe; Charlie Heb-do, Blinky Wind-so—'

Which was Audrey Woodington's cue to pull off her microphone, throw it onto the couch as she stood up, shake her head at Mick and then at Channing and Staveley, and storm off the set screeching, 'I'll have nothing further to do with this.'

She headed for the green room, picked up her coat and bag, shook her head again, this time at a trembling Ayesha, and made for the exit door where a crowd of protestors sprang into action, holding placards that bore anti-BBC sentiments and calls for Mick O'Shea to be banned.

Protestors who formed an orderly semi-circular huddled around Audrey Woodington as she stood before a young reporter with the Brit Talk logo on his microphone, enabling her to do a live link to London about how dirty she had felt sharing a couch with the despicable O'Shea. An interview which, like the crowd, had been pre-arranged. A nice, little, double-bubble earner, Audrey thought, when her lunchtime media work was complete.

8

MONDAY AFTERNOON

In the six months Sadie had worked at Harley Street's Hardman Clinic she had become an expert in the field of penises. We're talking Mastermind specialist subject level expertise thanks to her job of delivering Extracorporeal Shock Wave Therapy to affluent men with erectile dysfunction issues. They paid £350 to go into a sterile back room of the Hardman, take off their trousers and lay on rolled out paper on a leather treatment table. Then Sadie would glide in, surgically gloved up, lift the limp phallus, place several tissues underneath their shrivelled, armadillo-shelled nut sack, take hold of their shaft, grab a dildo-shaped handle wired to a Duolith SD1 Ultra Shockwave machine, and slowly pass it over the length of the flaccid member for twenty minutes, sending shockwaves through the skin in an attempt to break down atherosclerosis (a fatty plaque tissue that hardens the arteries) while encouraging the formation of new blood vessels, thus improving blood flow to the penis.

Complete a course of six visits to the Hardman for just over two grand and males previously found wanting in the love-making department would find themselves kicking down their front door, beating their bare chest and yelling, 'get up the stairs, love, King Dong's in town' before showing they were back to their youthful, pounding best. Well, that was the sales pitch anyway. But like everything else in the fields of experimental science, shock therapy and impaired sexual performance, results varied. Few of Sadie's clients were ever going to be doing a John Bindon—Princess Margaret's Cockney gangster boyfriend whose party trick was hanging five half-pint tankards from his stiffened joystick—in fact, few of the older ones were ever going to remotely live up to the name above the Hardman Clinic door. But none of them minded as they had nothing better to spend their money on than taking a punt at a miracle. At worst it was a nice half-hour spent in the company of an engaging young woman holding their cock as she gave it much-needed attention, while they laid back and fantasised. It certainly beat cultivating a prize marrow down the local allotment.

Some of them got off on the intimacy of the experience. Sadie could occasionally read in their twinkling eyes, as she held their manhood in her hands, the message: 'I know what you're thinking, missy: if you were a few years younger, you'd have that for lunch.' Which was not 100% inaccurate as Sadie was often thinking, at the time, whether to go for

SICK MICK

Pret a Manger's hoisin duck wrap or avocado and herb flatbread for lunch.

Others, embarrassed at putting on public show a todger whose virility was so impoverished it needed an electric shock to try to bring it back to life, couldn't wait for it to be over. The happy ending for them was pulling up their belted slacks and slipping on their tousled loafers when Sadie had left the room.

She never ceased to be amazed at the variety of specimens in the secret world of penises. Everyone seemed different, brimming with its own personality and back story.

Some were upward-curving like a banana, others arcing downwards like a chilli pepper. There were thick shafts and thin shafts. Some wide at the bottom and narrowing towards the top like a traffic cone, others slim-based and big-headed like a lump hammer. The small ones could look like acorns, gherkins or baby carrots, the big ones might be long and cold like a cucumber or thick and meaty like a salami. Some were as thin as asparagus, others as thick as an aubergine. Some were like deformed potatoes, ugly and lumpy, others like a chunk of gorgonzola, blue-veined and stinking.

She passed the time thinking up names for them. There was Michael Jackson, which had a different pigmentation from the rest of the body, and Eddie

Redmayne which was cute and freckled. A circumcised member was a Larry David, a shaved one a Bruce Willis and a hairy one, a Mick O'Shea.

She was thinking about Mick after finishing up with Donald Trump (fat, slimy with a discoloured head and a weird-looking foreskin that flopped about when a gust from the air conditioner hit it) and walking into the small garden at the back of the clinic with a freshly poured latte from the machine in the staff kitchen, to take a break.

It was a warm afternoon and the pocket of sunlight at the far end of the garden looked enticing, so she grabbed one of the comfy Lafuma recliner chairs, moved it out of the shade, dropped into it, kicked out the bottom bar with her heels and sank back into an almost horizontal position, letting the rays wash over her face like the first hit from a steaming power shower.

She had watched Mick on *Quays at One* on her phone, sitting alone on a bench in Regents Park, and thought the following: What a snooty bitch that Audrey Woodington is, Alan Staveley is on the spectrum, why would a woman who looked about forty wear red pigtails and a boiler suit? Who gives a shit how many kids Charlotte Channing has? And that Mick had definitely had a spliff before he went on. No doubt. The eyes. The overconfidence. The giggling.

SICK MICK

The turning of everything into a joke. She couldn't bear to look online to gauge the reaction, preferring to convince herself that he hadn't done too badly.

Sure, those who wanted him to lay prostrate on the studio rug begging for forgiveness would have been disappointed. But that was good, wasn't it? Made him look real. He had played for gags which probably wasn't the best move in the current, dark climate, especially the Blinky Wind-so bollocks. But hang on, he's a comedian, isn't he? Isn't that what he's supposed to do? Isn't that what he does all the time, whether he's on stage or off it? All these strangers ranting about him on TV, in the papers and on social media don't know him. They are judging someone they haven't got a clue about. They don't know that he spends most of his waking life trying to be funny because in his screwed-up head, being laughed at equates to being loved. With the upbringing he had, love was in short supply.

After his second year in infants school he had no mother to give him a hug, just a father whose heart, spirit, body and mind were broken, who couldn't show his only son how much he loved him. His dad's sister, Helen, did her best to help out, doing Vinny's shopping for him and cleaning the house, but she had her own family to look after and she worked as a carer. What affection she had to offer after a day filled with looking after everyone else, she gave to her own two sons.

So Mick had grown up feeling lonely and unloved with a father who adored his only child but, thanks to the soul-crushing hands that life kept dealing, had no way of showing him. Unless he'd had a few drinks and they would watch Father Ted or The Office together on the couch and he would hold his beaming son tightly to him as they rolled around laughing. That's why Mick associated laughter with love. He had seen how, when his dad was laughing, the shutters would drop and he could get close to him. He took that theory out into the world. If he could make the street, the class, the playground or the pub laugh, he'd be the popular character with all the mates. But at what cost?

Sadie had never met a more complex person. There were times that she could get him to open up, but once he felt he had given too much away, that he had allowed her to see too far inside him, an alarm would go off in his head and he would switch to self-deprecating humour. It was weird, she thought, seeing someone you know really well being characterised so inaccurately. This line they're throwing out about being a left-wing agitator could not have been further from the truth. Naturally, where he came from, he had no time for the people with power, whether that be the

SICK MICK

Royal Family, the Tories or that magistrate who gave him a suspended sentence for possessing a few grams of coke. But he was a working-class product of the most politicised city in England. What did they expect? When he could be bothered to cast a vote he gave it to Labour, but as he'd said to Sadie at the last general election, 'a serial killer could gun down every shopper in the frozen aisle of the Lidl on Park Road and he would still get elected round here if he wore a red rosette, so what's the point in me voting?'

Such apathy angered Vinny who, whenever he heard it, gave Mick a lecture about past generations of trade unionists who had sacrificed their jobs and their health to win rights and benefits that his cushy generation took for granted. Vinny was an old school socialist, his beliefs handed down to him from his father, Vic, who was a docker.

Ten years in the army diluted his socialism, but following his discharge after the Gulf War, where he was floored by shrapnel from a landmine that killed two of his mates, injured him in twenty-five places and required his left leg to be amputated from the knee down, the fire returned to his belly. As he was cold-shouldered out of the military, given a pitiful pension and told that his mental health issues were not down to Post Traumatic Stress Disorder but something lesser called Gulf War Illness, he questioned why he had ever been sucked in by all that For Queen and Country garbage. What had all that devotion to duty actually done for him? He became highly suspicious of the jingoistic voices on the right who spoke in bellicose tones and argued for aggression abroad, with no experience of the horrors of war. He developed a pathological hatred of Tony Blair when he joined George Bush in engineering another bloodbath in the Middle East. He grew to detest nationalist politicians like Donald Trump, Vladimir Putin, Benjamin Netanyahu and those Britain First enablers who perverted the notion of patriotism for their own ends, stoking the fires of hate against foreigners without knowing, or caring, about the consequences of their words.

Many times he had fantasised about showing these men, and they were nearly always men, exactly how their warmongering words played out. He would picture them alongside him in the desert with the Fourth Armoured Brigade chasing Saddam's Republican Guards out of Kuwait. They would be with him and his mates as they stampeded across the sand slaughtering Iraqis not much older than boys, howling like lunatics as they watched enemy tanks turn into bonfires of fire and smoke, hearing the pitiful screams from within the melting metal, swarming past corpses charred black through the effortless evisceration of the coalition's superior weaponry. They would then see a blast of white light and be thrown six feet in the air. And instead of Vinny's Geordie mate, Jezza, and his Scottish buddy, Alan, being blown to pieces, it would be the politicians. Instead of Vinny having his shin and foot torn from the rest of his leg and his body peppered with metal fragments it would be one of them, lying unconscious on the blood-drenched sand, their life ebbing away, only to be saved by courageous, quick-thinking comrades. Then being forced to live with the consequences of war for the rest of their lives.

These days, the loss of his leg was the least of Vinny's issues. Technological advances had given him a virtual bionic one. For the past few years stairs had become a doddle, there was no trace of a limp, he could jog. With enough whisky down him he'd even been known to attempt a Michael Jackson moonwalk. And if he ever wanted to jump a queue at a racecourse or an airport, he'd just whip up his trouser leg, frighten the officials with the sci-fi device staring back at them, and get the red carpet treatment.

When doctors in the early 90s had claimed he was suffering from Gulf War Illness due to anthrax and plague vaccinations before deployment, exposure to depleted uranium in tank shells, and inhalation of pollution from the burning Kuwaiti oil wells, Vinny just laughed. He knew that the cause of his illness was living with the guilt that he had survived while some of his mates hadn't. It led to unprompted aggression, constant debilitating fatigue, and moods so dark the shade of black had yet to be invented that could sufficiently describe them. He would have regular nightmares about being back in action, struggling to get away from a force he couldn't see, before waking up to find marks on his ex-wife Lynne's neck where his hands had been. Then the shame of what he had become kicked in and he would shut himself away in the upstairs box room, drinking to numb the pain. But that would only make tears gush from his eyes and fill him with an even deeper self-loathing.

A passing cloud blocked out the sun from Sadie's face and the fall in temperature made her sit upright and zip up the fleece she was wearing above her dark blue scrub top. She thought again of Mick's TV appearance, trying to recall the line he had said that had set alarm bells ringing. It came to her. Something about Long John Silver and pieces of eight. Why had he gone there? Why mention Vinny losing his leg? Great comeback but if Vinny had heard it the triggering could be lethal. Had he been watching the show, she wondered. She checked her watch. Ten past three. She still had five minutes before Danny de Vito (miniscule in length but wide, hairless and funny) arrived. She pulled out her phone, went to favourites and tapped on Vinny. She knew it was a long shot as he would be in the pub by now, especially as it was Mad Monday. The karaoke would be blaring in Ranelagh's or Lanigan's or whatever crazy house opposite Liverpool's Central Station he had wandered into. She let it ring eight or nine times before ending the call and putting it away. She knew there was no point ringing Mick as Ayesha had banned him from answering the phone. So she began texting to tell him to check on his dad, when the phone went off in her hand. It was Vinny.

'Hi, just seeing if everything's okay,' she said, as her right ear took a cacophonous blast, the most distinguishable part being a male voice strangling Rhinestone Cowboy in the manner of a Vic Reeves pub singer.

'I can't hear you, love. I'm just walking out the pub now,' Vinny replied, the background din diminishing with each step away from his table to the door, much to the relief of Sadie's stinging cochlea.

'I can hear you now. Can you hear me?' Vinny asked, and although she could still hear Glen Campbell being assassinated in the background, it was clear enough.

'Yeah, listen. Have you heard from Mick?'

'No. He didn't come back last night. He probably

stayed at Robbo's. Was he on the telly today?'

'Erm, I think so. Why?'

'Well, strangers have been coming up to me in the pub wanting to shake my hand, telling me he's a hero. I even got two whiskies sent over. What was he on?'

'I, erm, can't remember to be honest. Something in Manchester. Wouldn't worry about it. You know Mick. The usual bollocks. Anyway listen, I've got to get back to work. It's dead on that you're getting free drinks bought, but don't have too many, right? It's only Monday.'

'I'll be fine, love. Thanks for ringing.'

Sadie gave out a huge sigh of relief and thought about finishing the text to Mick, but time was against her so she went back into the clinic to fondle Danny de Vito.

Vinny sucked in a gust of air, letting the buzz from the whiskies course through his veins. There is nothing, he thought, quite like walking from a boozer into the afternoon sun in a busy city centre watching people rush past, head down, going back to work or about their sober business while you're on your way to being half cut. You want to stop them, tell them to slow down, lighten up and come inside for a drink because life is just too short. That made him smile. Life's too short. Oh, how he finally knew the truth of that throwaway phrase.

SICK MICK

The smell of vinegar-soaked fish and chips from the Lobster Pot filled his nostrils reminding him that he hadn't eaten all day. Or had he had a couple of slices of toast for breakfast? It was hard to keep track these days. He knew that Mick and Sadie believed he was in the early stages of dementia but they were wrong. It was worse than that. Getting worse by the day in fact. When he had been diagnosed with cancer after his visit to Broadgreen Hospital, surgeons had removed the prostate and hoped they had caught it all. But it had spread into his lymph nodes and bones and there was not a great deal they could do, especially when he refused chemo and hormone therapy.

That was why his mind wasn't there most of the time. It was wandering. To no place in particular, but mostly to the day when he would have to tell his only son he was about to die and he would be left on his own. The guilt consumed him. Vinny blamed himself for Lynne leaving Mick motherless and now he would be leaving him fatherless too.

He had good mornings, afternoons, even days when everything seemed back to normal. Then it would creep up on him again and he'd feel brittle and helpless and angry. It was as though he had fog on his brain which was stealing his sharpness and putting him two seconds behind everyone else.

Coming into town on the 82 bus that lunchtime, he

had panicked as the driver opened the doors and looked at him. He fumbled in his pocket for change but that felt wrong and he didn't know why. He pulled his wallet out to grab a note when the driver spotted the top of his seniors' bus pass in a leather compartment and told him he didn't need to pay. The guilt and the cancer was closing him down, stealing his thoughts and his dignity.

Vinny realised he was blocking the Ranelagh Street pavement, started to walk towards the Lobster Pot lured by that deliciously pungent smell, then remembered he was sitting with his mates in the pub, turned and headed back into the mayhem.

It's Now Or Never was being strangled by an old guy in a beige camel-hair coat, with long sideburns, a thin black tie, shiny brown brogues and a studded earring, who genuinely believed his gyrating hips were turning-on the female drinkers. Vinny walked back across a laminate floor made gluey and squelchy by too many spilled drinks and over-bleached mops.

He took his seat at a table with two of his mates, Macker and The Pellet (so-called because his dad, who always had a skinhead, was nicknamed The Bullet), necked a whisky which stung his throat, then took a long swig of his all-day happy hour Madri lager to soothe it. He placed his pint glass on a beer mat and licked his lips. God, he felt good this afternoon. So he was dying. So what? Everyone is dying. It's just that some people like him have an earlier date chiselled into their headstone. What can you do about it? Sit at home drowning in self-pity, dragging everyone close to you under? Or be here, partying like there's no tomorrow, in the Scouse over-50s Ayia Napa?

Macker, who was fat, bald and rarely unhappy, leaned over and told Vinny he'd missed a treat while he was outside. Big Carla, the pub manager, had taken her blouse off to reveal a red bra the size of a hammock, which was holding up her massive mammaries, and below them several rolls of flesh whiter than the Arctic. She had grabbed the mic and told the pub that her friend Ashley needed cash to send her son to America for a brain operation and demanded everyone stick a fiver in her bra, with a kiss given out for a tenner and a tongue for a twenty. She then kicked her shoes off and switched into Tina Turner mode belting out *Proud Mary*. In between choruses of 'rolling on the river' she fixed her glare on men who had yet to put their hands down her bra and yelled, 'get up her you miserable mingebags. Are you frightened of a real woman?' Before shaking her breasts a la Tina and making the notes tumble to the floor like autumn leaves in Sefton Park.

Vinny grimaced, then looked at the group of women laughing coarsely on the table next to his, most of them with big hair, big handbags and big voices. They would all have flexed their larynxes by tea-time, making the floor theirs without a hint of self-consciousness, and whoever could nail Patsy Cline's 'Crazy' would be queen of the pub.

Horses were racing each other on lush green grass on the large wall screens, with the sound off, a substitute commentary being offered by men who spoke in whistles due to dodgy dentures, mostly cursing their luck.

As Brendan, the pub stud, strolled confidently towards the karaoke machine, two of the women on the next table nudged each other and pulled a face that said, I would. Brendan was a plasterer in his mid-fifties who sported a powder blue suit with a navy polo shirt done up to the top button, hands like shovels, long grey hair and the kind of swaggering confidence an Old Etonian assumes when he breezes on to a Russian oligarch's yacht.

His bright blue eyes oozed charm and his body language spoke of a devil-may-care attitude that would keep him attractive forever to a certain type of working-class woman. He picked up the mic and went effortlessly and tunefully into *Born to Run* grabbing the attention of every female in the pub over fifty. Which was every woman except the barmaids.

Vinny leant over to The Pellet, a tall, one-time half-decent centre-half for non-league club, Marine FC, who had proudly kept his trim, muscular frame intact, and said, 'he's a big, posing tosser, him,' to which Pellet replied, 'and you're a big jealous tosser, you.' Their mutual laughter was interrupted by a whippet-thin, hollow-eyed, twitching young man in a puffer coat that was two sizes too big trying to flog razor blades, sports socks and fish fingers from a black bin bag. Vinny waved him away, stood up, said, 'same again lads?' and moved to the bar. En route, an intense man with the build of a middleweight boxer in a black Fred Perry shirt, shook Vinny's hand, pulled his ear towards his mouth and shouted over Brendan's Bruce Springsteen, now sounding ropey as the high notes had kicked in, 'I saw your Mick today on the telly. Brilliant, mate. Brilliant. Tell him to keep telling the truth about this screwed-up country.'

Vinny smiled, pulled away from him and carried on to the bar, bemused. One barmaid was taking a big order, working three taps and two spirits optics at the same time. Another had gone to change a barrel so Vinny tried to catch the attention of the young barman at the end of the bar, who was being shown folded-up tee-shirts in cellophane wrappers with slogans like 'Eat The Rich,' 'F*** The Tories,' and 'Hasta La Victoria Siempre' emblazoned under that famously defiant picture of Che Guevara.

Vinny did a double-take when he saw the black tee-shirt the salesman was wearing. He shuffled towards him and leaned in to study it.

'Do you like it, mate?' The salesman asked. 'We've literally just made these. Cool aren't they? This fella's a proper ledge.'

Daubed across the front in bold white capital letters were the words *Je Suis Mick* above the snarling face that had graced the front of that morning's *Daily Mail*.

'Friggin' hell,' Vinny exclaimed, 'that Jesus Mick doesn't half look like my lad.'

9

MONDAY AFTERNOON

Within forty hours of a routine stand-up session at Liverpool's Laughter Bucket, relatively unknown Mick O'Shea had head-butted his way into the national consciousness.

#SickMick had been trending on X since that morning's *Daily Mail* front page followed by #JeSuisMick after his appearance on *Quays at One*. Anti-monarchist groups had adopted him as a symbol of defiance, Irish republicans hailed him a groundbreaking rebel up there with James Connolly and pro-independence Scots were calling him the new Braveheart. Which was a comparison made easier by the fact his long, unkempt hair, mad beard and general mountain man appearance made him look like he had followed Mel Gibson, wailing and cursing, into battle against Edward I.

The darling of the Left had also become the bete noire of the Right, with think tanks such as The Campaign For Common Sense labelling him 'an ugly manifestation of the anti-patriotic cancer attacking Britain's soul,' and Jeremy Clarkson posting that he wanted to see him 'paraded through the streets in the nude then publicly disembowelled like one of my Diddly Squat chickens.' His infamy had even spread abroad with *The New York Times* hailing him 'the latest enfant terrible of English comedy who epitomises the cultural fissures in a deeply-divided post-colonial, post-Brexit Britain.' All of this had flown over Mick's head, partly because he never read his reviews, but mainly because Ayesha, sensing he was one bad taste gag away from self-destruction, had nabbed his iPhone leaving him incommunicado.

After the *Quays at One* show she took him to a nearby Costa Coffee and tried her best to explain what was happening, and how he should respond. Her take was that the media was currently starved of any real news outside of the duke's coma after going into the same blanket censorship mode it had done when Queen Elizabeth II had died. However, there were a couple of big differences between the two events. Firstly, the duke was still alive and, second, his death, if it happened, would not feel anywhere near as traumatic as the Queen's because she had been the national mother figure for as long as the vast majority of British people could remember. So, unlike last time, there was now room in the British media for other stories once the initial shock had passed.

And Mick had become more than a story. He was a polariser. Culture wars had been raging in Britain for the past decade, dividing down political and generational lines, with the Right believing the Left wanted to cancel any voice that didn't obey the Pronoun Police, accept diversity quotas, welcome asylum-seekers with the door keys to five-star hotels or admit the world was burning to a cinder, and the Left believing the Right was on a Ku Klux Klan-style crusade to cancel anyone who challenged traditional orthodoxies.

Ayesha pointed out that other comedians had been sentenced to hanging in the court of popular opinion for offences against the monarchy, citing Danny Baker's post of a chimp leaving hospital when Harry and Meghan's mixed-race son was born, Jack Whitehall suggesting that the Queen had remained standing throughout a Diamond Jubilee boat trip because she'd caught a urinary infection from Prince Philip, and Frankie Boyle joking on *Mock the Week* that the one thing you would not hear Elizabeth II say during her Christmas broadcast was, 'I'm now so old that my pussy is haunted.'

Staying with the royal genitalia referencing, which was the gravest charge against Mick, Ayesha described how David Baddiel had once asked panellists on the tea-time BBC Radio 4 programme, *Don't Make Me Laugh*, to discuss the fact that the Queen has had sex at least four times. To which

Russell Kane replied, 'For me this is just a quadruple representation of why inherited power is so dangerous. Four times we have to think of Republicanism as we imagine four children emerging from Her Majesty's vulva.'

All of which made the moralisers apoplectic and led to calls for these so-called comedians to be burned at the stake. But in each case the hysteria soon subsided.

As Ayesha talked Mick through her thinking and strategy, she noticed that he was looking more distracted and disinterested than usual. Which was saying something. For the past couple of minutes he had been staring with a sad expression, at a point in the distance behind Ayesha's head.

'Are you okay?' she asked, but received no reply.

'Are you listening to anything that I'm telling you?' Again, no response. He just kept on staring behind her.

'I get it. Why listen to your agent outline a survival plan aimed at saving your entire career? It's not like you're deeply in the shit or anything, is it?'

'That breaks my heart, you know,' Mick said, pointing at a table near the coffee shop door. Ayesha turned around to see a middle-aged Downs Syndrome man, holding what looked like his father's hand, staring adoringly into his eyes, as the dad wiped smudges of cappuccino from around his son's mouth.

She instantly turned back to face Mick, fearing her gaze was intrusive.

'You can tell by those streaks of grey in the lad's hair that he's what, late forties?' asked Mick. 'And his dad is in his seventies. Imagine how much time and affection and protection he's given that boy throughout all of those years. Imagine all that effort and worrying that turned his hair snow white. Just look at the devotion between the two of them. That's pure love, isn't it? The purest of loves. It's beautiful.'

As he leaned towards Ayesha and lowered his voice she waited for a punchline that never came.

'But what happens to the poor lad in a few years when the dad dies?' Mick continued, his voice reduced to a slow whisper. 'The chances are his mum has already gone or will go soon. So where does that leave him?' He paused for a few seconds, staring intently at a bemused Ayesha, waiting for an answer.

'How devastated will he be when he finds there's no-one around to look after him and treat him and make allowances for the fact he's still really a child in a man's body? How will he exist without the only love he's ever known?'

Ayesha saw tears welling up in Mick's eyes and realised the image had hit him hard. Did he see himself there, she thought, as he waved at the two men who were leaving, the youngest one waving back while his dad opened the door and led him out.

There was a painful five second silence broken by Ayesha saying, 'I'm sorry. I didn't realise what you were thinking. You're right. There are more important things than wankers inventing outrage over a few of your gags.'

'I heard everything you said,' Mick answered as he turned and offered his full attention. 'And I'm with you. I'll lay low. I'll ask Robbo if I can stay with him for a couple of nights. Can you text Sadie telling her I'm fine and might come to London to stay with her?' Ayesha nodded, grabbed his hand and told him, 'it's all going to be fine you know. We can sort this. Honestly.'

As he drove the thirty-five miles back to Liverpool, Mick tried to process all the madness going on around him. Okay, he thought, I may have gone over the top with the royal sketch but the worst part of it came in response to that quilt and his missus who had walked out, which sent me off on one. How did those few minutes of jokes lead to this? How have I become a national hate figure on a par with the Yorkshire Ripper? Is the country losing its marbles like my dad? Is that what it is?

When he reached the Dingle he drove slowly up the hill on Park Road past the derelict Gaumont cinema, the Ancient Chapel of Toxteth, Lidl supermarket, the vape shop, dog groomer, florist, laptop fixer and the countless takeaways where pubs used to stand, past the top of Moses Street where he could see a crowd outside his house, then carried on the short distance to Robbo's in Morton Street where he parked the taxi.

He nipped into Tesco for two litres of vodka and two large bottles of tonic, having been assured by Robbo that he had the stash and they were set for an afternoon forgetting about all this crap. Which, thanks to large vodka-and-tonics and Camberwell carrot-sized spliffs, was what the pair were able to do.

It was no cliche to say Michael O'Shea and James Robson were like brothers. They could not have looked more different, with Robbo standing a mere 5'8" with cropped sandy blond hair and a body kept athletic due to regular runs along the banks of the Mersey. But both had grown up in the Dingle, attended the same primary and secondary schools and Robbo was one of the very few people who called Mick by his childhood nickname of Osher.

Both had spent their teenage years with only one parent, Robbo's father dying in a road accident when he was eleven, and both left school at sixteen, with few qualifications, even fewer prospects, drifting into apprenticeships that never lasted and ending up living off their wits. Which mainly involved cheap flights to non-EU countries where they would smuggle back cigarettes and spirits for the black market, and trips to other European cities to relieve their shops of their latest designer sports gear, re-selling it back home for profit.

Eventually they tapped into Liverpool's burgeoning tourist industry after taking a ride on the Magical Mystery Tour bus when they were stoned, and realising how easy it would be to pinch the guide's script and set up their own Fab Four taxi business. Robbo took to Ticket to Ride with a far greater appetite than Mick, who was happy to play the role of guide but could not be doing with the admin side of the business. As his comedy career took off he handed his share of the firm, which comprised two Hackney Cabs, to Robbo, with the agreement that he could keep on drawing a wage as a guide, and use the spare taxi when bookings were low.

By the time they had finished their second joint, and third triple vodka, a good forty-five minutes into their crap-forgetting session, the buzz was kicking in. Robbo was spread out flat across the couch telling the ceiling, and possibly Mick, of his plans to buy a third taxi and do Sick Mick tours.

'It would probably be best if you killed yourself and left a letter saying how you couldn't live with all the pain you'd caused. Or even better if you were murdered, because everyone would love you. I could arrange that, if you like. I'd do a cracking speech at the funeral. And the tours would be dead cost-effective as we'd hardly need any petrol, what with your entire life story being in the Dingle. What do you reckon?'

But Mick was locked into a deep conversation with Morticia and Robbo's dad, Jimmy, about whether astronauts will eventually wipe out life on other planets through giving them venereal disease, just as the conquistadors did with New World natives in the 16th century. Although with Morticia being a cat and Jimmy being a framed photo of a dead man on the mantelpiece, it was something of a one-way conversation. Which was one of Mick's favourite reasons for getting stoned. He could launch into an effortless stand-up act without any hecklers.

Mick and Robbo's symbiotic relationship hit peak weird when the two were getting high together. They would both float off on a magic carpet to the outer limits of their imagination, talking at each other, but never listening. This could go on for an hour then, almost by telepathy, they would tune into each other's thoughts and take a trip down memory lane to some childhood experience and laugh so hard they could feel cement-mixers churning in their guts.

Then they would hug, tell each other of their fraternal love, before shouting in an American accent, a la John Lennon, 'Where are we going, fellas?'

'To the top, Johnny.'

'Where's that fellas?'

'To the toppermost of the poppermost. Riiiiiight.'

They had yet to reach that state of climactic euphoria, although Mick, who had attacked the drugs and alcohol far more ravenously than usual, was well on the way to forgetting about all of his hefty baggage. As he had said to Robbo when his best mate asked what he fancied doing that afternoon, 'Well, I may as well get off my face as I've been ordered to hide it.'

Robbo lived alone in the two-up, two-down terrace, having split from his long-term partner and childhood sweetheart, Becky, the previous year. It was amicable but it still hurt, especially when she took their five-year-old son, Ethan, to live with her back at her mother's. There were nights when he ached for familiar noises in his family home but all he could hear was silence and all he could feel was solitude. The knocked-through living room and kitchen was unmistakably owned by a man who hadn't changed a thing since his life was turned upside down. A giant flat screen television permanently connected to an Xbox dominated. There was a beige patent leather couch with a matching armchair, the arms of both scarred with black rings. Previously, wooden coasters decorated with scenes from North Wales bought during the week in Llandudno when Ethan was conceived, had withstood the damage wrought by hot cups. But they had long been binned. The glass coffee table had not seen a squirt of Mr Muscle for eighteen months, just the occasional half-hearted wipe down with a dishcloth, hence the permanent brown and white smears made by splashes of curry and lines of coke. There was a dead rubber plant in the corner that had long ago expired through thirst, without Robbo realising it had passed to the great botanical garden in the sky. A cream, stained rug in the shape of a skinned sheep lay on the laminate floor, with matching laminated blinds on the window, coated in a centimetre of dust. On the walls, a black-and-white print of the Manhattan skyline was hung next to one of Liverpool's Three Graces and the mantelpiece bore silver-framed photos of Robbo's mum and dad and him, in a suit, beaming as he held Ethan at his christening.

On the other side of a crumb-encrusted, granite-effect worktop lay a sink full of unwashed dishes, two 12" Domino's pizza boxes housing a few crusts and a fridge that was empty save for a slab of cheese, half a bottle of on-the-turn milk, a shepherd's pie ready meal, two pieces of pita bread and three bottles of Staropramen lager. A plastic bag full of old clothes that Robbo had meant to take to the charity shop last month but never quite got round to, sat by the back door. All-in-all it was a sorry depiction of a life on pause waiting to be re-booted.

Ethan stayed with him every other weekend, and had been there the previous day, which was why toys were still strewn all over the carpet and the coffee table. Robbo would leave them exactly where his boy had dropped them, for days, because tidying them up jolted him back to reality.

Mick had picked up two dinosaur transformers and was marrying them off to each other, pretending to be a priest with a speech impediment, asking, 'D-do you t-t-take this tr-tr-tri-ce-ceratops to be y-your lawfully-w-wedded-wife, til getting t-t-twatted by an asteroid y-you do p-part?' when he spotted a gun on the floor.

'Woh, mate, is this Ethan's?' he said, picking it up and examining it.

'Yeah, it's a cap gun,' replied Robbo, still flat out on the couch.

'God I used to love these,' said Mick, firing it at Robbo, causing a loud crack and a plume of smoke that gave off a familiar whiff of sulphur which made Mick inhale deeply and grin.

'Ah, that smell, man. Takes me back to being a kid,' said Mick, examining it. 'They haven't half changed though. We had shitty plastic cowboy guns that fell apart and you had to cock them back to get a sound. But this is, like, fake aluminium or something. It looks real. Like a proper hit-man's piece of metal.' He fired it again at Robbo, who clutched his heart and made his eyes go gozzy, pretending he'd been hit.

'Yeah, it's illegal that, Osher,' said Robbo, sitting up. 'My uncle Terry, who works the New York cruise ships out of Southampton, brought it back for Ethan. It's a proper replica of a Beretta. They outlawed them in America after cops had fired on kids who were playing with them. Thought they were going to shoot up their school or something.

'Same in this country now. Cap guns are only allowed to be sold if they have bright markings on them, so they can make out they're toys. You get caught with that baby on you, you're up on a charge.'

Mick had tuned out after he heard the word Beretta, throwing himself onto the laminate floor, rolling over, pointing the gun at the door and letting off two more smoky cracks.

'The caps aren't like the paper ones in our day. They're plastic,' said Robbo. 'And they sit in a magazine in the gun handle, so you don't need to pull back the cock and let it go to get a sound. You just pull the trigger.'

Mick stood up and slipped the gun into the back of his trousers, pulling his shirt over it. Then walked to the door, pulled the fake Beretta out in one quick action, turned around, trained it on Robbo and screamed in a Jimmy Cagney voice, 'Put 'em up you dirty rat. Or so help me God, I'll fill you full of lead.'

Mick examined it again. 'It would be great having this in a packed chippy, wouldn't it? You could just stroll to the front of the queue pointing it at everyone, saying, I think you'll find I was here first. Then turn it on the server and say, calm as you like, Now, good man, stop what you're doing and prepare me a half-and-half curry with fried rice, if it's not too much trouble.'

'Talking of which I'm starving. Fancy a Chinese?' asked Mick.

'I could murder a salt 'n' pepper chicken.'

'I'll get some gear from our house and pick one up from Chiu's on the way back?'

'Hang on, Osher, didn't you say there was a load of reporters hanging around outside your dad's?'

'Yeah, so what?'

'And your agent's told you to lie low?'

'How is me going to a drawer in my own bedroom to pick up a fresh pair of undies not lying low? I can handle them.'

'Okay, well you know you can kip here for as long as you want, don't you?' said Robbo.

'Thanks, mate. Ayesha's telling me to get out of Liverpool for a bit. Go and stay with Sadie in London until it all dies down. But I don't want to leave my

SICK MICK

dad.'

'Don't worry about Vinny, lad. He can look after himself.'

'Nah, you don't know what he's like lately. I've seen a change in him. He's always depressed and he's become really forgetful. In fact, he called me Robbo twice in the same conversation yesterday. I asked him if his eyesight was going and that's why he was mistaking me for an ugly little tithead, but he just stared at me. Didn't laugh or correct himself or anything.

'His mum had early onset dementia, you know? Went loopy while she was still in her fifties. So I Googled it and they reckon it's the one type of dementia that's most linked to your genes. I was going to have a word with the doctor this week, but with all this crap going on…'

His voice trailed off and Robbo stepped forward, gave him a hug and said, 'Listen mate, you need to sort your own shit out first.'

As Mick walked to Park Road then into Moses Street, the late afternoon sun that hung above the Mersey temporarily blinded him. He narrowed his eyes and looked down the left-hand side of the street to his house, where a comical scene involving a gang of teenage hoodies on mountain bikes and a dozen members of His Majesty's Press pack was unfolding.

One hoodie had done a wheelie with his bike onto the bonnet of a Vauxhall Corsa, and a man in a suit was shouting at him in a southern accent to remove it or he would ring the police. A cameraman with headphones around his neck was attempting to wrestle back a boom mic from another hoodie, as a woman in a dark suit ran from a car parked on the other side of the road to help him.

When Mick strolled past the big recycling bins at the top of the street and into general view there was a pause as all eyes turned in his direction. The hoodies began whistling and clapping, and five car doors opened with photographers and reporters rushed towards him.

'Have I missed something?' said Mick, getting out his house keys and barging through the scrum as cameras clucked and flashed, random questions were fired at him and a hoodie broke off from whistling to yell, 'Go 'ed Mick, batter the beauts. We'll help ya.'

Mick reached his doorstep, turned and, towering above the gathering ruck who were breathlessly thrusting recorders and cameras towards his face, said, 'I've been told to say nothing, folks. So I'm sorry, but I can't help you.'

'Just tell them to fuck off,' screamed the hoodie who had now de-wheelied from the Corsa.

SICK MICK

'Don't you think you should apologise to the Royal family, Mr O'Shea,' asked a reporter.

'I think they might have other things on their minds right now, don't you reckon?' Mick replied as he turned to put the key in the door.

'What do you say to those who are calling you sick?'

'I eat up all my greens so I haven't been sick for ages.'

'Are you too scared to answer to the public?'

He shook his head at that one, decided not to bite, pushed open the door and shouted, 'Dad, you home?' but his question was met with silence.

As he shut the door he spotted three envelopes, each with his name written on the front in biro, lying on the mat at his feet. He picked one up and, as he ripped it open, a card fell into his hand bearing the words: Harry Carlisle, Reporter, *The Sun*. In the envelope was a note that read:

We're on your side Mick and we are prepared to pay a lot of money for an exclusive interview with you. Give me a call. Thanks, Harry.

He threw it to the floor, his eyes and nose scrunching up and his mouth curling in disgust at the thought of spilling his guts to them. The offer of the bribe left him feeling violated, infected, like monkeypox had been spat through his door. He wanted to douse the hall in bleach and scrub it clean. But mostly he wanted to ram the card so far up Harry Carlisle's arse it would bleed.

He climbed the stairs to gather some fresh clothes and a toothbrush, the words 'are you too scared' ringing in his head, when the doorbell rang. Then rang again. Then a clipped and confident male voice, the kind that was very common in the apres-ski bars of Verbier but not that widely heard in Dingle's Holy Land, boomed through the letter-box.

'Mick, my friend, why don't you come out and give us your take on this story? We're here to help you. I'm not lying, mate. Come and tell us what you're thinking.'

He threw the kitbag he had pulled from his wardrobe across the room, kicked the bed and uttered in a low, angry voice as he wiped his sweating brow with a white hankie he'd found on the bedside table: 'Here to help? On my side? Tell us what you're thinking. O-fucking-kay fellas.'

He threw off his jacket, ran downstairs taking them two at a time, opened the door and burst onto the street, staring down at the Press pack as it moved towards him, then, waving the hankie, he launched into an impromptu impersonation of Al Pacino in *Dog Day Afternoon*.

He pointed at the nearest cameraman and

screamed, 'What's he doing? Go back there, man. He wants to kill me so bad he can taste it. Attica, Attica, Attica. Remember Attica, huh?'

The reporters and photographers scattered into the road, some hiding behind cars, struggling to comprehend the image of a deranged yeti bombing around the pavement, scowling and screaming the word 'Attica' at them.

They clearly weren't familiar with Sidney Lumet's body of work, so the impersonation of Pacino's classic improvisation scene outside the Chase Manhattan bank was wasted on them. Mick's shouting, plus the cheers from the hoodies, drew neighbours out onto their steps, giving him the audience he craved, encouraging him to shout 'Attica' even louder.

As he marched up and down the pavement, with the Press holding their ground on the road, he felt something uncomfortable in his lower back, reached for it and, realising it was Ethan's toy gun, fired the fake Beretta into the sky, giving off three loud cracks in time to his chants of 'Attica, Attica, Attica' as a plume of smoke hung in the air.

The entire Press pack ducked, two women reporters and one man screamed, then they stampeded en masse to the top of the road, most swearing and one shouting back, 'don't shoot, don't shoot!'

The hoodies were now having such a ball the centre

of Moses Street had turned into a mountain bike disco. They were doing wheelies, bunny hops, firecrackers and end-ohs, wailing like a pack of mad dogs in appreciation of Mick's spectacular floor show.

Seeing the enemy had fled, Mick put his arms in the air and yelled, 'yeee-ess' at the hoodies and neighbours who were now giving him a round of applause, before slowly walking back into the house, laughing.

At the top of the road, taking cover behind the recycling bins, the reporters let the shock subside then, one after the other, hit their phones.

10

MONDAY EVENING

Vinny jumped down from the 82 bus onto the pavement outside Tesco a bit too sharpish, the phantom pain sensation in his left leg shooting to his groin and making his head feel like it had been kicked by a horse. This confusion in nervous system signals between his spinal cord and brain had been regular in the first few months, after his prosthetic leg had been fitted and the nerves in his stump were rewiring, but rarely happened these days. Apart from when he was pie-eyed after a day on the lash and, instead of his brain registering that its owner was sixty-two with a fake lower limb, believed he was a young Michael Flatley inventing Riverdance.

The shock and soreness made him put less weight on his amputated leg so he limped as he crossed at the traffic lights on Park Road, forcing a middle-aged woman who knew him to ask if he was okay and a neighbour in his thirties offering to walk him down the hill to his house. To say everyone looked out for each other in this part of the world might sound as cliched as claiming there was a comedian born on every street corner, but it was true. The first bit of the sentence, that is.

Vinny, who had lived in The Holy Land all of his life, was widely respected for the uncomplaining way he had lost a leg fighting for his country and brought up a son on his own. It was a respect showered also on that son who had become something of a local hero for working tirelessly for the south Liverpool food bank, sitting for hours with the lonely, and raising the cash to buy dozens of new football kits for youngsters whose families were on benefits.

Vinny, having refused the kindly neighbour's help, limped the short distance to Moses Street, thinking he would need to take the edge off this pain with a good slug from that bottle of Grant's whisky in the kitchen, when he was confronted with a scene straight out of *CSI: Vegas*.

Two police vans blocked the street five houses from Park Road, and armed officers were preventing anyone from walking down either pavement. Between Vinny and the vans was a thirty-strong mob made up mostly of youths baiting gunmen in protective clothing, who pointed their automatic rifles at the floor. For a second he thought he was back in Belfast in the 1980s.

As he reached the vans, he could see that twenty yards further down the hill two more were parked, with officers stopping anyone getting past them, and in between were half-a-dozen crouched police in

Kevlar helmets, NOMEX balaclavas and goggles, pointing Heckler and Koch carbines at the door and windows of his house.

He pinched his neck hard to see if he was dreaming or had overdone his meds and was hallucinating, but all he felt was a sting.

Two officers moved slowly around their colleagues to Vinny's front door, one of them kicking it with his right boot while keeping his Heckler and Koch trained at chest height, yelling, 'Open up, armed police. Come out and show your hands. Do it now.'

Vinny pushed his way through the mob to the two coppers guarding the pavement and screamed, 'That's my house! What are you doing?' But one of them pushed him backwards, causing him to lose balance and fall to the floor, which in turn caused the mob to charge them, screaming abuse, and three teenagers to yell, 'That is his house!'

As two officers walked towards the front door with a red 16kg, hardened steel battering ram, the ruckus made Inspector Helen McAndrew, the senior Authorised Firearms Officer in charge of the operation, raise a hand to the ram-raiders and walk towards Vinny, who had now regained his balance and looked like he was about to swing a punch at the copper who had floored him.

'Let him through,' she shouted.

The two armed police parted and Vinny, dusting down the back of his trouser leg and giving the young copper who had knocked him over a death stare, limped towards the tall, thick-set Inspector McAndrew and asked, 'What in God's name is going on?'

'Do you live at number 15 Moses Street, sir?' asked McAndrew.

'Yes. Why?'

'Can you tell me your name?'

'Vincent O'Shea. Why?'

'Does anyone else live with you?'

'Yes. My son. Michael. Please tell me what is going on here.'

'Do you know where he is?'

'No I don't. Why do you want to know?'

'Oh, I'm a big fan of shoot 'em up movies and I'd like his autograph,' she hammed.

'What?'

'Mr O'Shea, I have a warrant to inspect your property. We have evidence that suggests someone fitting your son's description came out of your house this afternoon and used a firearm in the street.'

Vinny froze. Surely not, he thought. No way.

'What kind of firearm?' he asked with a nervous twitch.

'A handgun.'

Jesus Christ, thought Vinny. I've brought this all on

him.

'And have you, erm, found it?'

'No, because your son—if he is inside your house—isn't opening the door. Which is why we're about to smash it into pieces and ask those lovely teenagers up there if they want some early bonfire wood, unless you would like to open it for us.'

'Of course. Sure,' he said, fumbling through his coat pocket for his keys and limping towards the house, his body turning cold and his head feeling like the horse who kicked it before had brought a few equine friends around for a second go and they were hammering his skull with their hooves.

Vinny opened the door, shouted out his son's name in vain, walked down the hallway into the living room and sat down in his armchair, thinking through the possibilities, dreading them finding the gun, gobsmacked at Mick's stupidity.

The armed police split off in pairs and entered, rifles first, each room in the house, shouting 'clear' when no sign of activity was evident.

'Thorough search,' Inspector McAndrew shouted upstairs before following Vinny into the living room, seeing he had turned ashen, and asking if he was okay. 'I apologise if one of my men pushed you over just then but there was an aggressive crowd surrounding him and this is a serious situation.'

'I'm alright,' said Vinny.

'I noticed you were limping,' said McAndrew, her inquiring tone suggesting she was more than a little concerned about an ambulance-chasing lawyer contacting him to point out that where there's blame there's a claim.

'Yeah, it's this. I had a bit of a reaction before,' Vinny replied, pulling up his left trouser leg to reveal his prosthetic, and regretting it instantly when the follow-up question landed.

'Oh, I see. How did you end up with that?'

'Erm, an accident. A few years back. Don't like to talk about it, you know.'

'Of course,' McAndrew replied, the uncomfortable silence broken when one of the officers walked into the room holding up the fake Beretta in his gloved hand.

'Found it on his bed. It's a toy ma'am. A cap gun I think they're called,' he said as McAndrew stared at it, shaking her head and Vinny stood up, the relief making him grin like an imbecile.

'Bag it up and continue the search for anything dodgy or illegal that may have put him in the state of mind to terrify half the Northern Press pack,' she said.

'Illegal? What?' asked Vinny. 'Are you saying our Mick acting the goat with that toy gun is illegal?'

'It's an imitation firearm. Anyone using one in

public in a threatening manner, as your son was, can be looking at a few years jail. Do you know where he got it from?'

Vinny's relief subsided and he slumped back into his armchair shaking his head.

'Well if I were you, I'd try to find him and tell him to turn himself in before a man-hunt is launched.'

'A man-hunt? For having a cap gun? Jesus.'

The armed officers gathered outside the living room door and told McAndrew that the house was clean.

'Right, back to the vans. Tell the mob showtime is over and clear the street,' McAndrew said, before turning to Vinny. 'Where is he likely to be? Does he have a partner?'

'Yeah but she's in London.'

'Family?'

'He doesn't have any. Mother left. No brothers or sisters.'

'Friends?'

'Oh, he's got loads of them. Half the Dingle. Good luck getting them to help you.'

'Mr O'Shea, this really is serious. You'll be paid a visit from detectives very soon asking for all of his contact details. If you don't cooperate, or if you withhold information, you could be deemed an accessory to his crime. Which is why I recommend you make some phone calls to let your son know he has to hand himself in. There is going to be a lot of national publicity about this. Have you been watching the TV today?'

'No, I tend not to.'

She spied the remote control on the arm of the sofa, leant down and picked it up.

'May I?' she asked, pointing it at the television. Vinny nodded, she switched it on and went through the news channels until she landed on Brit Talk, which was showing an advert for a budget cremation plan.

'I think you'll find that all this channel has talked about for two days is your son and his comedy act. Wait until they cop a load of his latest Rambo impression. Good day, Mr O'Shea,' she said, putting the TV controls down, walking into the hall and out through the front door.

Vinny moved towards the window, opened a slat in the Venetian blinds, looked out to the street and watched for three minutes as the four police vans drove up towards Park Road, much to the disappointment of the youths who had enjoyed a good half-hour's cop-baiting.

He limped into the hall, put the bolt on the front door and painfully climbed the stairs before walking along the landing to Mick's room. He picked up his desk chair, took it back to the landing and placed it under the entrance to the loft, then stood on it and pulled down a handle which opened the hatch and sent down a ladder.

He moved the chair, climbed the ladder, wincing in pain as he went, before pulling a light cord, and crawling on his belly, each hand on a joist, towards a pile of cardboard boxes which he moved out of the way enabling him to reach a padlocked metal tool box jammed up against a rafter.

He grabbed the box, entered his four birthday digits on the keypad, 1411, and pulled the box open. The sight that greeted him made his head and shoulders drop with relief.

'Thank Christ for that,' he muttered, before grabbing the Browning Hi-Power, single action, semi-automatic pistol he'd smuggled back from Kuwait when his role in Operation Desert Storm had come to a sudden end.

'Thank Christ for that,' he said again before planting a kiss on the cold steel.

11

MONDAY EVENING

'Fuck, fuck, fuck, fuck, fucking fuckety fuck,' erupted Lance Fleury, kicking back his desk chair, standing up and lashing a stress ball bearing the words Poke Your Woke Up Your Ass at the person who had delivered the crushing news.

'Th-this isn't as bad as it seems,' stuttered Ivo, the cowering trainee Brit Talk producer, who looked like the resident punchline in a bad sitcom about young techno geeks.

'Of course it's fucking bad news you fresh out of Poxbridge tool. We had the bastard bang to rights. The ratings would have gone off the scale. And you drop this on me fifteen minutes before I'm about to go on air?' yelled Fleury, picking up a Taxation Is Theft ball from his desk and throwing it even harder at Ivo, hitting him flush on his retro, square-lensed, tortoiseshell glasses.

It was fair to say these stress balls weren't doing their job.

'Right, go and get Panda,' barked Fleury, sitting on the edge of his desk, face contorted into that of a mad-eyed Māori warrior mid-Haka.

'Sorry? Panda?'

'What?'

'Who is, erm, Panda?'

'Fucking Chi Chi from the London Zoo, who do you think, you dozy prick?' he screamed, his neck veins bulging and his eyes looking as though they were about to pop out of his face and baptise Ivo's pristine Stop Ocean Plastic tee-shirt with two trails of chunky slime.

'Pandora Fitzroy-Price. Tonight's star guest. Who the fuck gave you a job? Is pater's mate on the fucking board? Get me Panda then get Richard Hollister, a proper producer, tell him we have an emergency, then fuck off and glue your face to the M25 or whatever you net zero scruffy cunts do when you're not jerking off on Greta Thunberg.'

What had dropped was a statement from the Merseyside Police Press Office. It read:

> Following an incident today at 5.10pm in Moses Street, Liverpool 8, armed officers attended the scene where they recovered a toy Beretta gun from a property. We urge the individual who was seen using this imitation firearm in a public place to urgently contact his nearest police station.

Fleury stood up and paced around the small office that looked out onto the newsroom, adorned with framed photos of him shaking hands with Donald Trump, Vladimir Putin and Jair Bolsonaro, plus a huge Make United Kingdom Great Again election poster featuring starving Ethiopians holding begging bowls, with an X over each face, next to the slogan CHARITY BEGINS AT HOME, and a *Daily Mirror* front page whose headline asked, under a photograph of Fleury aggressively stabbing a finger at a female Albanian *Big Issue* seller in an Oxford Street shop doorway: IS THIS THE VILEST MAN IN BRITAIN?

Three minutes earlier he had been psyching himself up to deliver a show that, in his view, could have cemented his reputation as the king of evening TV. Possibly even won him a Royal Television Society Award. Or a knighthood.

When he and Panda had arrived from the Waldorf late that morning, they had worked out a killer game plan. Her poodle, Tory MP Adrian Jenkins, would be paid to announce, exclusively, that he was putting forward a motion in the Commons calling for an updating of the offence of high treason to be laid on the statute books, which would outlaw the kind of hate-filled attack on the monarchy that Mick O'Shea had delivered.

They would have had a general discussion on the couch about treachery, bringing in a trumped-up constitutional expert who would eventually admit that

O'Shea could have committed treason. The logic being that, due to existential threats currently posed to Britain by totalitarian dictators and Islamic terrorists, plus the violent verbal assaults on social media against critics of O'Shea at a time when national defences were low due to the ailing health of a senior royal, he was undoubtedly a traitor.

When the Brit Talk cameraman sent over a video at 5.15pm of Mick firing his gun in Moses Street as the fleeing media ran for their lives, Fleury thought all his Kristallnachts had come at once. There was now no doubt that this deranged individual was a danger to society. That he was evidently someone who despised everything about this country and wanted to destroy our way of life.

A Modern Day Lord Haw-Haw. Or, as Fleury was now christening him, after patting his own back so much it became numb, Lord Ha-Ha.

He could see the headlines in tomorrow's *Express, Sun, Mail* and *Telegraph,* praising him to the heavens for his genius in capturing the zeitgeist with that moniker and his exemplary piece of public service broadcasting in forensically analysing why O'Shea should be tried for high treason. Only for the police to kill the story.

It didn't make sense. Brit Talk technicians had blown up stills of the pistol and hired what they believed was an expert to confirm it was undoubtedly a Beretta 84FS Cheetah semi-automatic. So how could the police claim it was a toy?

Were they in on it? Had they planted the fake gun to get O'Shea off the hook for fear of inciting the notoriously irascible residents of Liverpool 8 into a riot? He wouldn't put it past them. Would they soon be taking the knee at a Scouse Comedians Matter rally? Bastards, he thought. They've done this to screw me over.

Panda breezed through the open door looking the epitome of calm. 'We've got this,' she told him.

'Really? It doesn't feel that way.'

'My contact in the north tells me O'Shea has gone on the run. Police are trying to track him down, but no-one is giving him up. He's now looking at jail time for possessing an imitation firearm. The longer he goes without handing himself in the worse it gets for him. But the better it is for us because until they charge him, we can say what the hell we like about him.'

Fleury sank into the blue, armless reception couch and rubbed his chin. 'You know, you might just be right. We can still call for the treason law to be updated, still ask our expert if they believe he is guilty of it and still say this guy needs to be locked up. Because he's shown he literally does. In fact, wait a minute, William Joyce went on the run too.'

'Who?' asked Panda.

'Haw-Haw. He went into hiding in North Germany after Hitler killed himself. Stayed there until British soldiers shot him in the leg. Then dragged him back home where he was hanged for treason. So, of course it still works. Yes. Lord Ha-Ha is on the run. And we're going after him. We're geniuses, Panda. Geniuses. How long until we're on?'

'Just over ten minutes.'

'Right, I'll rejig my intro, you get Hollister to bring the other guests up to speed. We need to own this, own this, own this,' he barked, banging the desk three times.

'So why don't we offer a reward for information leading to O'Shea's arrest? We'd be the first to do so,' said Panda.

'Great idea. I can't see Hollister agreeing, though. He'll need to get that signed off upstairs in triplicate. Why don't we do it off our own bat? Great publicity for the show and your website. Besides, you never pay. You just bullshit whoever informs on him that you knew about it already.'

'Sure, why not?' Panda said hesitantly.

'Right, let's get the bastard. Go.'

Up in Liverpool, Vinny was seated on a hard chair at the Formica table in his darkened kitchen, slugging his third Grant's whisky, pushing an unwanted ham and piccalilli sandwich around a plate and trying to make sense of what was left of his life.

The detectives had called around but he was of no help to them. No, Vinny didn't know where Mick had got his cap gun from, where his thirty-year-old adult son now was, what he intended to do next, or if he had any more inflammatory anti-royal material planned. But what he did know, he told them, was that somewhere in the city there was probably a mini-market being held-up, or an innocent drinker in a pub being shot at as they spoke, and the arseholes doing the firing were using real guns. Shouldn't you be out catching them?

To be fair to the detectives, they appeared embarrassed that they were trying to track down the owner of a kid's gun. Their presence hadn't bothered Vinny, but the words from Inspector McAndrew about him being a potential accessory to his son's crime had. How little she knew. Of course he was an accessory. Everything he'd done since coming back from Kuwait had shaped Mick's fate for the worse.

He had been an accessory to a boy's life deprived of normality. Because he had turned into a selfish, self-pitying shell incapable of dealing with emotion. His mood swings, his despair, his self-loathing had denied his son a mother, a father, a home. That's why he is out there screaming for attention. A lovely lad whose only crime was wanting the affection his parents couldn't give him, trying to get it the only way he knew. Acting the fool. And look where it got him. A few years in jail, that police woman had said. But he had only months left. Would Mick be inside when he died? Would he be sat in the front row at Springwood crematorium, handcuffed to a prison officer, unable to wipe away his tears. I'm an accessory, all right, thought Vinny. An accessory to screwing up the life of the only person I truly love.

The hard seat was making his back ache and the sandwich didn't interest him, so he picked up the bottle of Grant's and his glass, climbed out of the chair like an old man in a care home, limped from the kitchen into the living-room and fell into his armchair.

He placed the whisky bottle on the floor, picked up the TV controls from the arm of his chair and turned up the volume to hear a jazzed-up version of Jerusalem accompanying the opening credits to Brit Talk's Lance Fleury Tonight. A memory came back of the policewoman telling him that all this channel had been talking about for the past two days was Mick. So he poured himself another and watched.

In the blue studio, Fleury was seated behind a desk with a screen to the left of his head which bore the same snarling image of Mick that had been plastered on the front of that morning's *Daily Mail*, which Vinny had seen in the pub on the tee-shirt. Above the snarl were the words: SICK MICK GOES TONTO.

Seated to Fleury's right, on a blue couch, were Panda Fitzroy-Price and Darpita Harper, a lecturer from the online law degree company The University of Chambers, who was billed as a constitutional law expert, but was mainly a regular on Brit Talk because she was Asian (thus offering a shield to white presenters denouncing immigration) very attractive (large breasts that hadn't seen surgery, flirty eyes, glowing skin, never off her Peloton) and would basically say anything they wanted her to as she was grateful for the exposure.

Despite Fleury having been interviewed about Mick three times since Saturday, and posting a running social media commentary of his various states of anger, this was the first time he'd had the chance to devote a full show to the subject.

He repeated a few of the worst-taste gags from Mick's Laughter Bucket set and played a clip on the screen from Quays at One which ended with the 'potato, po-tar-toe; tomato, to-mar-toe; Charlie Hebdo, Blinky Wind-so...' and Audrey Woodington storming off the set.

'I can't tell you how much this enraged me,' Fleury bawled at the camera. 'Audrey Woodington is not just a personal friend and a revered politician who has served her country with distinction, she is a seventy-five-year-old lady. Look how upset the yobbish O'Shea has made her. I have never seen anything so sickening on the television since a member of the Sex Pistols called Bill Grundy a dirty old man, then repeated it using the b-word.

'What was the BBC thinking, a mere thirty-six-hours after O'Shea had launched an obscene attack on a potentially dying senior royal? Even worse, in my eyes, why did they provide him with a lefty lecturer from the university of Toytown to back up his filth, leaving Audrey Woodington outnumbered, intimidated and bullied. Small wonder she stormed off, too upset to carry on. Yet again the BBC has a lot to answer for. As do the police. Watch this. Here is O'Shea around five o'clock today outside his house in Liverpool.'

The camera panned back to the screen showing footage of Mick doing his shoot 'em up Attica act in Moses Street as journalists fled in panic, their screams made louder by Brit Talk engineers for added effect.

'In any civilised country, somebody inciting hatred against the head of state and his family, who then acted in a bizarre manner, seemingly under the influence of mind-altering substances, before putting the fear of God with a gun into reporters who are simply doing their job, would by now be behind bars and made to stay there for a very long time.

'But because we live in Woke Britannia, the only time hate speech is deemed to be an offence is when it is spoken by those of us on the right of politics. It is an absolute disgrace. Just look at this statement from Merseyside Police about O'Shea, issued in the past hour.'

The statement flashed up on the screen and he read it out. Then repeated the final sentence in a tone somewhere between a nursery school teacher telling off a toddler for eating plasticine and a supermarket announcer asking a member of staff to open till six: We urge the individual who was seen using this imitation firearm in a public place to urgently contact his nearest police station.

'It's as though he's left a tube of Pringles at a train buffet counter and the guard has come on the Tannoy asking him politely to go back and pick it up,' said Fleury. 'It's pathetic. Pathetic. Merseyside Police should be scouring the streets for him, because regardless of whether the gun he brandished was fake or real, he has committed a serious offence punishable by prison. And he is a danger to society on more than one level.

'You see, just as I don't believe this so-called comedian should have been free to terrify journalists with a fake gun, neither do I believe the BBC should have been allowed to invite him on to a show to justify his warped hatred towards the monarchy at a time of public grieving.

'I believe he should have been arrested when a great friend of this show, Pandora Fitzroy-Price–' He nodded warmly in her direction, the camera panned to her and she blushed, '–who, I'm pleased to say is with us tonight, broke the story on her excellent Pandora's Box website on Sunday morning.

'I believe that O'Shea should have been held in a police cell and an application made to the Criminal Prosecution Service to charge him with high treason. Yes, high treason. Because we have to take a stand against the out-of-control leftie hate mob who despise patriots like you and I, and are a grave threat to the safety of our great country. And if we can't take a stand now, when they mock the physical well-being of The Nation's Great Grandfather, with the British people raw with shock, then when can we?

'Thankfully, I'm not alone in thinking this. We have a sane voice in the Commons who agrees with me and wants to do something about it.'

Fleury swivelled around in his chair to the screen showing a middle-aged man with a pale, jowly face and a downbeat expression that suggested he'd experienced a life full of knock-backs, dressed in a pinstripe jacket and blue tie, sitting in the box room of his Guildford home flanked by a pair of Union Jacks with a framed photograph of Margaret Thatcher behind his head.

'Welcome to the show, Andrew Jenkins MP. Now I believe that first thing tomorrow you are presenting to the House of Commons an Early Day Motion asking for the Crown Prosecution Service to study this case and see if it can bring a charge of high treason against O'Shea?'

'That's right, Lance. Enough is enough. Why should we have to put up with this constant barrage of vitriol from the Left, much of it arriving under the protection of so-called humour, a lot of it, I am ashamed to say, being facilitated by our state-run broadcaster the BBC. It doesn't just cause tremendous hurt to British people, it destabilises the very institutions that make this country work.'

Vinny was on the brink of lashing his whisky bottle at the TV when his mobile phone rang. He looked at the screen, saw Sadie's name flash up and answered it, turning down the TV volume.

'Hello love.'

'Hi Vinny. You ok?'

'Yeah, not bad? Has Mick been in touch?'

'Yes. The friggin' eejit doesn't know where to turn. He can't hand himself in yet as he's still off his tits on weed and vodka, so he's borrowed the taxi off Robbo and driven off to get his head together.'

'What? Driving when he's high and pissed? Has he completely lost it?'

'He said he wasn't going far. Just somewhere to sleep for the night, then he'll go to the cop shop tomorrow and come clean when the drink and some of the drugs has left his system. Robbo's given him a burner phone, that's how he rang me. He told me he's been trying to get you but you're not picking up.'

'The phone's been going berserk. I'm only picking it up when I see a name I know.'

'Well I'll text you his number after this call and you can speak to him. He's mortified at the trouble he's caused, Vinny. Says he didn't know it was a crime to let off a toy gun in the street. His head's been all over the place since Saturday night. I think we need to help him now, you know?'

'I know love,' said Vinny, giving off a long sigh. 'I just don't know how to. The more I'm watching the likes of this wanker on the telly calling for Mick to be charged with treason the more angry I'm getting.'

There was a three second silence before Sadie asked, with fear in her voice, 'Are you watching Lance Fleury?'

'Is that what they call the tosser?'

'Vinny, don't watch him. Please. Yes, he *is* a tosser.

SICK MICK

A shit-stirring tosser is all he is. Please don't watch him. He'll only get you riled.'

'Ok, love.'

'I'll text you Mick's number. Give him a ring, please. He's not in a great place right now.'

'Ok, love. Will do. See you.'

Vinny put the phone down and turned up the sound on the television, where Fleury was well on his way to whipping his audience into believing that Mick should be facing a hangman's noose.

Panda was finishing off announcing that her sources in Liverpool were telling her that O'Shea had gone into hiding and there was a search on to find him, but with the police being stretched and locals unlikely to give him up, it was dubious they would get a result.

'So, let's get this straight,' said Fleury. 'A traitor to Britain, who spreads hate at a time when its people are on their knees, has gone on the run from justice. That is precisely what Lord Haw-Haw was, and did, at the end of World War II. Ladies and gentlemen, we have a modern day Lord Haw-Haw on our hands, or as I like to call him,' he span round in his chair, 'Lord Ha-Ha.

'Yes, Lord Ha-Ha is on the run. But this haha situation is not in the slightest bit funny. As you already know, to my mind he is guilty of the most grievous of offences: high treason. Let me bring in our constitutional law expert, Darpita Harper, from the University of Chambers, to discuss this.

'Darpita, can you tell us what the charge of high treason is and whether O'Shea's actions have at least merited the CPS considering prosecution?'

'Well Lance, it's interesting that you should mention Lord Haw-Haw, as William Joyce was the last person to be found guilty of high treason in the UK and executed back in 1946. But more than 670 years after it was introduced, The Treason Act still remains law in this country, now punishable with a tariff of up to life imprisonment, and is defined as the crime of disloyalty against the Crown,' said Darpita, flashing Fleury a smile that said, 'take it away, baby.'

'Well, I think we can all agree that O'Shea is guilty of that,' said Fleury, his eyes lingering longer than they should on Darpita's bare calf and knee as she crossed her legs, causing her short skirt to ride up her thigh. Pandora wasn't impressed.

'Well possibly. But if you dig deeper, it becomes more difficult to prove. Theoretically, to be charged with high treason an offender needs to be perceived to have been plotting the murder of the sovereign, committing adultery with the sovereign's consort, the sovereign's eldest unmarried daughter or the wife of the heir to the throne, undermining the lawfully established line of succession, levying war against the sovereign or giving succour to the sovereign's enemies, either through aid or comfort.'

'Well, we have him hook, line and sinker,' yelled Fleury. 'Giving succour to the sovereign's enemies through comfort. Isn't that precisely what O'Shea and all of these leftie comedians and commentators do when they undermine the monarchy with their vile attempts at humour? Do you think the Russians, or the Islamic State, North Korea, China and, yes I'll say it, the European Union, weren't comforted to hear O'Shea's act and the grief it has caused in this great country of ours? And what about all the sovereign's internal enemies who wish to see the monarchy abolished. He's giving them succour on stilts, isn't he?'

'Well, put like that it is not inconceivable for a case to be made. Back in 2014 the Government looked at considering high treason charges against British citizens who had travelled to Syria and Iraq to fight with Islamic extremists, but there wasn't the political will to see it through,' said Darpita.

'Well knock me down with a pacifist's white feather. Our parliament lacked the political will to protect its people from home-grown Jihadists by dealing with them as the traitors they are? Dearie me, I'm shocked, shocked I tell you,' said Fleury in a mocking tone.

'So, in short, Darpita, am I correct in saying that it is

possible to assume, if the political will was there, that O'Shea may have committed high treason?'

'With the right political will it is certainly possible to assume that, yes.'

'And that is from a constitutional law expert, folks. Darpita, while I have you here, can we clear up the definite charge O'Shea is facing: possession of an illegal firearm.'

'Well it is illegal to carry and display an imitation firearm in public, especially one as realistic as that.'

'Will they throw the book at him? I've been hearing ten years.'

'That is the maximum tariff. But bearing in mind he wasn't using it in a robbery, or to resist arrest, it is highly unlikely he would receive anywhere near the maximum sentence.'

'So what kind of stretch are we looking at?'

'It depends on what defence he offers, any previous convictions and the judge, but people convicted recently for the same offence have served between one and two years. It is considered very serious.'

'Well, clearly not that serious, if you look again at the statement from Merseyside Police, who apparently have better things to do than arrest a maniac who looks in need of help.'

'But I assure you, we're taking it very seriously. Which is why I can exclusively reveal, on *Lance Fleury*

SICK MICK

Tonight, that Brit Talk, in conjunction with Pandora's Box, the website that pricks the Westminster Bubble, are offering a reward of £10,000 for any information leading to the arrest of Mick O'Shea.'

'Lord Ha-Ha is on the run, folks, and we intend to find him. And when we do, we will be lobbying heavily for the charge of high treason to be considered, which, as you've heard our constitutional law expert confirm tonight, is a charge that cannot be ruled out.

'We have a great opportunity to draw a line in the sand here,' said Fleury, the camera homing in tight on his face as he launched into his nightly patriotic diatribe, deluding himself that the world was hanging on his every word when, in reality, less than one per cent of the British population were bothering to watch.

'The luvvie Left have declared war on Britain, attacking every patriot who draws breath on this sceptred isle. How far are we going to let it go? Why do we let them get away with all of their hate?'

'Do you remember when I was attacked during an election walkabout by a protester throwing eggs and a comedian said on the BBC that she'd wished it was anthrax? Nothing happened to her. She still works there. I said at the time that she was guilty of incitement to hate. That she was indulging in terrorism of the mind. I was called an attention-seeker. Sure, an attention-seeker who, ever since, has been advised to hire a bodyguard when I'm out canvassing or reporting for Brit Talk.

'As I will be from tomorrow, when I meet the crowds who are gathering in London, awaiting news of our royal hero's fight for life as a nation wills its Great Grandfather towards his 100th birthday. I will be out there with them every day until His Grace pulls through, interviewing the very best of British patriots and bringing you the very latest news on his condition.

'But where will Lord Ha-Ha be? Where is he now? People must know. Indeed I appeal to those who are closest to him, his family, to turn him in for the greater good.

'But you won't, will you? You're probably laughing along with him, saying–' He puts on a very bad Scouse accent. '–well done, Mick, we're proud of ye, la.

'If so, you need to take some of the blame here. This may be your adopted country with a name like O'Shea, who knows? But you live in Britain and you have allowed someone to grow up detesting this country.

'You may see patriotism as an alien concept. You may not know the price in blood that men and women have paid in the name of our king or queen to give the likes of you–' he points at the camera '–the freedom you enjoy today.'

SICK MICK

Back in his armchair in Moses Street, the bottle of whisky now empty, Vinny stared back at Fleury's image, and for the first time since he had been told he was dying of cancer, the brain fog cleared to reveal total clarity.

He saw a man who had never faced combat trying to cover himself in the glory of war, issuing threats to him and his son. A son who had devoted his life to looking after someone who had lost his leg for his queen and his country. A son who had given a broken soldier a reason to live. And now this vile opportunist was trying to make a name for himself by pushing his son over the edge.

Vinny lifted himself from the chair and limped into the hall then back up the stairs to his loft muttering, 'I'll fucking show him the price you pay for patriotism.'

12

TUESDAY MORNING

It looked like a scene from a low-budget TV show called *I Dropped Out of The Rat Race and Live in a Taxi Next to a Motorway*. Inside the Hackney Cab, which had spent the night in the car park of Knutsford Services, a hobo-esque figure lay sprawled across the back passenger seat, his pale, hairy belly protruding through his unbuttoned shirt, with Coke bottles, Ginsters Scotch Egg wrappers, bags of Pom-Bears and Walkers prawn cocktail crisps, a near empty packet of Rolos, plus the contents of a box of Maynards Bassetts Liquorice Allsorts strewn across the floor (except for a pink, circular allsort which was stuck to Mick's beard) and quivered in time to his snores.

Actually, make the title of the show *I Came Down From Being Stoned Off My Head and Had the Worst Attack of the Munchies Known to Humanity*.

Ayesha peered through the steamed-up windows, dreading to think what had caused the condensation, and knocked on the glass for a third time. But he was out cold. She checked her watch. It was almost 10am and the car park was filling up with workers and travellers who had been on the road for hours. She took out her phone and rang the number Mick had texted her the night before.

A muffled ring tone came from the pocket of a jacket lying between the Scotch Egg wrappers and the Pom-Bears, causing Mick to reach out too far, overbalance, fall off the seat, land with a heavy thud on a bed of liquorice allsorts and jump up startled, his fists going up and his eyes racing around the interior of the cab as though he was searching for a burglar.

He saw Ayesha, creased-up with laughter, on the other side of the window, rubbed his face, got to his knees and opened the locked door, the thunderous rush of car engines from the M6 making him cover his ears and usher her inside.

'Jesus Christ, Mick,' she said, covering her nose with her hand to block out the rancid smell of processed meat and body odour. 'It's a miracle you haven't gassed yourself to death. It smells like you've shat a dead skunk.'

'You know what they say, lady? She who smelt it, dealt it,' he replied, opening the windows.

'And you've got a liquorice allsort stuck to your beard,' she said.

Mick felt for it, picked it off, stared at it and sighed: 'Yay, the coconut one. My favourite,' before sticking it in his mouth.

As Ayesha pulled a flask of black coffee and a bag

of Danish pastries from a holdall, Mick spotted a litre bottle of Buxton water, grabbed it and slugged on it until it was half empty before letting out the relieved gasp of a man who had slaked his thirst in an oasis in the Kalahari Desert.

'How are you feeling,' Ayesha asked, filling the flask lid cup with strong black coffee and handing it to Mick.

'Not bad considering what I did,' he replied, taking a gentle sip of the thick, steaming liquid and sitting back in the seat, kicking the debris away from his feet.

'Er, 'did' being rampaging through the streets with an imitation firearm, or the amount of drugs and alcohol you put into your system?'

Mick ignored her as he reached into the bag of pastries, grabbed an apple slice and started munching on it.

'So what's the plan? I tell the lawyer to head to Admiral Street police station, we drive there, and you hand yourself in?' asked Ayesha.

'I dunno. The vodka has worn off but if they test me for weed I'm done for. Better give it a few more hours.' Ayesha looked at the floor, frowning. 'Listen to me. I sound like a serial killer who's coughing for twenty-three murders when all I've done is let off a cap-gun outside my own house for a laugh,' said Mick.

'Well, some people definitely see you as the new

Fred West,' said Ayesha, pulling three of that morning's national tabloids from her bag, all carrying a photo of Mick, arm in the air firing the gun, his open mouth and blazing eyes twisted into a crazy smile reminiscent of Jack Nicholson in his 'here's Johnny' moment from *The Shining*.

The Sun went with: ROYAL-BAITING COMIC GOES GAGA IN STREET while *The Star* opted for the more punchy SICK MICK GUN TERROR. *The Mail*, meanwhile, took its lead from Lance Fleury by asking in its main headline: WHO WILL STOP HATE-FILLED LEFTIE LORD HA-HA?, with the subhead saying, 'Vile comic who mocked duke's coma fires gun and goes on run.'

'Lord Ha-Ha? What's that about? Do they think that I'm Dingle aristocracy and I was out on my estate firing a gun into the air trying to hit a partridge for my tea?'

Ayesha explained the pun before taking him through last night's Brit Talk show, filling him in on how Lance Fleury had been after him since Sunday morning and he now wanted to see him charged with high treason.

On the plus side, she pointed out that, because Fleury was so widely despised, Mick had become a hero to half the country. The Attica clip had so many hits on TikTok and X that sites had almost crashed, and the phrase Sick Mick had gone viral, with Gen Z loving how the Boomers had failed to understand that the word 'sick' also means cool. She had received many dozens of emails from media organisations around the world asking for interviews and offering him work. Every major US chat show wanted him and NBC even offered to fly him out to New York for that week's prestigious *Saturday Night Live*.

'So it's not all bad,' she said. 'You just need to own up to the imitation fire gun charge, and…'

'I'll be booked for a residency in Strangeways for the next couple of years,' Mick chipped in, popping Ayesha's good vibe balloon, and making them both stare out of the window.

Things could be worse, he thought, watching the sales reps and white van men jog towards the services for a leak as they tried to dodge the light rain that had started to come down. He could have a proper job. He could be wearing a cheap suit heading to a meeting in a Telford head office where he had to clinch a deal to be the sole supplier of paper-clips to Ramsbottom & Son. And when he failed, due to the phoney with the vice-like handshake who had promised the deal to someone he knows in his golf club, it would mean he would have missed one too many targets and would now be sacked, causing his wife to walk out with the kids as he could no longer afford the mortgage. Given the choice, he thought, he would genuinely prefer being the resident comedian in Strangeways for a couple of years. Think of all the new material that would come to him. Especially in the showers.

Imagine doing any other job than entertaining, he thought. Where was the buzz? Imagine going to work knowing exactly what you were going to say to people who you mostly wished serious harm to, and knowing how they would react to your meaningless banalities? Imagine being told to stop making people laugh when they are trying to work and to take that pointless job more seriously? What would be the point of living? Who would choose to do just enough to pay the bills and take one fortnight a year in Majorca until their pension kicked in and they could spend the day watching adverts for equity release or funeral plans on TV? Who could possibly want such a beige life?

'I'm guessing you probably don't know the answer to this, but what were you thinking when you started shooting that gun?' asked Ayesha.

'Honest to God, I didn't know I was breaking any law. Robbo reckons he told me it was an offence to carry it, but I just can't remember him telling me. I was stoned and messing around with his lad's toys.

'It was when I heard one of them reporters lying through the letterbox that he was on my side that I just flipped. But I was only arsing around with them. I thought they'd get that it was a toy gun.'

'Is Robbo mad at you?'

'Wasn't best pleased, but he's a diamond. He lent me this cab, gave me a few quid to tide me over and this burner phone.' He reached into his jacket pocket and checked the screen. There was one missed call from five minutes ago, which he guessed was Ayesha, and one message that was sent last night at 10pm.

He opened the message and, as he read it, his head shot back as though he'd been hit square in the face with a mallet. He threw the phone onto his lap, ran his hands through his hair, breathed out and said, 'Shit.'

'What's up?' asked Ayesha.

Mick handed her the phone and she read out the text message: Don't worry, son. Me and my little faithful are on the case. That bastard who wants you hung for treason is getting it.

She looked at Mick and asked, 'Your dad?'

Mick nodded. There was a silence as both tried to decipher the message and their own thoughts.

'His little faithful is the pistol he brought back from the Gulf War that he keeps locked in a drill box in the loft,' said Mick.

'Tell me you're joking,' said Ayesha as Mick shook his head. 'Then the bastard who wants you hanged who he's saying he's going to kill has to be Lance Fleury?' she added.

'Nah, there's no way he'd know about him. He would never watch that channel and he never buys a paper. Probably just a coincidence. He's losing his marbles, getting stuff mixed up. Give it a couple of hours and he'll be in The Irish House getting bevvied, forgetting any of this happened,' said Mick.

The phone rang. Mick recognised Sadie's work number and answered it. She was in an over-excited state, talking fast in a high-pitched, agitated voice as she told Mick she had just rang Vinny and she could make out from an announcement in the background that he was on a train heading to London Euston.

Mick filled her in on Vinny's text message, telling her he couldn't believe his dad was going after Fleury as he was convinced he wouldn't have a clue who he was. Which is when Sadie told him she had spoken to Vinny the previous night and he told her that he was watching Fleury.

A loud rapping on the back door window interrupted the conversation, with Mick telling Sadie he would call her later. Standing outside the taxi was a bald, bespectacled man in his fifties, wearing a shirt and tie under a kagool.

'Oh, I forgot to tell you,' said Ayesha. 'Fleury has put a ten grand reward on your head, so tread carefully.'

'Really? Is that all? Hardly Britain's Most Wanted

SICK MICK

then, am I?'

The man knocked again, Mick wound the window down and asked, in a caricature of a Northern Irish accent, 'Can I help ye, fella?'

'Hopefully. I'm taking the wife to Liverpool next month and was thinking about surprising her with a Beatles taxi tour. Can you tell me how much it costs?'

Mick looked at Ayesha and grinned mischievously. 'It'll cost ye an arm and a kneecap if you pay on the day, but if you book in advance I can give ye a bit of a discount, so I can.'

'Well, erm, I haven't yet finalised the itinerary,' he replied.

'Just get the phone number off the side of the taxi and ring up to book when you have. They're very reasonable,' said Ayesha.

'Will do. I hope they give it a good clean out,' he said, pointing to the floor of the taxi and grimacing.

'Oh, the mess,' said Mick. 'We're just rehearsing that time John had a mental breakdown for a special *When The Beatles Went Loco* trip I've been booked to do later.'

'Really? When was that?' asked the bald stranger.

'Just before he wrote 'Help!' He went totally off his rocker. Drove away from home with loads of sweets and crisps and stuff singing 'help me if you can I'm feeling down'...etcetera, etcetera. Proper deep depression so it was. He ended up like Alan Partridge in Dundee, getting fat on bumper bars of white Toblerone. You'll hear all about it on the tour.'

'Wait a minute,' said the man, studying Mick's face closely. 'Don't I know you from somewhere?'

'No, I'm just a humble Beatles tour taxi driver practising a full-on John Lennon breakdown. You're probably mistaking me for *Harry Potter*'s Hagrid. Many people do.'

'No, it's someone else. Who is it?'

'Did you get the number? Only we're really busy,' said Ayesha.

'I'm trying to get into full doolally character as John. You're a distraction so you are, fella,' said Mick, closing the window. The man stepped back, pulled out his phone and tapped in the number on the side of the taxi, peered hard again at Mick, then walked away.

'Come on, let's go to the police station and face the music, this has gone on long enough,' said Ayesha.

'You're joking,' answered Mick. 'I've got to find my dad. He's got a gun. He's losing his mind. Join the dots will ya?'

'No. You need to hand yourself in. That's what you need to do. Then go after him.'

'What if they don't let me? What if they hold me? Do I tell them there's another O'Shea out there with a gun, only this time it's real. Then request a family suite at Walton?'

'You won't need to. You'll get bail.'

'I can't risk it.'

They each stared out of a different window in silence. I've had some tough gigs in my time, thought Ayesha, but this was shaping up to be the hardest. There was the middle-aged National Treasure game show host who was such a voracious paedophile the joke was that he demanded a ball-pit and a slide as his dressing room rider. And there was the Perrier Award winner whose hedonistic appetite was so insatiable he made her have his coke dealer and pimp on speed dial. But nobody had been dominating the front pages for having an act so sick they were perceived to be a traitor; none were looking at a nailed-on jail sentence and none had decided to go looking for their gun-toting dad with a price on their head.

Yet, human being wise, she struggled to think of a client who had been in the same class as Mick. It was rare, she thought, to work with someone so special, as a talent and a person. He had earned her loyalty. She owed him a strategy.

'So, what's your excuse for taking days to hand yourself in? That's going to go down well with the judge when you end up in court,' she said.

'I'll say I had a breakdown. That all the pressure was getting to me and I went into hiding because I was depressed and couldn't face the world. I've already got a history of it. I've been on antidepressants since I was fourteen and saw a psychologist for three years, not that it did me any good. It'll be a piece of piss getting a shrink to back me up. I need to worry about my dad first.'

He tapped Vinny's number into his phone but no-one picked up. They sat there in silence.

'Ok, so tell me exactly how you think this might pan out?' Ayesha asked.

'I drive to London.'

'Oh, that tiny hamlet of twenty people called London, where you will definitely find him straight away. Good luck with that.'

'Did this Fleury fella say where he was going to be for the next few days?'

'Standing with the crowds outside Buckingham Palace or wherever they are gathering, I think.'

'Big crowds?'

'There's already thousands of them queuing up.'

'Queueing for what?' Mick asked.

'To walk past an easel that carries the note that says he's in a coma.'

'Seriously? I'm accused of thinking up sick gags about this brain-washing farce, when the people in charge are churning out rip snorters.'

'They're laying flowers and stuff as well, but look,

you don't need to worry about…what do you mean rip snorters?'

'A laugh that's one step down from a Mount Everest. Anyway, forget that. Did Fleury announce on telly last night that he would be with the crowds?'

'Yeah. He bragged about how brave he was, not needing a bodyguard when he meets the people. Why?'

'Ah, so that's why my dad, the old desert fox, is so confident. He knows there's a couple of days to size him up and pick his moment. I need to get down to London and sort the mad old bastard out before he does.' Mick went to get up but Ayesha stopped him.

'Hang on. That fella asking about the taxi tours almost recognised you. If you step out in London, anywhere near the mourners they'll be on to you.'

'Good point, Batman.'

Ayesha tapped a question into Google on her phone then looked up at Mick. 'Right they've got showers at these services. I'm going to the nearest Boots to get you an electric shaver, some scissors, sun glasses and soap. And you're going to go into those showers to shave your beard and hair off.' Mick burst out laughing and shook his head.

'No way. I don't suit the emaciated Japanese Prisoner of War look. Haven't really got the figure for it.'

'After that I'm going to a charity shop and buying you a bobble hat and some clothes that look nothing like your stage gear.'

'Ah brilliant. I always go for the Special Needs look when I go to London. Can you get me a helium balloon with a cat's face on too?'

'Then I'll get you a new burner phone and deodorant which—you really fucking need to use if you're aiming to mingle with crowds. The alternative being I just drive away now and wash my hands of you forever.'

'What? When *Saturday Night Live* want to book me? You can't kid a kidder, kid.'

'Do we have a deal or what?'

Mick scratched his beard then leaned forward, picked the Rolo packet up from the floor, which had one left inside. He unpeeled the wrapper, pulled out the chocolate toffee sweet and offered it to Ayesha.

'I love you so much, Fagin, I'll even give you my last Rolo.'

'God, you're a wanker O'Shea,' she said, taking the Rolo and sealing the deal.

SICK MICK

13

TUESDAY LUNCHTIME

It was the perfect time of year to be in Sadie's favourite spot in London. Late May, peak bloom season, seated on a bench in Queen Mary's Gardens in Regent's Park, the vast kaleidoscope of dazzling, multi-coloured rose beds, the medley of hypnotic fragrances unleashed by delphiniums, peonies and begonias and the soothing birdsong combining to make her feel more zen than a Buddhist monk on the road to Nirvana.

Why do people pay a fortune for aromatherapy sessions, she thought, when nature lavishes its bounty so generously, and you can bathe your senses and clear your brain with a prawn mayo baguette on your lunch break, sheltered from the noisy city by a barrier of stiff poplars and a timeless carnival of beauty?

Naturally, she realised that not everyone worked or lived a short distance from such a lavishly-planned and religiously-preserved paradise. Sadie had fallen on her feet on both fronts. She had become friends with Connie, an office intern at the Hardman, whose parents had bought her a flat in Weymouth Mews, a five-minute stroll from the clinic. When Connie told Sadie she was planning to spend nine months travelling across the world, asking her if she would like to flat-sit, rent-free for the duration, she almost bit off the Trust Fund Babe's manicured hand as she showered it in grateful kisses.

If Sadie was not exactly head-over-heels in love with her job in Harley Street, she could not have been more ecstatic at its proximity to her beloved Regent's Park, which had been built in the early nineteenth-century for the pleasure of very wealthy families who lived in the elegant white Georgian mansions that overlooked it. You could imagine Mary Poppins flying kites with the Banks children here.

In terms of calmness, it was undoubtedly a step up from the Belfast parks of her childhood. Especially during the marching season, when a completely different array of colours and noises would play havoc with the senses.

The calmness was helped by dogs being banned from the gardens. Not that Sadie harboured Cruella de Vil instincts, apart from against some of the tiny, yappy, designer pups she wanted to kick into next week. But without the canine barks and haranguing humans, the only noise was the background chirping of reed warblers, sparrow hawks and stonechats.

You could hear yourself think, as her granny Ellen used to say, when urging her to work things out for herself on the grounds that, 'you should believe nothing you hear outside your own head and only one half what you see.'

Sadie never understood that, but then neither did she understand some of the other old Irish sayings her granny came out with such as, 'She's like the crows. She's got high notions,' or 'put a devil on horseback and he'll ride to hell,' or 'I'm not saying she's a crook but she's got two fingers the one length,' or 'That fella's so tight he could peel an orange in his back pocket wearing oven mitts.'

Oh, how she needed time to think, now. Oh, how she was struggling to believe everything she was hearing and most of what she was seeing. She had repeatedly rung Vinny but reached voicemail every time, and each time she left variations of the same message, telling him she may have been mistaken but she was sure she heard a train announcement during her previous call that sounded like he was on his way to London. And if he was, would he like to meet up for a drink?

She knew in her guts that, having alerted Vinny to her knowledge of his unplanned journey, he would now not speak to her in case she gleaned other clues to his whereabouts. But still she tried.

Mick had rung Sadie back when Ayesha had left him to buy the instruments needed to execute his identity-transforming makeover. He told her his theory on why his dad was heading to London and how he had no choice but to delay handing himself in to police and going in search of him.

She railed against him at first, relishing the chance to hand out yet another bollocking for bringing this ton of horseshit down on everyone's heads, before slowly coming round to his logic.

Sadie was more convinced of Vinny's early onset dementia than Mick, and worried that he may be so confused by events he was genuinely capable of killing Fleury. Especially after he had openly taunted him about not knowing the meaning of patriotism and the price men and women have paid for it on the battlefield. Vinny had never spoken to her about his wartime experiences but Fleury's unprompted attack seemed to her like tossing a hand grenade at his good leg and laughing. If any taunt would tip him over the edge, it was that.

Ayesha had warned Mick not to stay in Sadie's flat as there was a good chance it was being watched either by the police or the tabloids. His plan, he'd said, was to sleep in his cab and he would text her the location on his new burner phone that night if she fancied a bunk-up in the back seat.

When she told him to go screw himself, he replied that he'd probably have to, but if she had a rethink and fancied jumping in the cab, he would be generous and knock the night-time rate off her fare.

SICK MICK

She looked at her watch, which told her she only had fifteen minutes left of her lunchtime, so rose from the bench and gulped in her last hit of paradise, hoping it would sustain her through her walk back to Harley Street.

After she had climbed the five stone steps and held her pass over a scanner by the side of the heavy black front door, allowing her to enter the clinic, the receptionist told her that Grace Fairfax, the manager, wanted to see her in her office right away.

Sadie's face turned an even whiter shade of her freckled pale. Had she found out she was employing the girlfriend of Britain's Most Wanted, she thought? Gemma, the firm's accounts manager, was the only person in the clinic who had met Mick but she was on holiday. Surely she wouldn't ring Grace from her Crete sunbed to grass her mate up? Maybe the police had been in, but why, after they had called at her flat last night and she had convinced them she didn't have a clue where he was? Was it a sackable offence going out with a comedian who has a sick sense of humour and a penchant for firing toy guns in public?

She walked tentatively down the corridor on the plush Dartmoor Barley Twist carpet until she reached the manager's office, knocked on the door and was told to enter by a middle-aged woman with the voice of a 1950s BBC continuity announcer.

'How are things with you, Sadie, good?' asked the expensively-suited, raven-haired, matchstick-thin boss.

'Grand, aye,' Sadie blurted out in an upbeat tone which was as forced as her smile.

'Good to hear. We're very pleased with your work.'

'Brilliant.'

'In fact that's why we're having this chat. You haven't had a VIP before, have you?' Sadie gave Grace a puzzled look, not sure if she was supposed to be laughing at a joke, and answered, 'Well there was a local radio DJ back in Belfast who groped me very inappropriately at a school disco, if that counts?'

'What?' replied Grace, not sure if she was supposed to be laughing, offering sympathy, or phoning the police. 'No. You misunderstand. A VIP client. Here. In this clinic?'

'I don't think so, no.'

'So you've never wondered what goes on in the annexe room at the back of the garden?'

'Not really, no. I just reckoned it was used for overspill or something.'

'Well, we offer a service to men who are in the public spotlight, where we promise — or rather sign a confidentiality contract in which we agree — not to mention to anybody, not even our family, that this famous person has undergone sexual performance enhancement. You can understand why?' asked Grace fondling the eighteen-carat diamond on her glittering white gold necklace.

'Aye, sure. But I would never give out the names or discuss the details of any client of mine, whether they were famous or not.'

'Of course you wouldn't. I know. You're a professional.'

'Totally. Always.'

'And that's why you're perfect for our latest client, who you will be attending to in ten minutes time. The procedure is no different from normal, except I will take him into the room and prep him, and he will be wearing an eye-mask and headphones and there will be no conversation between you. Simply give him the treatment as normal and tap him three times on the shoulder when you have finished. Then leave. When he is dressed, he will exit through the annexe door that leads onto Devonshire Mews West, the cul-de-sac directly behind us.

'I will give him his own keys to enter the clinic from the mews, and for your follow-up appointment you can sit in the garden and he will buzz you to enter when he is ready. He will know the prep routine after today, so all you need to do is go straight to the shockwave machine and begin therapy. With no small talk, or talk of any length at all. Does that make sense?'

'Erm, yeah. I guess so.'

'I cannot over-stress the need here for total discretion. Most VIPs have enemies who will go out of their way to expose private information and, well, we know how low the Press can go.'

Shit, thought Sadie. Was she telling me she knew all about Mick but was saying nothing? That this was the deal? I have dirt on you that you don't want me to know so keep schtum about this VIP or I'll cause trouble? Was this a threat? Probably not. Probably a generalisation about the press. I'm just being paranoid, she told herself.

'All good then?' asked Grace.

'Ay, sure.'

'No questions?'

'If it's Jamie Dornan, can I ask for a selfie, even if he keeps his mask on?' she nervously joked, hating herself the second the words left her mouth, her boss's stern expression confirming that she was right to.

Grace handed her the confidentiality agreement, and told her to wait outside the annexe in the garden until she was buzzed in, reminding her that if it leaked out, and it was proven that the leak had come from the clinic, she would know the leaker had been her as she was the only other person in the organisation who knew the identity of the VIP being treated. Sadie nodded and left the manager's office.

SICK MICK

Well that was weird, she thought, walking towards the locker room to undress down to her scrubs. Gemma had once dropped the phrase 'top secret' into the conversation, then quickly changed tack, and when Sadie asked her to elaborate, she waved it away and moved onto something trivial. Now she knew why.

She couldn't see what all the fuss was about. It made no difference to her whose limp penis she was handling. A cock's a cock when all's said and done, she thought, then laughed at the prospect that she may be about to give a dick a celebrity name that actually belonged to the same celebrity. Maybe Grace would sack her if she knew she'd been telling people about Donald Trump, Danny de Vito, Eddie Redmayne, Larry David or Bruce Willis. Oh, and Mick O'Shea, now that he was partially famous. Well, one hundred per cent a prick, at least.

Sadie walked into the garden, grabbed her Lafuma seat, took it to the annexe door and reclined into it. After a couple of minutes she heard a loud buzz from the room, gave it ten seconds in case there was a yell about a struggle with a trouser leg and, when none came, she walked inside and gave the VIP—who was laid on the treatment table, with an elevated back putting him into a semi-upright position—the once over.

On his head sat a black baseball cap bearing a logo of a Y interlocked with an N in a distinctive font. It was a New York Yankees cap, but Sadie didn't recognise it. A large, padded navy-blue mask covered his eyes and he had Air Pods in his ears. Behind the camouflage she could see tufts of grey hair.

He wore an olive crew-neck jumper on top of a rust windowpane check shirt, and at the bottom of his bottle white legs were maroon Paul Smith socks. Placed over a Corby press in the corner of the room was a pair of fern green cord trousers with oxblood brown brogues placed underneath, and a quilted dark-sand coloured Barbour coat with a suede collar, hanging from a peg on the wall. Landed gentry come in from the country by the look of him, Sadie thought, her brain rummaging through reality TV shows that had been set on rural estates trying to put a face to the body. But failing.

She wheeled the Duolith SD1 Ultra Shockwave machine to the side of the treatment table, pulled up her chair, lubricated the massage probe, set the dial to a medium pulse wave then, using her left surgically-gloved hand, gently lifted the sheet of kitchen roll from his penis and began to slowly run the probe up and down his pink and flaccid shaft.

'Jesus wept,' he shouted, his bare knees trembling and maroon-socked feet twitching, causing Sadie to remove the probe. He pulled out an Air Pod and said: 'Sorry, nurse. I didn't hear you come in. That was a bit of a shock. That's all.'

'It's on a medium setting right now, but I can take it lower if you like?' said Sadie.

'No, that's fine. The higher the better. I can take it,' he replied, giving off a false, raucous laugh.

His posh, gravelly voice sounded familiar, as did his large, stained teeth and the deep, raspy laugh that seemed to come straight from his lungs.

'Okay well tell me if it gets painful,' said Sadie, hearing Fleetwood Mac coming from his loose Air Pod. He stuffed it back in his ear and gave her the thumbs up, giving her permission to return to action.

Sadie picked up his penis again and fished for a nickname. It was on the smallish side, thin with a wide bell shape at the top. She already had a jingle bell, so couldn't call it that. As she placed the probe at the front of the shaft she noticed, on the back of it, a few dots near the bell. It's a toadstool, she thought, and began singing in her head *I Wan'na Be Like You* from the Jungle Book, almost exploding with laughter when she got to her new line 'a toadstool VIP.'

She gently lifted up his testicles and penis, nursing them in her left hand, as she moved the probe down to the perineum, that small section of the anatomy where most of the erotic nerves and pelvic floor muscles sit, that Sadie believed perfectly summed up a male. As in it was halfway between an arsehole and a ballsack.

The sensation of electric waves hitting his G-Spot made the VIP's upper thighs shudder slightly and he gave off an involuntary, pleasured groan. That drew Sadie's eyes to his face and she lingered on it for a few seconds trying to work out, from the uncovered features, who this mystery celebrity was.

She looked all over for clues, asking herself in her head, in a Keith Lemon voice, 'who lives in a cock like this?' But she couldn't quite place him. He must be a minor politician, probably a Lord, she thought.

She carried on massaging the perineum, then moved back up to his shaft, her mind drifting to Vinny, which gave her a knot in the stomach. The VIP was relaxed now, the waves travelling through his penis and the thought of what this might mean to his sexual performance stripping away all fears he had about undergoing the treatment. Indeed, he was so relaxed he began to join in with Fleetwood Mac.

'Now here you go again, you say you want your freedom. Well, who am I to keep you down?' he belted out, which caused the probe to fall out of Sadie's hand.

'Sorry,' he bellowed, 'that must have shocked *you*. Didn't mean to sing there. Just feeling very relaxed. I'll shut up. You carry on.'

But it wasn't the sound of his singing voice that

made Sadie's hand, like her knees, go limp. It was the way he had aggressively spat out the word 'freedom' that set off an alarm in her head.

Sadie now believed she recognised the voice, and a careful study of his facial features that weren't hidden convinced her. It was the same voice she had heard on last night's TV before going to bed in a state of panic. The one that had been talking about the price in blood that men and women had paid for our freedom. It was Lance Fleury.

How apt, she thought, that he had a toad's tool.

14

TUESDAY NIGHT

Vinny was on to his third can of draught Guinness and his thirteenth shout of 'bastard' at the small Samsung TV attached to the pale blue Travelodge wall. He was laid back on the double bed, his prosthetic off, headboard and pillows taking his upper body weight, watching highlights of that day's royal grieving events with Craig, a mate from his army days, who was seated on the hard desk chair in the small gap between bed and window, also drinking Guinness and also shouting at the TV but inserting the words, 'creeping, arse-licking, hole-tonguing, brown-nosing and scabby,' before the word 'bastard.'

The focus of their ire was the BBC'S Royal Correspondent, Norman Green, a balding redhead with a ghostly complexion, who was presenting the highlights package with a unique style of unquestioning subservience that he had elevated to an art form.

Green had spent four decades bowing, scraping and tugging his forelock so hard you could almost hear his balls burst through the TV screen when he was in the presence of royalty. That's despite the family he devoted his journalistic career to flattering, treating him like a mediaeval groom of the stool by dousing him in crap at every opportunity.

'You'd never tire of smacking that face, would you,' asked Craig, a bald, squat, burly East Ender who had served with Vinny in the 4th Armoured Brigade in the Gulf and, four years later, without him in Bosnia. The pair, both sons of dockers with a gallows sense of humour, had stayed mates since Kuwait but their catch-up visits in recent years had been few and far between.

'I'd never tire of smacking all the phoneys he fawns over, who struggle to move with the weight of those medals on their chest,' answered Vinny, taking the litre bottle of Famous Grouse whisky from Craig and glugging down a mouthful.

They had met a couple of hours earlier in the Royal George pub opposite Euston station, but Vinny had decided three sips into his pint of San Miguel that it wasn't for him. A gin-soaked hen party from Stafford had tumbled off a southbound train and proceeded to hold an impromptu shrieking contest that threatened to shatter the Prosecco bottles that littered the tables. The last straw for Vinny was being hit on the head by a pair of testicles attached to a huge, pink, inflatable penis after the chief squawking hen spotted him throwing a filthy look in her direction.

They bought a carry-out from an off-licence and

SICK MICK

headed across the busy Euston Road to the Premier Inn hotel that Vinny always stayed in when visiting London. Mainly because it was a short dawdle from Euston and the sausages they served up in the eat-all-you-want buffet breakfast were, as he told everyone in the voice of a pretentious chef, 'to die for.'

'Do you know how many medals that little tit Prince Edward wears when he's in full military dress?' asked Vinny.

'Dunno. Four, five?' Craig replied.

'Six. Half-a-dozen medals for a whopper who spent five minutes in the Marines before running home crying to his mum. Then she goes and gives him honours that the lads who finished their training had to lay their lives on the line to get. Sums this country up,' said Vinny.

'And what about this duke?' asked Craig.

'How do you mean?'

'Have you seen the metal on his chest? For doing what? The only fighting he ever saw was playing battleships with his nanny at bath-time. They're calling him a war hero for going out a few nights in the Blitz with his security guards and a film crew and helping people into shelters. Gullible bastards.'

'Why did he never serve?' asked Vinny.

'Failed the medical with his twitchy eyes I'd guess.'

'Are you sure he wasn't a Nazi-lover like his uncle

Edward?'

'Probably,' said Craig. 'Eh, remember how they tried to pass off that picture of him doing a Hitler salute as a teenager by saying the sun was hurting his damaged eyes. Fuck off.' They both laugh and shake their heads.

'Still, he's the People's Duke ain't he?' said Craig. 'So all's forgotten. What is it they call him? The Duke of all Our Hearts. What bollocks.'

They were back in familiar territory now, in a shared place they could only ever talk about with each other because those who had never been there had little chance of comprehending the words and emotions it would conjure up. It was a place that lived in their heart every waking moment and in their nightmares most sleeps. There in the thick of the action. Lost in the filthy fog of war, their senses overloaded with the sounds and smells of bullets, shells, fear and screams. Young men with fire in their bellies but shit in their fatigues. Every particle of them focussed with a ferocity on their job, their survival, their comrades, their regiment and their folks back home. But not for their queen or king. For these two, it was never about all that.

Talking to each other was a release. Vinny had seen dozens of therapists and psychiatrists, but he untangled more mental knots in ten seconds with an old comrade like Craig than a week spent with any mental health professional. As for strangers, even family, trying to get inside his head and understand what fighting in a war was like, was impossible. How can you begin to describe the full horror of seeing the face blown off someone you had been joking around with at breakfast? How could you begin to describe a fit, fourteen stone, six foot, musclebound, intensely proud, battle-hardened man pleading for his mother as his life drained away?

How could you articulate your irrational hatred for young men you had never met, based solely on the grounds that if you didn't kill them they would kill you? How do you describe the primal scream of relief that leaves you when your bullet or your bayonet shatters the body of the human being that has been classified as your enemy and you know that's one less opportunity for you to lose your life?

The answer is you can never truly explain it, and when you attempt to, and inevitably fail, the sense of self-loathing the next day is crippling. So you try not to go there, even with people you love.

It's the same with survivors of disasters or terror attacks. Only when you are with a fellow survivor does conversing about the event that mentally scarred you forever make any sense. Only then are you speaking the same language as the person listening.

Only then do you feel safe that what you are saying will not be perceived as being spoken to win you attention or, even worse, pity.

'The biggest joke is the only two royals who earned their medals through seeing action—Harry and the sex abuse silencer—are banned from wearing them,' said Craig, pointing at the TV when their conversation hit a lull.

'No, the biggest joke is that they only have to squeak in public for that ginger beaut on the BBC to say the eyes of the world are on Britain when the only people with their eyes on this shite are nutters and rubberneckers who haven't got a life,' said Vinny.

'And you're down here to join them?'

'That's the plan. Did you bring what I asked for with you?'

'Yeah,' said Craig, reaching inside his jacket, pulling out a small plastic bag from a pocket and tossing it at Vinny who opened it, looked at its contents and gave his mate the thumbs-up.

'Right, that's my part of the bargain, so come on, spill the beans, why are you really down here mingling with the nutters and rubberneckers as you call them?'

Vinny took a gulp of Guinness, followed by a sharp intake of breath before telling him he had terminal cancer and would struggle to see another Christmas.

That led to Craig hauling himself off his chair, leaning over the bed and giving him a silent bear hug that lasted minutes, before reminding him that he was a born fighter and he had to battle his diagnosis to the end. Craig told him that his sister had gone private and been given the all-clear from breast cancer, and that he would organise a whip-round among the lads from the regiment and get his old pal to see the same surgeon.

'No mate, I've accepted my fate, and the last thing I want now is saving,' said Vinny. 'I've lived with so much pain since Kuwait that, if I'm honest, dying seems almost like a relief. My only thoughts now are for my lad. I'm worried how he'll cope losing another parent.'

'He can look after himself, Vin. You should just be thinking about getting better.'

Vinny raised a hand and told Craig, 'I'm doing the speaking,' then moved on to tell him about Mick's stand-up routine, the media hounding and the shenanigans with the toy gun. All of which Craig knew about but was waiting to hear from Vinny's mouth before bringing up.

He told him about Lance Fleury not just going after Mick, but him, questioning his patriotism live on TV, asking if the O'Shea family were aware of all the sacrifices that had been made for this country.

'How dare he lecture me about sacrifices made for this country? How can I let him get away with that?'

'Okay,' said Craig cautiously, wary that Vinny didn't want to be interrupted. 'So you still haven't told me what brings you down here to mingle with all the nutters?'

'Well my first thought was to shoot him.'

'What, are you serious?' asked an incredulous Craig.

'Yeah, I thought I'd give him one in the shin with my old Browning to let him know what a blood sacrifice feels like.'

'I can't believe I'm hearing this.'

'I said that was my first thought. Then I sobered up the next day and, well, I sobered up. My next thought was I still had to get him back somehow for our Mick. My final chance, if you like, to say that my mind may have seemed miles away but I was always there for him. Right to the end.'

'Okay, so how is that going to work,' asked Craig, squeezing his empty can into his fist.

'Well he's going walkabout with the crowds isn't he. So I want to get close to him, win his trust, then expose him as a fraud and a shithouse while the cameras are rolling.'

'How?'

'I want to see fear in his eyes when he finds out who

I am.'

'Like I said, how?'

'Haven't decided yet. Might take my empty pistol and…'

'What? Do seven years for carrying a weapon you were supposed to have left in the Gulf?'

'Well I probably haven't got seven months, so what does it matter?'

'It matters plenty. How's that going to help Mick, who's facing a stretch for doing the same stupid bleedin' thing? They'll tell the judge, you can see where he gets his trigger happy habit from. Send the pair of them down!'

'Okay. No gun.'

'Good. You don't need a gun, mate. Just shoot the fucker down with your words. There's plenty of ammunition to use if you want to show everyone he's a phoney. He sold Britain down the river with Brexit and he's been taking backhanders off the Chinese for years. Ask him how he has the cheek to question anyone's patriotism.'

Vinny pushed himself up, grabbed the prosthetic that lay by his side, attached it to his lower leg and eased his body off the bed. He picked up the bag Craig had given him, walked to the wardrobe where he grabbed a pair of light grey chinos and a dark blue blazer, then reached into his holdall, pulled out a small box and walked towards the bathroom.

Craig said nothing. He swallowed a mouthful of whisky and looked up at the ceiling, angry at the news Vinny had delivered, concentrating on the need to stop the tide of tears that were welling up behind his eyes.

Five minutes later Vinny emerged from the bathroom wearing the grey chinos, blue blazer, white shirt, blue regimental tie and the gift Craig had brought him — a green ceremonial beret with the distinctive black rat badge that had been their regiment's insignia since the days when Monty's men were chasing Rommel across the North African desert during World War II.

On his chest were pinned the Northern Ireland General Service medal with its purple and dark green ribbon and the Gulf War medal with a sand-coloured broad central stripe on a ribbon flanked by narrow stripes of dark blue, red and light blue.

He clicked his heels together as he stood to attention, then gave Craig a salute.

'What do you reckon? Will I pass, muster?' Vinny asked.

'You look absolutely glorious, mate,' answered Craig, his will defeated as tears streamed down either cheek.

SICK MICK

15

WEDNESDAY MORNING

He had only been awake for fifteen minutes, but Lance Fleury could already tell this was going to be one of those days that Hitler would describe as a bit of a Kampf.

The radio alarm by the side of his king-sized Waldorf bed had come on at 7.15am, a BBC presenter on the *Today* programme announcing that a YouGov poll claimed 70% of Britons now believed Brexit had been an economic disaster, with 52% seeing it as the most embarrassing mistake made in this country since Decca Records turned down The Beatles in favour of Brian Poole and The Tremeloes in 1962.

Fleury muttered, 'well piss off back to Islamabad then, you communist bitch,' at the esteemed Leicester-born journalist of Asian heritage, threw back the duvet, put his feet into his leather slippers, walked on the deep shag-pile carpet to the door in his silk pyjamas, and picked up the six national newspapers that lay outside. He strolled into the lounge section of his suite unleashing a loud fart, pushed the buttons on his DeLonghi coffee-maker that produced an Americano, sank into the green velvet Gallotti and Radice sofa with a yawn and began to peruse the papers.

The Times were leading on news that the banished Prince Harry was now intending to visit his favourite great-uncle, the duke, in hospital and do a walkabout with the people, leading to a possible security nightmare following the Taliban ordering a fatwa against him after he repeated the claim in his autobiography that he had killed twenty-five of their number.

Above that story was a headline that made Lance spit his coffee all over the photo of a distraught woman reaching through railings at the Palace of Westminster trying to touch the easel. The headline read: MP calls for Fleury Chinese links probe.

'They're joking? The front fucking page?' said Lance as he read how a Labour MP, using parliamentary privilege, had alleged in the Commons that Fleury had pocketed £750,000 from Beijing for three guest appearances on the state-sponsored China Central TV channel.

In a quote to the Press Association, Lance had laughed off the suggestion as 'fake news,' adding, 'our beloved Grandfather of the Nation is in a coma, our people are in deep shock, and all the Labour Party can do is dig up ancient slurs against me,' and reckoned the story would be lucky to make a few paragraphs at the foot of page eight. Instead, *The Times* had valued it as the second biggest news of the day.

'What a leftie rag this has become,' Fleury shouted towards the bed where Panda was still asleep, before lashing the paper on the floor. 'Almost makes me want to get a cat so I can use it to line its shit tray.'

As he sipped on the Americano, his bladder sent a message to his brain telling him it could do with another emptying, but he recalled that he'd been four times that night, the final trip half-an-hour before he got up, so chose to heed his doctor's advice to stare it down with brute willpower.

He flicked through the *Daily Mail*, searching for the China story, and saw to his delight that they had buried it in three paragraphs on Page 23. The *Daily Express*, whose pages Lance often graced because he was more than happy to share his rabidly right-wing opinions for free, hadn't touched it. 'Good chaps,' he said.

Then he picked up the *Daily Mirror* and his day took another considerable turn for the worse. They were leading page five with the China bung story, under the headline: SHAME OF JINPING'S POODLE, illustrating it with a photo from a rally Lance had attended the previous night in support of his friend, Robert Watson, who was standing for leadership of the UK Freedom Party.

A quick-thinking *Mirror* photographer had

managed to frame Lance's head, in rabble-rousing mode, between Robert Watson's Christian name and surname which were written large on the podium poster behind him. A sub-editor on the same wavelength as the photographer had cropped out ROBER and SON from the poster leaving only T and WAT, with Lance's ranting head filling the gap in between the letters.

'Jesus aitch fucking Christ,' he yelled, throwing the paper into the air and attempting to volley it but only managing to smash his shin into the glass coffee table, forcing a scream that woke Panda and probably half the guests on that floor.

'What's happened?' she yelled, sitting up in the bed, watching Lance roll around the shag-pile bellowing obscenities as he held his leg.

'Those twats at the *Mirror* have called me a twat,' he screamed.

'Is that even allowed?' Panda asked.

'It is when some dozy arsehole in Freedom's press office failed to realise that there's a twat in Robert Watson's name and they placed me slap in the middle of it.'

Panda threw off the duvet, put on the white, fluffy Waldorf bathrobe that was draped over the chaise longue at the foot of the bed, and walked over to Lance who was in a foetal position on the carpet, clasping his shin and muttering dire threats. She knelt down, hugged him and kissed him gently on the forehead making the kind of shushing sound nannies employ to soothe tantrum-throwing toddlers.

The loving embrace only darkened Lance's mood as it reminded him why he had gone to sleep last night in such a foul state of mind. When he had tried to make love to his mistress his erection had stayed strong for less than a minute, causing him to panic, withdraw his shrinking member and fall onto his back cursing his dysfunctional penis and the Hardman Clinic for their inability to get his soldier to salute.

'Come on, this is your big day,' said Panda.

'Is it?'

'Yes. It's not every day a man gets to be—'

'What? Called a twat in a national newspaper?'

'The face of Britain as the nation rallies in support of its royal family.'

'Hardly the fucking nation with *Brit Talk*'s viewing figures, is it?'

He brushed Panda away, giving her a withering glance which said the last thing he wanted to be was an object of sympathy, pulled himself up, sat back on the sofa and asked her to make him another coffee and add a dash of whisky from the decanter on the spirits tray next to the DeLonghi machine. As always, she obeyed unquestioningly.

'I'm so going to bollock those morons at Freedom for screwing me over. It's a schoolboy error. Absolute basic stuff. I'm sick and tired of being let down by incompetents,' he said, reaching for his phone after hearing that a WhatsApp notification had landed. The message from Richard Hollister, a senior producer at *Brit Talk*, turned his mood even darker.

'What the hell is this I'm reading?' he yelled at Panda. 'You went on Sophie Atkins' show last night to give an update on Mick O'Shea? How the? What the? This was supposed to be our story, Panda, you treacherous bastard.'

Sophie Atkins was Lance Fleury's nemesis. The right-wing rottweiler that Brit Talk's rival channel, Voice of Britain, set against him in the peak-time evening slot, who had managed to achieve the impossible: being more hated by lefties than him.

The failed reality show contestant found her mojo as the scourge of liberal thinkers on daytime TV where she famously defended Britain First activists who had put bacon through the letterbox of a Bradford mosque, saying they would have done the country more of a favour if the bacon had been coating a pipe bomb.

That led to her being offered a column in a downmarket tabloid where she positioned herself as the only true voice of the working-class despite her being a public school-educated snob who despised everything about the 'lower orders' especially their names, teeth, tattoos and the fact they 'love to wear clothes that have words on.'

She was sacked as a columnist following a record number of complaints to the Independent Press Standards Organisation over an article in which she had described asylum-seekers heading to Britain as 'lice in human form' whose boats should be sunk by a new branch of the Royal Navy called the Anti-Parasite Task Force.

She was then given a slot as a night-time shock jock on LBC where, in just one show, she defended far-right terrorist Anders Breivik (who killed sixty-nine members of the Norwegian Workers' Youth League at a summer camp) on the grounds that someone needed to stop these dim, young snowflakes growing into bleeding-heart politicians who would pollute the world with their history-rewriting, called for a Final Solution for gipsies and said she'd like to release a celebratory single to mark the 50th anniversary of Enoch Powell's Rivers of Blood speech by turning the lyrics of 'Rivers of Babylon' into a tribute to the racist MP, called Rivers of Birmingham.

Lance's visceral hatred of her stemmed from the fact that she garnered more love than he did from the extreme right of the political spectrum, especially after tweeting that she could never join his Make the United

Kingdom Great Again party as it was too centrist. That was days before she was kicked off that social media platform for remarking, during a world heavyweight title fight, that black men make the best boxers because the average negro's brain is smaller than a Caucasian's and thus the extra layers of membrane at the front of the skull act as a protective shield.

Atkins and Lance were joined at the political hip. The pair had famously been the subject of a *Guardian* newspaper cartoon, with Lance as Hitler and Atkins as Eva Braun, swinging dog-whistles and duetting to *Tomorrow Belongs To Us*, with a think-bubble coming from their pet German Shepherd, Blondi, asking 'how do you apply to be ein rescue dog?'

He detested her so much because he recognised her as the mirror to his soul but when he looked at her reflection he saw his own weakness: an insatiable political ambition which stopped him from saying what he truly believed in case he became a leper in the mainstream media.

He didn't mind being viewed in some quarters as a panto villain but he knew that, unlike Atkins, he had to remain the star of a panto that parents were not too frightened to take their children to.

'Since when did I have to check my every media appearance with you?' Panda said coolly, placing the Johnny Walker-laced coffee on the table in front of

Lance. But he was too busy clicking on the video link to a clip from last night's show to reply. When it started playing, he placed his phone on the coffee table and let it play.

'Let's move on to the story that has enraged the nation in its hour of grief,' said Atkins, her dead-eyed, pitiless features and dyed-grey, severe wedge haircut giving her the look of an accomplished sniper.

'That Scouse scumbag, that leftie loser, that crappest of comedians, that fat, feckless effwit who abused our royal family then went on the run like the coward he is after waving a pistol at reporters, Mick O'Shea. God I feel soiled just mentioning the inbred's name,' she said, pulling a disgusted face.

'Anyway, to give us an update on the big turd's whereabouts, who better to ask than the journalist who broke the story on her website, Pandora Fitzroy-Price.'

The screen split to reveal Panda sitting at home in a white-walled room with bookshelves full of political biographies, historical novels, Margaret Thatcher and bulldog figurines, plus a huge Pandora's Box logo behind her head.

'Hi Sophie,' said Panda with a smile.

'Hi Sophie,' repeated Lance in a mocking, childlike voice. 'How do you like your snake? Medium, rare or well done?'

'So do we know where this waste of space is?' Atkins could be heard saying on the phone video. 'My guess would be in a sleeping bag in a Greggs doorway in Bootle, waiting for it to open so he can barge ahead of the early morning benefits wasters and fill that obese gut of his with half-a-dozen steak bakes,' Atkins added.

'Well Sophie, the police don't appear to know, possibly because they aren't looking that hard. But the word from my sources in the north is that he's lying low in Liverpool waiting for it all to blow over.'

'Ooh, sources plural is it now,' mocked Lance. 'My sources in the North sounds like a shit remake of a shit telly show,' said Lance. 'Who are your sources in Liverpool out of interest? Derek Hatton, Ken Dodd's fucking Diddymen or, more likely, daddy's mate who owns half of it, the Duke of Westminster?' Panda grabbed the phone, closed the link and threw it into his lap.

'Fuck you, Lance. Who do you think you are?'

'I'll tell you who I thought *you* were. Someone who was loyal.'

'So it's loyalty you want to talk about is it? Well if I were you I wouldn't pick that hill to die on.'

'What does that mean?'

'Look at the papers,' she said, picking a few up and tossing them at Lance. 'Where was your loyalty to Brit

SICK MICK

Talk when you were moonlighting on Chinese TV? Sorry, where was your loyalty to this country when you were grabbing fistfuls of dirty yellow lucre?'

'That's a lie and you know it?'

'Do I? Funny how you can never disprove it though.'

'I don't need to. And how dare you question my loyalty to Britain?'

'Okay, forget Britain. Let's question your loyalty to me? You string me along, promising to leave your wife, promising my own show on Brit Talk, but neither ever materialises do they? You're just a bullshitter, Lance.'

'What have either of those situations got to do with loyalty?' Lance replied, laughing.

'Well let's take it back a step. What about loyalty to your wife? The one you've cheated on for thirty years while shagging everything in a skirt who naively believed you could help them get on.'

'Is that why you spread your legs for me then?'

'Dunno. I've forgotten. It's been so long since there was any point in spreading them,' replied Panda dismissively, the barb arrowing straight into the bullseye of Lance's ego, forcing his head to jolt backwards.

'I'm sorry. I didn't mean that,' said Panda, reaching out to touch him, but Lance slapped her hand away, walked towards the coat stand, pulled a packet of Rothmans Original and a lighter from his inside pocket. He stormed out onto the small balcony, slamming the doors behind him.

From his view on the eighth floor he could see out across the Strand towards Cleopatra's Needle in the Embankment Gardens and, beyond that, Whitehall and Westminster's Big Ben tower. The bright morning sun bounced off the Thames making London look so resplendent it almost gave him a lump in the throat.

He gripped the iron rail, closed his eyes and sucked in a gust of air, which he had to admit smelled much cleaner than it used to, just as he had to admit the rush hour sounded a lot quieter. Maybe there was something to the congestion charge and electric cars, he thought. Then made a mental note to never admit that publicly in case the Tarmac-chewers used it on placards at their next Just Stop Oil protest.

He pulled out a cigarette, tapped it on the packet, placed it between his lips, then sparked a flame from his gold lighter which lit his Rothmans' and flooded his bloodstream with a sweet, woody nicotine hit that sent a wave of pleasure to his brain.

He blew the smoke out from the side of his mouth, leaned back on the wooden door and, for the first time that morning, felt relaxed. He drew again, even deeper this time, and filled his lungs with smoke, thinking to himself that this was one of the last true manly pleasures not to be outlawed.

What kind of a man was Lance Fleury? he asked himself, as his gaze switched from London's skyline to his own soul. The last ten minutes had once again left him feeling small and vulnerable, wondering what the point of his life was if all he appeared to be doing with it was provoking hate. Does everyone see me as a traitor, a poodle, a poisonous twat? These bouts of self-doubt were becoming more regular for Lance.

He had always suffered them despite the public believing his skin was thicker than a pimp's wallet and that he thrived on animosity. He was only human. He wanted to be, if not loved, then admired. Especially as he grew older and began to assess what he had really achieved in a lifetime of politics.

His eldest son, Stanley, who was now twenty-eight, had cut off all ties with him. The breaking point came when he became engaged to human rights lawyer Shanaya Perera, whose Sri Lankan-born parents had refused to attend the celebration dinner as they could not bear to break bread with Lance.

He fell into a dark rage when Stanley broke the news. Lance responded, in sentences peppered with racist expletives, that they should be thanking Buddha that they were allowed to move to Britain not insulting one of their adopted country's leading political commentators. Shanaya, sitting in the next room, heard every word and, through tearful sobs, told Stanley he had to choose between her or his father.

His son's rejection felt like a blunt kitchen knife slashing his heart. What was the point in being famous if it earned you a reputation so toxic it would bar you from your son's wedding? What was the point in crusading for your country—even if you believed 100 per cent in that crusade—if it created a caricature of yourself that was so despised it would stop you from picking up, and holding, your first grandchild?

Sometimes he contemplated packing it all in and going back to work in property. Or even, when he suffered a particularly neurotic episode, slinking off to anonymity, maybe working for a charity in deepest Africa. Which was a prospect so absurd it never failed to shake him out of self-loathing mode and drag him back to reality.

He peered inside the room through the lace curtains and saw Panda reading the *Daily Telegraph* on the couch. The sight of her long, toned legs and tanned body, naked beneath the dressing gown, gave him a stirring below. Bit late for that old chap, he thought.

He reassured himself that it was early days with the shock therapy. Five more trips to the clinic and all would be well. He'd show her then. There's no point in spreading your legs for you, she'd said? He'd satisfy her so well that in a few weeks those legs would tremble at the thought of sleeping with Yours Truly.

He regretted over-reacting in such a vicious way to her appearance on Sophie Atkins' show. Panda had done nothing wrong and, more importantly, he needed to keep her onside with this O'Shea stuff. He couldn't afford to let her waltz off in a huff and hitch her wagon to someone else. Especially if that someone else was Atkins. The wise move was to swallow his pride, lose all of this maudlin self-pity, and creep.

He took one final drag on his cigarette, tossed it over the balcony rail onto the street below, blew out a huge gust of smoke then walked back inside, sat down on the couch next to Panda and picked up his whisky coffee. She cracked first.

'I really am sorry. What I said was below the belt. Shit, there I go again. Sorry.'

'It's okay. You're right. I am having problems in the below belt department. It's the stress. But I'm taking steps to sort it out. It's in hand if you'll pardon the pun.'

Panda laughed. Lance leaned across and kissed her.

'I'm sorry too. I was wrong to attack you for going on the Atkins show. You're right. This is your story and it's a great chance to build your brand. It just cut me deep because, because, it's…her.'

'Well, you didn't watch the clip in full. If you had, you'd have seen how she tried to undermine me.'

'What do you mean?'

'She basically used the interview as a platform to slag off all northerners by unleashing a slew of rehearsed gags, and looked down on me as if to say why are you wasting your time chasing such a scumbag?'

'You see,' said Lance, grabbing her hands, 'she's not like us. She's only interested in herself. The story has to be all about her,' he told Panda without a hint of irony.

'Do you really think he's lying low in Liverpool?'

'That's what Jason Garlick says, and he's been speaking to people in the city for the past two days.'

'Could he be somewhere else?'

'I've got a freelancer watching his girlfriend's flat in Marylebone and another outside his agent's house in Didsbury. They've seen no sign of him.

'Well get yourself up to Scouseland this morning and be in situ when he rears his ugly head. I'll book a cameraman to contact you and you can do a live link to the show with an update. How does that sound?'

Panda thought for a few seconds then nodded. Lance kissed her cheek, ruffled her hair and walked towards the bathroom taking his pyjama top off. Then turned around and said as he clicked his fingers. 'Oh, maybe put on some shades when you leave the hotel. There's bound to be a pack of vultures chasing me for a reaction to this Chinese nonsense. Don't want to give them any more ammunition.'

Panda gave a sarcastic laugh and shook her head. 'God, you know how to make a girl feel special and wanted, don't you? I'm just ammunition, am I?'

'Come on darling. Let's not go there again. You know I didn't mean it like that. You know you're so much more and when all this stuff blows over I'll—'

'Lance,' Panda said, interrupting him.

'What?'

'Fuck off, eh?'

16

WEDNESDAY LUNCHTIME

The Ticket To Ride taxi was illegally parked half on the pavement and half on the white zigzag lines at the approach to the zebra crossing. Mick stood outside the cab, one hand gripping a can of Fanta lemon, the other shading his eyes from the blinding midday sun as he stared across the road at the two-storey white Georgian townhouse that was home to the most famous recording studio in the world.

There were a couple of dozen tourists worshipping at the Beatles shrine, some taking photos outside the studio, others writing their names or messages of love on the white gate posts of the gift shop. Twenty yards down from the studio, they queued to walk across the zebra crossing that appeared on the cover of the Abbey Road album.

A small Japanese woman had her phone on the end of a selfie-stick and was videoing herself as she slowly retraced the steps of the Fab Four on the crossing, causing an angry BMW driver who she was holding up to beep his horn and flick two fingers at her.

The woman mistook it for a peace sign, stopped in the middle of the crossing and bowed in gratitude at the driver, giving him the reverse two fingers back, which caused a white van man, who was stationary in the opposite lane, to stick his head out the window and shout, 'Oi, Yoko, get a bleedin' move on, will ya.'

Not everyone around Abbey Road was in the mood to give peace a chance.

There had been a change of plan concerning Mick. In the hours between Ayesha leaving Knutsford services car park and returning, she had thought through her fugitive client's planned trip to the very place where the nation's media would be gathered, and ruled it out.

She told Mick that after he had shaved his head and face he should drive to London but stay out of sight, away from the centre. She would travel down, hand photos of Vinny to two of her trusted colleagues in their Soho office, and all three would stake out the queues for the duke's easel at Westminster and also outside the Palace to find his dad. The offer from *Saturday Night Live* had turned heads among the top brass at the Grin talent agency and they were on board with protecting what could turn out to be a very hot property. The plan was that if Ayesha or her team spotted Vinny, she would call Mick and he could swoop in and talk him out of his deranged assassination plan.

Mick had reluctantly agreed to keep a very low profile after Ayesha had given him £500, three sim cards for his burner phone, a sleeping bag, laptop and, crucially, his new outfit from Barnardo's charity shop in Knutsford: a double-breasted Prince of Wales check jacket that was two sizes too big, a light brown grandad collar cheesecloth shirt and a pair of rust-coloured cords with elasticated waist. 'You win. There's no way I'm walking around the centre of London dressed like a kiddie-fiddling geography teacher,' he had told her.

He had driven down to the capital the previous evening and turned right at the end of the M1, onto the North Circular Road, with the vague idea of heading to Wembley. From what his mates, who were football fans, had told him, you could always find somewhere to park a mile from the stadium. Plus, he had looked at the map and miscalculated, thinking it was quite close to Sadie's flat in Marylebone, so if she did take him up on his offer of a steamy bunk-up in the back of his cab she wouldn't have far to travel. It's good to put others first, he'd thought.

However, a few miles along the North Circular he spotted a McDonalds drive-through which alerted his growling stomach to the fact he had eaten nothing since his Scotch egg and liquorice allsorts buffet breakfast. He turned off the North Circular, ordered a Big Mac with bacon meal and extra fries, pulled into the car park, ate it, then decided he would stay parked there until a smiling jobsworth with a nametag on their apron told him to have a nice day somewhere else. But no-one did. So at 10pm he crawled into his sleeping bag, stretched out in the back seat and slept like a very full log.

He had spent that morning in McDonalds having a double sausage and egg McMuffin for breakfast and a Big Mac for an early lunch, his logic being the opposite of Paul Newman's when the film star was asked if he was ever unfaithful to his wife. To Mick's mind, why go looking for steak when there's hamburgers at home. And this north London McDonalds felt so much like home he even cleaned his teeth and had a swill in the toilets.

In between meals he drank cups of coffee and studied his laptop. His head was now clear of all drugs and alcohol and he could properly appreciate the national celebrity he had become. #WheresMick was trending on X; Netflix and Apple had been snowed under with requests to show *Dog Day Afternoon* after Mick had put Pacino's Attica scene back on the map, and *The Guardian* had run an article documenting the support he had received from Millennials and Gen Z, asking the question, 'Is This The Anti-Hero We've All Been Waiting For?'

The *Mail*, *Sun* and *Express* on the other hand were demanding to know (a) how long the police were going to allow this anarchist to laugh in the nation's face (b) when the BBC would announce they were banning him for life and (c) if he was the most potent symbol yet from left-wing culture warriors that they wouldn't stop until all of Britain's institutions were torn down. No answers were forthcoming.

He searched for any link between himself and Ticket To Ride tours but nobody had made the connection, which came as a big relief. He had assured Robbo that if he was arrested while driving the taxi he would claim to have driven it off with a spare set of keys he had found in his mate's house and that Robbo had known nothing of the vehicle theft.

When Mick tired of wallowing in his new-found celebrity he checked out Google Maps to see how far he was from Sadie's Marylebone flat and was disappointed to discover it was nine miles away. But something else caught his eye that was much closer to his new home: Abbey Road.

He studied photos of the studios and the zebra crossing and came upon a website advertising dozens of different London Beatles tours. Astonished that these tours were not confined to Liverpool, Mick spent two hours engrossed in the details of the Swinging Sixties' sights and stories they had to offer.

After sinking a cheeseburger he decided, out of curiosity, to head over to Abbey Road and check it out.

Which was how he ended up illegally parked across from the studios, studying the crowds.

His shaved head and face made him unrecognisable from his Giant Haystacks stage persona. With his two black bushy eyebrows being the only hair left above his chest, he now looked like Gru from *Despicable Me*.

He glanced away from the studios towards the zebra crossing where he saw a traffic warden heading in his direction, so jumped back into the taxi. Just as he was about to drive away a blond, bespectacled man in his forties stuck his head into the window and asked in a German accent, 'Are you free to do for us a tour?'

Mick looked behind the man at his wife and teenage daughter, who had pleading looks in their eyes, then towards the traffic warden who was now closing in with intent, and instinctively replied, 'Jump in.'

'How much do you charge for a party of three?'

'We can work it out,' said Mick, warming to his Beatles theme.

The man opened the door and let his wife and daughter go ahead before stepping inside. As the door shut, the traffic warden rapped on the passenger window but Mick just waved back, shouted, 'Say goodbye, folks, to the lovely meter maid,' then shot away from the pavement and through the zebra crossing almost wiping out half-a-dozen selfie-stick waving pensioners.

SICK MICK

As the Germans jolted back in their seats, their shocked looks questioning whether they had made the right move, Mick shouted into his mirror, 'Welcome to Ticket To Ride, the toppermost of the poppermost tour around. My name is Mal. What's yours?'

'Erm, I am Klaus, my wife is Ella and my daughter is Annalise,' the man said nervously as he strapped his daughter into her seat belt, his wife looking relieved that the cab had slowed down. 'So what form will the tour take?' asked Klaus.

Mick pressed a couple of buttons on the car's sound system and as the brass fanfare at the beginning of *Magical Mystery Tour* started up, he joined in the lyrics. 'Roll up, roll up for the magical mystery tour, step right this way.'

'How long will this mystery tour last?' Klaus asked.

'That's the biggest mystery of all,' Mick replied.

'And how many pounds is it?'

'However many pounds you think worth it is,' said Mick, drawing an affronted look from Klaus, which implied that his teutonic sense of order had been insulted by such a random measurement.

'Where are you guys from?' Mick asked, as he headed south past Lords cricket ground.

'Hamburg,' answered Annalise.

'Wow, thank you so, so much,' said Mick.

'For what?' asked Ella.

'For giving the world the greatest food ever, the hamburger. And for turning the Beatles from boys into men. Do you know what George Harrison called Hamburg?'

'No,' all three answered.

'The dirtiest city in the world. That's because he lost his cherry there to a fraulein of the night.'

This caused Annelise to cover her face as she laughed, Ella to frown and Klaus to reply frostily, 'Hamburg is now very clean. Unlike this taxi,' before picking up an empty Maltesers McFlurry carton off the floor and holding it up to the driver's rear-view mirror.

'Sorry, I had a kinders' party before you got in and I didn't have time to tidy up,' he said, silently thanking Ayesha for cleaning out the back-seat bombsite at Knutsford and putting in an air freshener.

'So, are you to show us the Beatles' sights of London?'

'Oh ja, ja. I'm going to tell you stuff you would never pick up from the other tours, because I'm from the south end of Liverpool where all the Beatles are from. You're not going to believe this, but mein father was Ringo's cousin and he told me so much stuff, you know, insider stuff,' said Mick tapping his nose.

'Such as?' asked Ella, triggering Mick into improv mode.

SICK MICK

'Well,' he said, scanning the road, spotting the big Gothic church of Our Lady of St John's Wood on his left and pointing to it. 'Paul and George, who were the two Catholics, would sometimes walk there from Abbey Road and say a prayer for inspiration when they were struggling to write songs. John tagged along one day because he was bored and noticed a four-foot statue of Jesus near the altar. He went up to it, leaned his arm on the statue's head, bent over so he was looking him in the eye, slapped his cheek and said, 'Holy father in heaven, I never knew you were a dwarf.' George and Paul fell about laughing and it became an in-joke among the group. And that was what inspired John to say that The Beatles were bigger than Jesus Christ, which landed them in so much scheisse when it got taken the wrong way. Anyway, let's make you feel at home.'

He pressed a few buttons, on came the German version of *She Loves You* and Mick started singing, 'sie liebt dich, yeah, yeah, yeah; sie liebt dich, yeah, yeah, yeah.'

Annalise and Ella joined in, and Klaus reluctantly followed them as Mick swung the taxi into Baker Street and past the Sherlock Holmes museum. He thought about telling them that Paul once read a story about Sherlock's missus dumping him for a man from the penny-farthing trade, which inspired Macca to write *She's Leaving Holmes*, but decided to store away the woeful pun for future use.

It made him grin though. He'd missed this. The testing of his comedy brain under real-time pressure. The public stage. The audience hanging on his every, nonsensical word. The not knowing what was going to leave his mouth next or in which direction the comic journey, or in this case the physical journey, would go. The living on the edge. The sense of infallibility. The buzzing on fear. The pure adrenaline rush. The sense of utter bewilderment when something you didn't even know that you knew was uttered to a rapturous reception. If there was a better feeling in life, he couldn't imagine it.

The taxi was backed up in a queue at the traffic lights at Marylebone Road, where a group of chanting football fans in England shirts were waiting to cross to The Globe pub to carry on getting tanked-up before that evening's game at Wembley.

'Schau, da ist der fiend,' said Annalise looking out of the window.

'What,' asked Mick.

'Sorry, she is joking. She said, look there is the enemy.' Said Ella. 'Germany are playing England tonight at Wembley.'

'And we have tickets,' said an excited Annalise.

'I see. Right,' said Mick. 'Let's get you in the mood

for Wembley.'

He fiddled with the buttons on the sound system, changing the track to The Beatles' German version of *I Want To Hold Your Hand*, wound down the windows, pumped the volume up to maximum and urged the family to start singing. They were reluctant to oblige but Mick soon picked up the chorus and was bellowing it towards the mob standing on the nearby pavement, 'Komm gib mir deine hand, komm gib mir deine ha-a-a-and, komm gib mir deine hand.'

The fans at first looked stunned, then realised they were being taunted by Germans prompting two of them to run towards the taxi shouting, 'Get the facking Krauts.' Mick put the windows up and hit the door locks, telling the petrified family not to worry as they were 'little dick men' with no lives.

Realising that they were not going to make it into the taxi, a pair of snarling, overweight, middle-aged men banged on the windows and chanted, 'Two World Wars and one World Cup, doo-dah, doo-dah,' which inspired Mick to wind down his window on the opposite side to them and yell back a line he'd heard German comedian Henning Wehn slap down an English heckler with, 'Four World Cups and one World Pope.'

The window-banging pair were joined by six of their mates who attempted to navigate the traffic and get to Mick, but the lights changed, and he pulled away singing, 'Deutschland, Deutschland uber alles' as he repeatedly punched his horn.

Annalise was now crying in the back seat, and as her mother comforted her, Klaus exploded. 'What in God's name was that about? Were you trying to get us killed?'

'All part of the tour. You see, it's what The Beatles would have done.'

'What?' snapped Ella, who had finally run out of patience with her eccentric guide.

'They hated war. That's why they handed their MBE medals back to the Queen as a protest against Vietnam.'

'I thought they were protesting against Biafra,' Klaus sniffed.

'Yeah, that too, and Vietnam, and *Cold Turkey* slipping down the charts,' Mick replied, for once being 100% accurate.

'This is not a tour, it is a farce. I don't believe you know anything about The Beatles,' said Klaus as Ella spoke to her husband, in an agitated mode, in German.

'We would very much like for you to drop us off here, please,' said Klaus.

'You sure? I was just getting warmed up.'

'We have heard all we want to hear from you, thank you.'

SICK MICK

'Okay, the customer is always king,' said Mick, pulling up just before Portman Square.

'How many pounds, please?' asked Klaus.

'It's on der house,' Mick replied, waving him away.

'No please, you must take something or we will feel like we are insulting you,' Ella said, but Mick shook his head.

'Danke schon, Herr Gru,' said a laughing Annelise.

'What did she say?' asked Mick, but the family had left the cab and were standing on the pavement.

'One last nugget of information and this is for free,' said Mick through the open window. 'Do you see the rooftop of the building behind you?'

'Ah, let me guess. That is conveniently where the Beatles gave their live performance after the *Get Back* album was finished, no?' said Klaus, as Mick smiled, pointed at him and tapped his head, saying, 'you're good, you're very good' before telling them. 'No. It's got really nasty pigeons who shit on your head, so don't look up. Auf wiedersehen, pets.'

He turned back to his wheel, moved slowly into the Baker Street traffic and said out loud, 'It never leaves you, kid. Talent never leaves you.' Then looked at himself in the mirror and said, 'Who the hell is Herr Gru?'

SICK MICK

17

WEDNESDAY AFTERNOON

It was becoming pretty clear that Panda Fitzroy-Price and Liz Morgan would not be meeting at six for mojitos. Panda had arrived at Liverpool Lime Street train station at noon, armed with an overnight case, a laptop and a host of preconceptions about a city she had never been within thirty-five miles of because, well, why would she? In her eyes, the North of England was an alien country and Liverpool was its capital, that viewpoint proven to be fully self-justified when she attempted a conversation with a cabbie and found herself scrawling through Google Translate on her iPhone looking for a language called Scouse.

But as the taxi headed up Mount Pleasant and took a right into Rodney Street, she was pleasantly astonished by the fine Georgian houses, their red-brick fronts glowing an attractive shade of terracotta in the late Spring sun.

The Hope Street Hotel also wooed her. Not just the stripped-back, pink Cheshire brickwork, iron pillars, pitch pine beams and cherry and walnut furniture, but the civilised staff. They almost seemed, well, educated. Who knew there were schools up here?

However, her Damascene conversion to Liverpool's

charms lasted as long as it took her to settle into The Quarter cafe opposite her hotel, order a pot of Twinings Earl Grey tea, ring Merseyside Police to ask why they had failed to arrest Mick O'Shea and be put through to Liz Morgan.

It was Liz's final day after sixteen years in the press office. The native Liverpudlian was moving to the Lake District to run a crafts shop with her carpenter husband, and to say she was demob happy was very much to understate how much she pined for her freedom. Escaping the evil worlds of murderers, wife-beaters, rapists, armed robbers and, worst of all, journalists, made her positively orgasmic.

The office whip-round had produced £400 in John Lewis vouchers, a card full of heartfelt messages about how she would be missed and how she would always be welcome back (that wasn't happening) plus a sumptuous, hand-made, white vanilla cake which she planned to share with her colleagues that afternoon after buying a round of Starbucks coffees. But the icing on her retirement cake was the phone call from Pandora Fitzroy-Price demanding to know, in a voice that sounded like a 19th century Dowager Countess reprimanding a scullery maid for over-boiling her breakfast egg, what the hell she was doing about Mick O'Shea.

Liz had stopped Panda, mid-lecture, to ask which

media organisation she was from, and when she replied that she was the proprietor of the Pandora's Box website, Liz had taken pleasure in saying, 'so, you're not really press then, are you?'

The frosty conversation took on an Antarctic plunge when an affronted Panda ran through her CV, regaling Liz with the ground-breaking reportage she had produced on the *Daily Telegraph* diary, as a think-tank lobbyist, a blogger who was featured regularly on Brit Talk, and her crowning glory: co-writing a diary with a minister about his struggles to sort out the Covid pandemic, whose emails she sold to the *Sunday Times* once the book was finished, which caused him and his family so much shame he tried to commit suicide. Liz's response? 'Yeah, so still not really press then?'

There followed a stand-off, during which Panda screeched the standard cliches of an entitled individual who was accustomed to getting their own way, culminating in, 'I demand to be put through to your superior.' This handed Liz the leaving present she could only have dreamt of, and could only have responded to in the style she wanted as she was safe in the knowledge that this would be her final day in press office hell.

'Have you ever heard of the practice of going off the record?' Liz asked.

'Of course I have, don't patronise me.'

'Would you like me to?'

'Only if you have something of relevance to the situation,' Panda replied.

'Oh, it's very relevant to the situation. Very relevant. You see, my superiors are rather busy right now. They were told last night that the lovely Prince Harry is going walkabout in London, meaning Merseyside has to send officers to high security locations to look for men with bombs who might kill innocent people. Sadly, that means we don't have the available manpower to look for a comedian with a toy gun who put the willies up a few journalists with nothing better to do than hound him for trying to make people laugh.

'A press release was issued three hours ago explaining how Merseyside would be sending these officers to cover key targets, which you obviously missed. Which is very surprising seeing as how you're a top, top news hound. Now, unless you need me to spell any of the words I've just told you, I'd quite like to get on with looking forward to not having to speak to the increasing number of stuck-up, phoney shitehawks like you who mistakenly believe they are journalists.'

The phone was slammed down before Panda could unleash her rage. Instead, after five seconds staring at her iPhone in disbelief, she punched in Jason Garlick's number, heard him pick up and was about to yell, 'Where the hell are you?' when he appeared in front of her saying, 'Hi, how's it going?'

'It's not going,' Panda replied, before launching into an attack on Merseyside Police in general and Liz Morgan in particular.

'First they decide it's not their job to arrest a lunatic in possession of a firearm, then they call the journalist who broke the story that alerted the world to said lunatic, a phoney shit. Oh I'm going to enjoy writing a blog on this and exposing them on Lance's show.'

'Was in possession,' Garlick said.

'What?' asked Panda.

'The police recovered the gun from his house so he hasn't got it.'

'Is that really the best you can come up with? What am I paying you for?'

'Well, you're not paying me, are you?'

She ordered Garlick to sit down at her table, then asked him to fill her in on where he was up to in his pursuit of Mick. He told her he had spent that morning and all of yesterday driving around the Dingle, touring Mick's favourite haunts such as The Florrie community centre, staking out the homes of his friends, asking around at the charities he did voluntary work for, but turned up nothing. It was the same story when he went to The Laughter Bucket last night. He has either vanished or he is still in Liverpool hidden away, he told her.

Panda asked about Vinny but Garlick replied that he, too, was nowhere to be seen. After telling her stringer once again that she did not know what she was paying him for, and Garlick expanding on his last reply by pointing out she had not paid him anything for six months, her phone rang. It was Lance Fleury. And his brain was boiling like a freshly-caught lobster in a chef's pot over the Merseyside Police press release which, thanks to Liz Morgan, she had been made aware of.

Such was the volume of his fury, Garlick could make out every expletive-ridden phrase, despite Panda holding her iPhone close to her ear and turning her back on him so he couldn't see her wincing face. Which, taking out repetition, translated roughly to: Merseyside police are lazy, bent bastards, the Home Secretary is a knee-jerk arsehole, Harry is a little cunt, ISIS can go fuck themselves and Panda had better find that leftie twat in that leftie shithole she was in, or not bother coming back to London.

She put the phone back on the table and tried to regain composure by draining the pot of the Earl Grey into her cup, hoping her face was not as red as it felt.

'There is one lead I haven't followed up,' said Garlick, before explaining that Mick was not much of a drinker but often popped up in a pub further down Hope Street called The Casa.

'It's a bit of a do-gooders hangout owned by sacked dockers,' explained Garlick, causing Panda to raise her eyebrows and stifle a mock yawn.

'They give out free legal advice, hold community meetings, run a foodbank, put on political plays, that kind of woke crap,' Garlick continued. 'And O'Shea often pops up there to help out. Crucially, there are upstairs rooms once used for offices where comrades without a bed can stay. It's the perfect hideout. And if he needed to come downstairs there is no chance of anyone who spotted him getting in touch with the police.'

'So you think he's doing a sort of Anne Frank?' Panda asked.

'Bit of a leap, that. But if you want to put it that way, yes, it's possible.'

'Oh my God, imagine if we catch him in there, and he lies about where he's been hiding? Think of the headline: 'Sick Mick in Holocaust Denial Shame.' Total proof that he's a Jew-hating Corbynista. I love it. What are we waiting for?'

'Well, I thought you said you would treat me to lunch,' said Garlick.

'My God, when you're not pestering me for financial handouts you want me to feed you. Why are you turning into such a self-pitying victim? You really must leave the North.'

'Well, if you followed up on your promises I might have the means to.'

'Come on,' she said, standing and throwing a five pound note on the table. 'Let's go catch the Scouse Anne Frank.'

Panda and Garlick walked down Hope Street, out of the shadow of the longest cathedral in the world, past the art deco Philharmonic Hall and the ornate Philharmonic Dining Rooms, until they reached the three-storey Georgian terrace that housed The Casa pub. They climbed the four steps to the entrance, and as Panda walked through the open door she had her worst suspicions confirmed. With its framed black-and-white shots of old dock scenes, trade union banners, busts of Tony Benn and Nye Bevan, posters advertising an am-dram production of 'The Ragged Trousered Philanthropists' and an exhibition of photos and memorabilia from the Spanish Civil War, it was a shrine to working-class solidarity. Or a museum of mawkish over-sentimentality, as Panda preferred to put it.

The Godolphin & Latymer-educated daughter of a minor aristocrat could not have felt less at home if she'd stumbled into Kellingley colliery miner's welfare soup kitchen in 1984, been thrown a tea towel by Anne

Scargill and pointed to the sink.

For an early Wednesday afternoon, The Casa was relatively busy. Two middle-aged drinkers stood at the bar, one examining the *Daily Mirror*'s racing pages, another scrawling through his phone.

In one corner of the square lounge sat Tony Dolan, a sixty-four-year-old former convenor on the docks, built like a tenement block with eyes that said backing down from anything was not an option. But today those eyes were full of pride. The self-trained legal advice councillor was breaking the news to a school dinner lady—who had been sacked three weeks earlier for having a sly drag on a Benson & Hedges Blue outside the kitchens—that she was being reinstated.

Tony had arranged a meeting with the school headmaster, where he told him that he knew exactly what he was playing at: cooking up some disciplinary excuse to slash costs by sacking non-teaching staff. He then asked how he'd feel having a picket line outside his main gate for a month, with teachers and parents forced to walk past placards saying 'School for Scabs' and, one the old Pink Floyd fan was particularly proud of, 'Dark Sarcasm in the Head's Room.'

'You're back in on Monday with all pay reinstated,' he told the dinner lady, before giving her an uncomfortable hug when she burst into tears.

Three tables along from Tony, Anthony McGrory

was sorting out the pile of tins, packets and cartons that people had dropped off to be redistributed to food banks. [In Catholic Liverpool circles the name Anthony, like Paulie in New Jersey mafia circles, is given to 50% of the male population. As well as Tony and Anthony there was also an Ant, a To, a Tone and an Ant'nee who drank in the Casa].

On the tables next to the window that looked onto Hope Street, a meeting of The Spirit Of Ebro—a group of retired men who kept alive the memory of left-wing volunteers who fought fascists in the Spanish Civil War—was in progress.

The Casa had become an unofficial International Brigade museum, its walls decked out with photos of young idealists resting and preparing for battle in late-1930s Spain, alongside reproductions of maps, letters and newspaper cuttings. Pride of place was given to a three-foot square roll of honour, listing every one of the 200 or so Merseyside volunteers, the places they fought, and where twenty-eight of them died. The group named itself after the Battle of Ebro where Liverpool-born Jack Jones, the formidable trade union leader, had been wounded. Lately, with an increase in far right groups feeding off perceived white, working-class alienation, and attacking asylum-seekers in their hotels, the Spirit of Ebro had made itself a focal point for anti-fascist activity in Liverpool. It was a kind of

SICK MICK

Dad's Army Wing of Hope Not Hate.

Standing up, addressing his men, was The Spirit's political commissar, Ray Moon, wearing a black beret and a black roll neck jumper which sported pin badges of Jack Jones and Tom Mann (the trade union leader who led the 1911 Liverpool General Transport Strike and had an International Brigade unit named after him). Ray was dapper in a mock-revolutionary, ancient Citizen Smith kind of way: short with gleaming skin and bright eyes that suggested he took his five-a-day, and a lean body suggesting he took full advantage of his David Lloyd pensioner discount. The seventy-four-year-old was a retired politics lecturer from John Moores University, a nurturer of socialism, an expert in Merseyside's industrial history, and the proud nephew of an International Brigade volunteer who had survived the battle of Jarama and passed on to him his beret. When he spoke people listened, mainly because they couldn't shut him up. Although, you did get the occasional heckler, like the near-deaf ex-docker who told Ray when he was in full Fidel Castro mode that he should be ashamed to wear that beret as the nearest he'd got to fighting in Spain was offering out a Benidorm barman who'd over-charged him for a pint of Guinness.

Garlick ordered a half-of-lager for himself, a sparkling water for Panda, and paid the barmaid. He also gave her no tip. As you would expect.

Panda told him she was going to take a look around, asked Sarah the barmaid where the toilet was, and followed her directions down a corridor that led to a large back room. She walked past the ladies loo, pushed open the swing doors and scanned the darkened function room, peering under tables, on top of stacked-up chairs and scouring the stage for any evidence that this was the home of Scouse Anne Frank. None was found.

She left the room as Tony was entering it and, surprised to see her, asked if he could help. She told him she had lost her way looking for the toilets, then blurted out: 'This is such a lovely, big building. Are there rooms to rent upstairs?'

'No, love. Why do you ask?'

'I'm just looking for somewhere to stay that has a bit of, well, character. Somewhere that's, I don't know, down with the workers?' She almost had to physically prise her facial features back into place as she heard those words leave her mouth.

'Down with the workers, eh?' Tony replied, laughing at the juxtaposition of her accent and that phrase. 'No, love. We don't rent rooms. But if you're a bit skint we can try to sort something out for you.'

As it dawned on Panda that Tony thought she was a well-off, professional Leftie who had fallen on hard times, her expensively-constructed face felt like it had been slapped with a packet of foodbank pasta.

'No, I'm good. Very good. But thank you,' she replied.

'So what brings you to the Casa?' Tony asked without the slightest hint of suspicion.

'I'm, erm. Well, we. We are a production company who are trying to find the comedian Mick O'Shea to make a documentary about him. Have you ever heard of him?'

'Mick, yeah. Sound lad. Does a lot of good work in the community.'

'Have you seen him lately?'

'He was in last Monday, I think it was. Picking up supplies for families in the Dingle. But he hasn't been in this week. Give me your card and I'll pass it on next time I see him.'

'Of course,' Panda replied, reaching inside her Mulberry bag, then realising she could not possibly pass on her Pandora's Box card, pulled her hand out.

'No, I haven't got any with me. Sorry. But it's okay. I'm sure I'll track him down,' she said, shaking Tony's hand and walking back down the corridor, past the toilets.

'You've just gone past the ladies again,' Tony yelled after her, causing Panda to turn on her heels and walk into the toilet, pulling a 'silly old me' face, dreading to think what aromas she might smell or sights she might see beyond the door.

When Tony returned to his seat where he had been poring over paperwork, his mate of fifty years and fellow ex-docker, Frank Monaghan, was at the table with a half pint of mild and a single whisky. Frank was a few years older than Tony, and thanks to forty cigarettes a day and a series of cancer operations that had removed half of his organs, he looked it. But a voracious reading habit kept his brain vinegar sharp.

'I can't put my finger on it,' Tony said, 'but I just bumped into a woman by the toilets and there's something not right about her. She's nervous. Deffo hiding something,' he told Frank, whose attention was now sparked on an otherwise boring Wednesday lunchtime.

When Panda walked back into the room and stood chatting with Garlick at the bar, Frank gave her the once over, telling Tony that he thought he recognised her but couldn't place where. He walked to the bar, ordered a bag of peanuts from Sarah and listened to the conversation between Panda and Garlick which sounded very terse, and the voices, especially the woman's, very posh. The penny dropped when Frank heard her say, 'Lance.' It was the way she pronounced it. As in Laans. He pretended to squint past her, focussing on something outside the window, gave her a close inspection and concluded that the face matched the voice. He handed a pound coin to Sarah, grabbed his peanuts, and headed back to Tony.

'She's a fucking Tory reporter off the telly who's in cahoots with that Brexit fella, Fleury. I've seen her slagging off Mick with him,' Frank babbled so quickly Tony told him to slow down and repeat what he had said. When he did, Tony nodded and replied: 'She must think he's hiding here. That's why she was asking about renting upstairs and sneaking around the back room.'

'Well it'd be a shame to disappoint her, wouldn't it?' said Frank, before shouting over to Panda: 'Eh, love, come here. I believe you're looking for someone.'

Panda glanced around to see if Frank was addressing Sarah, realised it was her he was talking to, and walked over, with Garlick, to their table.

'Tony says you're looking for our Mick,' said Frank.

'Yes, that's right. We have a proposition for a documentary type thing,' she replied.

'Oh, a documentary-type thing, eh?' he said to Tony, raising his eyes in mock surprise. 'I'm sure he'd love to meet you. But, you do know he's a bit of a marked man at the moment, don't you?'

'Well, yes,' said Panda.

'There's a shower of right-wing wankers on the telly and in the papers calling for him to be hanged, isn't there?'

Panda and Garlick nodded furiously.

'We have to be very careful who we talk to, don't we?'

'Sure. I can see why,' said Panda.

'So, before I tell you where he is you'll both need to put your hands on Tony Benn's head over there, repeat after me the words to the Red Flag, then take a socialist vow never to reveal his whereabouts.'

Panda and Garlick looked at each other in terror, before Panda replied, 'Of course.'

'Absolutely,' said Garlick with a nervous twitch.

Tony could no longer keep a straight face and burst out laughing. Frank joined in. Panda and Garlick just stared at them with a frozen expression, unsure what reaction to give.

'Nah, I'm only kidding you, love,' said Frank. 'No oath needed. I can see you are very trustworthy people. So here's the deal. Give us a hundred nicker donation for our foodbank and I'll tell you where you can find him.'

There was a short silence, broken by a squirming Panda asking, 'Nicker?' Frank telling her it meant pounds, Panda telling Garlick to cough up, Garlick saying he had no cash, Frank asking Sarah to bring the card machine over, Garlick holding his bank card over it and stumping up £100, and Panda asking for Mick's whereabouts with her natural air of confidence restored.

'When you walk out of here, turn right and straight ahead you'll see a big building shaped like a wigwam.'

'The Catholic cathedral?' Garlick asked.

'Very observant,' said Frank.

'What's he doing there?' asked Panda.

'He's sought sanctuary.'

Garlick looked at Panda and shook his head while Frank attempted to look offended.

'You don't believe he'd do that? With a good Catholic name like Mick O'Shea? I'm telling you, that's where he is. No skin off my nose if you don't believe me.'

'Okay, let's say he is there,' said Panda. 'How would we go about contacting him?'

Frank tutted and replied: 'And there was me thinking you sounded educated and knew your Victor Hugo from your Hugo Boss.'

'Sorry?' asked Panda.

'Just go inside the cathedral, find a priest and tell him your name is Esmerelda and you're looking for Quasimodo.'

Tony collapsed into a heap of laughter saying he couldn't take any more, as Garlick turned on his heel and walked to the door with Panda following, shouting, 'bastards.'

Frank stood up, did an impression of a hunchback, lifted his whisky, and screamed after them: 'Aren't you going to get me a drink Esmerelda? I'm on the Bells, the Bells.'

SICK MICK

18

WEDNESDAY EVENING

The British love to tell themselves they do a certain kind of state occasion with more panache than any other race on earth. After every monarch's death, an ancient royal etiquette machine comes into its own, churning out a meticulously-planned, lying-in-state extravaganza in a stark 11th-century Westminster Hall surrounded by pomp, circumstance, a diamond-encrusted crown and men in tights. Outside, Old Father Thames spews its brown spume under those famous, ancient bridges, and crowds of loyal subjects queue as far as the world's TV cameras can pan, for days on end, to do their patriotic duty: gape at a coffin covered with a flag.

But right now, with a ninety-nine-year-old venerated duke in a coma following a serious blow to the head, and showing no signs of springing back into life, the nation was in a state of emotional limbo, unsure whether, when, or how to open the floodgates of grief. So, it staged a rehearsal for the big one. A semi-final that was fast approaching the penalty shoot-out.

The familiar gold-trimmed, wooden easel that Buckingham Palace places inside its gates to announce the birth of royal babies had been put up outside The National Hospital for Neurology and Neurosurgery in London's Queen Square, to offer updates on the duke's condition. However, the hospital could not cope with the ensuing pandemonium; there were major roadworks outside Buckingham Palace and the government's popularity was sinking in the polls, so it decided to give the Prime Minister and his despised Cabinet a chance to mingle with the masses and be seen spreading their empathy thicker than strawberry jam, by placing the easel inside railings at St Stephen's Entrance to the Palace of Westminster.

On show, from 8am to 8pm, was a framed message informing grievers that The Nation's Great Grandfather was gravely ill, but all was being done, including by God, to save the duke. Although the Palace was refusing to answer if God had been contacted to see if he was chipping in with his world-class saving skills.

As with Queen Elizabeth II's lying-in-state, long queues snaked their way along the banks of the Thames to catch a glimpse of the royal easel. Mothers with big coats and watery eyes, clutching bemused children whom they had dragged out of bed at dawn to drive 150 miles to be 'part of this island's story' told interviewers, through broken voices, that something on high drew them to return the love that Blinky had bestowed on them.

There were complete strangers making 'friends for life' with like-minded ghouls, grown men in Union Jack suits and England cricket jumpers hoping to be snapped for the front page of tomorrow's *Daily Telegraph* and middle-aged women armed with supplies of tea, sandwiches, anoraks and royal biographies.

Scores of villages across this green and pleasant land were deprived of their idiots as they had gone off to brag for the rest of their lives that they were there. The queue to see the easel had begun the previous night when the most devoted grievers/attention-seekers camped outside Westminster to be the first to set eyes on the framed note.

By now, Wednesday evening, the queue wound away from the Palace of Westminster along the north bank of the Thames towards Lambeth Bridge. It was big in number but only Donald Trump could claim the queue was anywhere near as long as the one for the late Queen.

The focal point for the assembled media was Victoria Tower Gardens, that small, triangular patch of greenery that borders the pavement by the side of the Thames between the Houses of Parliament and Lambeth Bridge.

Dozens of journalists from across the world had

donned their finest black attire and raided their thesauruses to steal every grief synonym on offer for first person pieces to camera, interviews with royal experts and vox pops with any queuing mourners prepared to say they had once met the duke when they were a child, preferably in their impoverished Third World village, and he had given them a generous smile that has never left their heart.

A scrum had developed around one mourner in particular, former England football captain Darren Merton, who had turned up unannounced (that's if you don't count his agent tipping off every TV and newspaper in London) to 'be with the people' in 'paying my respects to a top, top gaffer whose life was a game of two halves, but who, at the end of the day, like me, stepped up to the plate when the heat was on, and gave his all for his country.'

Merton's presence in the queue had nothing to do with the fact that central to his post-football career brand strategy was the securing of a knighthood, which he had been close to receiving one year after spending a week helping to build a village hall in Burkina Faso for relief charity Who'll Speak for the Children? A selfless task which was documented by his own ten-man film crew for release on Channel 4. However, his chances were blown when an email to his former agent was leaked in which the one-time darling of English football revealed how incandescent he was that actor Ben Kingsley had been knighted ahead of him, asking why, and this is how it read in the *Sunday Mirror*, 'that baldy c*** who as done nothin since f****** Gandee as been given the top f****** gong wen Ive ad to make do wiv a f****** CBE? Well f*** them all. I aint doin no f****** charity s**t ever again.'

So here was Merton seeking redemption, hoping his act of solidarity with the people would erase all memory of that email, and the king, whom he had done a few gigs with for England, would soon be saying, 'Arise, Sir Darren.'

The good news for Merton was that he now looked almost saintly compared with daytime TV golden couple Will Bloomfield and Ali Summerbee. They had been outed for jumping the queue by joining a separate Palace of Westminster VIP Lane to see the easel, under the guise of being journalists. The nation of fair play had been left apoplectic and the couple were crucified in the court of public opinion because, in Britain, you can cripple the people by lying to them about the need to cut economic ties with your biggest trading partner or deceive them about the necessity to take part in a pointless middle-Eastern war that will kill legions of innocents and spawn countless terrorists, but jump a queue and you are dead to the world.

That was the topic Lance Fleury was discussing with two middle-aged women as he strode alongside them in Victoria Tower Gardens, holding a Brit Talk microphone in front of them, going live to what he liked to pretend was 'the nation.'

'It's just not on, is it?' said one of the women wearing a red, white, and blue hair slide and holding a framed photo of King Charles looking miserable on the day of his wedding to Diana. 'I mean, we've travelled all the way from Wednesbury in Staffordshire, getting up at … when was it, Jacqui?'

'Six o'clock, Sandra,' said her friend, who had a matching hair slide and was holding a framed photo of Charles looking miserable as he walked behind Diana's coffin at her funeral.

'Yeah, six o'clock. And we've been queuing here for how long Jacqui?'

'Hours, Sandra.'

'Yeah, hours. Yet because they're celebrities off've the telly they get to just walk in as easy as you like. It's one rule for one, isn't it Jacqui?'

'And one rule for the rest,' said Jacqui.

'We used to love Ali and Will, but we've really gone off them, haven't we, Jacqui?'

'We have, Sandra.'

A producer's voice bellowed in Lance's earpiece that the couple were TV death and that he needed to grab some better-quality grievers, causing him to thank them before turning back to camera.

'As you can tell there is plenty of anger aimed at Summerbee and Bloomfield for disgracefully jumping the queue and going straight to the royal easel as VIPs, while ordinary folk have had to wait for hours to do their patriotic duty. One chap said to me, 'their halos are broken forever,' and another said, 'it's at times of grief when people really show their true colours.'

'And how right that last chap was. He could as easily have been talking about our police force, who have decided to virtually give up the search for sick leftie comedian Mick O'Shea who slandered the royal family to a treacherous degree then terrorised journalists with an illegal weapon, all because Prince Harry is honouring us with a trip from California and they fear Islamic terrorists may target him.

'Now, if the camera can just move around a little,' Lance said, pointing past the gardens and down the queue, 'you can see just how many police are here today. It is swarming with them, absolutely swarming. But I have to say, I don't know what good they can do because if someone with evil intent wanted to smuggle a bomb into a rucksack or a holdall then this is the perfect cover because most people are carrying one. So, it strikes me that if we do have a terrorist incident the police will once again be reacting *after* the event.

Meanwhile O'Shea is out there somewhere, looking on and laughing at us all.'

The Brit Talk cameraman swooped his hand-held lens down the five-deep line, which was moving slower now as it neared its final destination, and thirty yards away he picked out a man wearing a beret holding up the queue as a group in the crowd stopped to listen to him. The cameraman did not linger on him, instead pulling up and looking out across the Thames. Had he done so, his camera would have revealed Vinny showing his prosthetic leg to a small group in the crowd and Craig telling them that his old army pal was feeling tired having stood for six hours, so could he please be allowed to step in ahead of them to honour the family he fought so valiantly to protect. In truth, the pair had been scouring Westminster for an hour hoping to find Lance Fleury, and now they were within eyeshot of him they realised they needed to get in line.

'Thank you so much,' said Vinny, dressed like an Armistice Day veteran, his regimental tie and beret complimenting medals that glinted magnificently in the dying embers of the evening sun, exaggerating a hobble as he entered the throng.

'It's an honour to stand with you, sir,' said a man in his thirties with a Cornish accent, offering him the brown, steaming tea he had just poured into a plastic beaker from a flask which Vinny graciously declined.

'Do you mind me asking, sir. Did you lose your leg in war?' Vinny would normally have replied, 'No, I slipped on a banana skin, what do you think, what with these medals and this beret, you thick git?' but not wanting to cause a row he simply nodded and turned away.

He was in no mood for small talk as the adrenaline was starting to kick in. The target was in his sights, twenty yards away, which forced him into observation mode. Fleury, wearing a black suit and tie, was talking in an animated fashion into a hand-held camera, pointing at the crowd and thrusting his microphone under the chin of his latest interviewee.

Was he really going to do it, Vinny asked himself? Did he still have the nerve he had when he was young and focussed, and taking on the enemy had become second nature to him? When going into battle without a scintilla of guilt felt like the entire point of his existence?

'Are we going to make it?' Vinny asked impatiently.

'Hard to say,' said Craig, staring at the time on his phone which read 18:50. 'The next show is at seven. Depends on how many more he wants to interview.'

'Remember Plan B.'

'Roger that,' replied Craig.

As Vinny drew to within fifteen yards of Fleury it

dawned on him just how small he was. For the record, five foot seven before you throw in an extra inch for the specially built-up heels. It's so true what they say about small men and their syndrome, Vinny thought. If only all males had grown to his height of six foot one there would have been no Napoleon, Hitler, Mussolini, Stalin, Franco, Putin, or Boris Johnson. Although, to be fair, there still would have been a Donald Trump.

When he reached within ten yards of Lance, he was surprised to feel the nerves kick in and his hands become cold and claggy. He tried to remember the last time they had felt like that but couldn't.

When he moved to within five yards, he was aware of small beads of perspiration forming on his upper lip and his throat becoming tight and dry. A flashback to his first tour of Northern Ireland zapped into his mind, heightening his senses. There was that tightening knot in his stomach that he had felt as he jumped out of his armoured truck onto a West Belfast Street full of smoke and panic. There was that smell of his own fear rising from his sweating armpits and filling his nostrils. There was his heart once again pounding into his chest like a sledgehammer.

'Well, I'm afraid the clock has beaten us, folks,' Vinny heard Lance Fleury say into his microphone, which prompted him to nudge Craig in the back, then move out of the queue and kneel down pretending to tie a shoelace. As agreed, Craig carried on walking towards Fleury, not looking back.

'I have been talking you through the first evening of the royal easel standing outside Westminster informing us of our glorious royal hero's condition and acting as a point of national grieving. And I tell you, if these huge queues are anything to go by, and the outpourings of love that I'm feeling from this crowd, then they will remain huge for the coming days.

'This is Lance Fleury handing you back to the Brit Talk studio for the seven o'clock news, reassuring you that with patriotic people like these ones behind me, our country's future is in safe hands.'

As he took out his earpiece and gave a double thumbs up to the cameraman, Craig stepped out of the queue, prodded his finger at Lance and yelled, 'How have you got the balls to come over all patriotic you bent bastard?'

Lance Fleury was no stranger to being abused in public places. He had been doused in paint and milk, had eggs and tomatoes splattered all over his suit, been spat at, manhandled and wrestled to the floor and been called every curse and profanity known to man. He had even had the steaming contents of a chamber pot poured onto his head from a first-floor window in Brighton as an elderly lady shouted down at him, 'Here's some more shit for you to chew on.' But never had any of that happened as he stood beside a queue of gentle folk waiting to mourn a gravely ill duke.

'What on earth are you talking about, man? Have some decency for God's sake,' replied a confused and startled Lance.

As Craig lifted a clenched fist Fleury put up his arms to protect his face, Vinny leapt from behind, rugby-tackled his mate to the grass and pinned him down with his weight, saying, 'Cool it, okay?' as the body below him squirmed and struggled to be free.

There were gasps from the crowd. Lance patted down his hair and adjusted his tie trying to regain his composure. Four police officers arrived at the scene. One dragged Vinny off Craig, two others picked Craig up and held on to him, while the fourth asked Lance what had happened. After he explained, Craig was escorted to a police van and Lance picked Vinny's beret up, examined it, and handed it to him.

'Wow, saved by a real-life Desert Rat, eh? Thank you so much for stepping in but I could have handled him. You soon get to realise these guys are all mouth and no trousers,' he said.

'It was pure instinct, Lance. You don't mind me calling you Lance, do you?' Vinny asked.

'Of course not. I'm honoured. And your name is?'

'Eddie,' said Vinny.

'So, tell me Eddie, what did you get these for?' he asked, pointing at Vinny's medals.

'Tours of Northern Ireland and Kuwait. First Gulf War. Came home with a nice little present from Saddam,' he said, pulling up his left trouser leg and showing Lance his prosthesis.

'Wow. And you leapt on that guy to protect me. I'm in the presence of a true hero.'

'As I say, it was nothing. Just an old soldier's instinct kicking in.'

'Don't be modest. You are the finest of us. The best of British. And you're no doubt here tonight out of your love for king and country?'

'There's no finer love,' Vinny lied.

'Listen Eddie, I really have to run now, otherwise I would love to have taken you for a pint to thank you and to hear your stories.'

'That's okay. I'm getting back in this queue if they'll let me.'

'But it just so happens that on Friday evening I'm doing a special show live from the Cenotaph, on a kind of patriotic, for king and country theme.

'I don't know if you'll be around as you sound like you're from the North, but if you are, I'd love you to be my special guest. What do you say?'

'Well, I'm staying down for the week, so I'll still be here. So, yes. Why not?'

'Perfect. It starts at six. At the Cenotaph. Get there fifteen minutes early for a briefing and a getting to know you chat. I'll see you there,' said Lance, extending his hand.

'I wouldn't miss it for the world,' Vinny replied, grabbing his hand and giving him the firmest of handshakes as he stared hard into his eyes.

19

THURSDAY AFTERNOON

Mick was bored. Very bored. As in sitting in his cab in a North London McDonald's car park on a grey Thursday afternoon playing I Spy with himself bored. The only distraction from the abject tedium came when his little eye spied the illuminated sign bearing the McDonalds menu, which was a magnet to his stomach; its force field pulling him inside the golden arched pleasure dome, to feed his ballooning salt and dopamine habit. Mick was definitely winning Customer of The Week, although not having any nice days.

He had just finished a call with Sadie who was refusing to let him travel within a mile of her Harley Street workplace or her nearby flat, having curtly ruled out the prospect of her cuddling up with him between greasy wrappers and cartons in a North Circular Road fast-food car park. I've been served a restraining order, he thought. The calls to Ayesha were equally disappointing. Neither she, nor her team, had made any sightings of his dad, the spotter charged with shadowing Lance Fleury at 7pm last night having clearly knocked off early and gone to the pub.

'What if he's come to his senses and gone home?'

Mick had asked, only for Ayesha to tell him that Robbo had been watching the house in Moses Street and it was empty.

She told him to keep on keeping his head down, to stay patient and if Vinny had no intention of shooting Fleury, he had nothing to worry about. He could just hand himself in when the fuss died down, play the mental breakdown card, and take what was coming on his newly shaved chin.

'By the time you find my dad I'll have turned back into a hairy yeti,' he replied, before asking his agent if she fancied taking him for a drink in a very quiet pub where he would be on his best behaviour. She laughed loudly at him. A road digger almost. He was missing that.

He decided to go for a drive. He wasn't sure exactly where he would drive to, but he had liked the look of Camden Town when he had taken a nose around there yesterday and picked up a cool, peaked biker's cap, just like the one Marlon Brando wore in *The Wild One*. Maybe he could take another walk down by the lock, go back to the market, have a quiet pint in one of those pubs that Amy Winehouse used to get mental in.

That had been the idea, but it wasn't how it panned out. En route to Camden, when he was stuck in traffic halfway down Chalk Farm Road, he spotted a sign outside a pub which said: Open mic afternoon - today.

SICK MICK

Ignore it, was his first thought. Maybe just sit in the corner and check out the talent, was his second. I need some company and some laughter and Ayesha won't find out so sod it, was his third and winning thought.

The Antelope & Turnip was a former double-fronted furniture shop that had been stripped back to brick and wood, the cheapest and tackiest contents of several Camden antique shops thrown onto its walls like yellowing confetti, a bar with taps serving craft ales from independent breweries installed in one end, and a stage at the other, with upturned barrels and stools spread out in between.

Mick, wearing his Brando cap and shades despite being indoors, and the sky outside as cloudy as the pint of Wicked White Weasel 6% IPA he had ordered, was seated in the corner at the barrel table furthest away from the stage, an old tin-plated advert for Oxo cubes next to his head, trying to look inconspicuous. But looking like an extra in a Hell's Angels movie.

A woman in her early twenties had the mic, doing a sketch about the pitfalls of life at university, which Mick thought about as funny as being kicked in the balls by a randy bull, but she had the three front tables filled with her mates, and they were forcing out laughter. With one man, who Mick guessed was a loser trying to get off with her, howling like a wolf in an Alaskan mid-winter. Virtually all the other tables were empty.

He began to play a game he always played with Sadie whenever they were out: Celebrity lookalikes. That was their favourite pub pastime. That, and diving in on seats that had just become vacant, which other drinkers had been enviously eyeing up and were about to pounce on to. Oh, and playing Spot the Biggest Gobshite. But they dropped that a while back when Sadie complained it wasn't fair as Mick was winning it every time.

He decided that the two bar staff looked like Velma and Shaggy from *Scooby Doo*, but then deducted the points from himself after conceding that was the case in every stripped-back craft ale pub. He then decided the game didn't work without Sadie, polished off his Wicked White Weasel and walked to the bar for another pint.

This time, the brew that most grabbed him was a pale ale with a cartoon drawn on the pump handle of a busty woman giving a naked old man with popping eyes a massage, called Hoppy Ending. He threw down a fiver and three pound coins as he winced at the price, remembering that outside of Liverpool you don't say 'take one yourself,' as they usually take enough to put down a deposit on a flat, and returned to his barrel.

There was a double act on stage now. The same

double act you see in every pub back room during the Edinburgh Fringe. A couple of 6'3" ex-public school am-dram merchants who met at university as Brideshead Revisited extras, wrote sketches together, and were handed the finance by their parents to take their pitiful, laugh-free show filled with patronising attempts at portraying working-class people up to the Scottish capital for a month. Because they see their work as philosophy as much as it is comedy, they are usually called something like École Normale Supérieure (Jean Paul Sartre's Parisian alma mater) and put on a show entitled Allegory of The Cave (an essay from Plato in which he compares the effect of education or the lack of it on our nature). And five minutes into the show you realise you would be laughing more if you were sitting in the nearest launderette, staring at the round window of a washing machine, watching your dirty clothes tumble around the suds while a lonely, middle-aged man sits on the bench next to you talking you through the reasons he now lives on his own. His acute halitosis having already given the game away.

In the audience will be a couple of ex-public schoolgirls who fancy the Brideshead am-dram merchants and are the only punters finding the act remotely funny. But the women don't actually laugh at it. One just says to the other, 'that's rilly funny,' and her friend replies, 'Yah, and, like, rilly clever.' When it is not remotely either.

They will play to ever-diminishing crowds which, by the third week, will consist of the pub's barmaid on her way from the lounge to the cellar to change a barrel of Tennent's. They will, if they are lucky, receive one review, two paragraphs in the *Leith Gazette* or the *Airdrie and Coatbridge Advertiser*, saying the pair are embarrassingly derivative and should not, on any account, give up their day jobs.

They won't, of course, have day jobs yet, but that miserable summer will end up on their curriculum vitae as, 'I was once one half of a cutting edge comedy double act which starred at the Edinburgh comedy fringe and wowed the critics,' enabling them to appear zany and charismatic as a counterbalance to their intellectual brilliance as evidenced by their first class degree, thus getting on the shortlist for a safe Tory seat.

It began to dawn on Mick, as he instinctively found himself moving four barrels closer to the stage with his pint of Hoppy Ending, and studied the full tables at the front, that they were all students from nearby University College, and the acts were indeed rehearsing for their Edinburgh summer run. As the École Normale Supérieure duo were politely applauded off, with a couple of whoops from the front seats, the MC grabbed the mic and asked, 'any more for any more?'

He may as well have said, 'oi, you, fatty, with the gay pride hat and sunglasses look, what are you waiting for?' Because to Mick's ears that question was a dare for him to be the centre of attention and that was something he could never turn down. One of his earliest memories places him as a five-year-old at the front of the school assembly watching an old boy, who had gone on to become a singer whose group had made the charts, return to play an acoustic version of his hit. When the song ended and the applause died down, the singer asked if any of the kids knew someone who was famous. Nobody put their hand up, so Mick did, and was called on to the stage by the singer who asked him who he knew who was famous.

'Me dad,' answered Mick.

'Oh, yeah and what does he do?'

'He's a singer in a group like you.'

'Has he had any hits?'

'A few, yeah.'

'What's the group called?'

'Echo and the Vinnymen.'

'You mean Echo and the Bunnymen?'

'No, sorry. I mean Vinny and the Vinnymen.'

There was a short silence then the singer burst out laughing and the entire school, apart from Mick, joined in. When the singer said, 'I think we might have a famous comedian of the future here, guys,' a huge smile lit up Mick's face. From that day on he knew his destiny was to be standing on a stage looking down on laughing faces, being bathed in love. And there he was again, that Thursday afternoon, in Camden's Antelope & Turnip, holding what was left of his pint, putting on an aristocrat's voice to tell the MC his name was Lord Hercules Spondoolicks, not having a clue where that name or voice came from, why he was holding the mic, and what Ayesha would do to him if she could see him now.

'How are we today, chaps and chapesses?' he asked, getting no reply.

'Yes my name is Hercules and I'm a Lord from the Berkshire branch of the Spondoolicks clan, but you can call me Herc.'

'What about Herrcccgh,' yelled one of the students, feigning a vomit, which raised the biggest laugh of the afternoon thus far.

'Look, old boy, I get why you might want to donate your brain to science but shouldn't you have waited until you died?' Mick replied, getting an even bigger laugh, then following it up with, 'now why don't you toddle off to the far corner and finish evolving, there's a good fellow,' which saw the heckler's face turn vermillion as his friends pointed at him and jostled

SICK MICK

him.

'It's ok, I understand. I was a student once, you know,' Mick carried on, saying to the heckler, 'Oxford. You may have heard of it. On your rejection email. Which is why you're studying in London. Here's a tip. The secret to getting into Oxford is having Latin as your second language. Not, as in your case, Twattery.'

That punchline turned the road-digger into an ejector seat and pushed the heckler to the point of tears. God, he was loving this. Like a heroin junkie injecting fire back into his veins after days without a hit, Mick began to float.

The pub manager, who had been sitting at the bar reading *The Guardian* newspaper on his tablet, had turned to watch Mick when he heard a rare sound for these afternoon open mic sessions: uncontrolled mirth. Ten seconds later he had left his stool, walked behind the bar and pressed the record button on a camera that was positioned half-way down the room on a bare ceiling beam, focussed on the stage.

The laughs were coming thick and fast now, as he dressed up some of his material in a posh voice and realised it still worked. He even managed a rip-snorter (when hands fly to faces as stuff comes out of noses) doing the sketch about a support group for sex-starved men who deliberately harm themselves so they can be admitted to hospital for twice-daily bed-baths.

'Are any of you going to the vigil in Hyde Park tomorrow for our very ill duke?' Mick asked the small audience. 'One was given a VIP ticket, but looking at some of the new money that has been invited, like that Californian actress and her ginger bitch, I'll probably stay at home and whip the staff as they clean out the moat. Well one has to give them some fun occasionally, doesn't one?

'On the other hand, one may attend. I hear on the QT that Boy George may be doing a rendition of Coma Chameleon.'

As the laughter rang out, he spotted the MC at the side of the stage signalling for him to wind up, and signed off with, 'Here's one final piece of advice for any budding comedians. The second you start talking about the horrors of pineapple on a pizza is the time to become a chartered accountant.

'I've been Lord Hercules Spondoolicks and you've all been educated. You're welcome.'

20

LATE THURSDAY AFTERNOON

'Why on God's earth have they begged that wizened-up old hag to come out of retirement? Where's their goddam dignity?' A trouserless Lance Fleury screamed so furiously into his phone that the square paper towel on his groin fell away to reveal his limp penis.

So consumed with rage had he become at the announcement that Brit Talk's main anchor at tomorrow's Hyde Park Vigil for the Duke would be Jane Goodwin, the BBC's former royal correspondent, and not him, that he failed to hear Sadie knock three times on the Hardman Clinic door, the agreed signal for entry when the client had forgotten to buzz in the therapist.

Lance looked at her from his upright position on the treatment table as she walked in, pleased to be finally putting a pretty face to a delicate hand, then recoiled in horror as he felt the mask on his forehead and dragged it down over his eyes. He lay there as cold and stiff as a corpse in a Siberian blizzard, fearing all was lost and his face would soon be plastered over the front of every tabloid with puns about his inability to stand for erection.

Sadie walked towards the Duolith SD1 Ultra Shockwave machine, saying nothing, then wheeled it towards the side of the treatment table and sat down on the hard chair. As she lubricated the massage probe and set the dial to a slightly higher than medium pulse wave than Lance's previous visit, she gave him the once-over. There was no baseball cap this time and no Air Pods. Instead of his crew-neck jumper he had a white open-necked shirt with a brown pin-striped check and his socks were still Paul Smith, but this time with the classic three-stripes.

She removed the paper sheet, which he had hastily pulled back over his faulty machinery, gently picked up his toadstool with a surgically-gloved hand and slowly ran the probe up and down the only part of Lance's body that did not appear to have gone stone rigid.

'I've upped the intensity of the pulse so let me know if it's too strong,' she said.

'The stronger the better, please,' he replied, relieved that she had broken the uncomfortable silence, and human contact could drown out the humming of the shockwave machine.

'Sorry, I have to ask this, after my own stupidity: Did you recognise me when you walked in and saw me without the eye-mask on?'

'No, I didn't,' said Sadie. 'Should I know you?'

'Well, most people do,' he replied in a tone that was more miffed than relieved.

'So you're famous then?'

'Well, yes, I suppose I am.'

'Don't worry, we get a lot of famous men in here. To tell the truth it's not your face I'm looking at.'

Lance laughed and replied, 'Yes, of course.'

There was a long silence before Sadie thought she would have some fun, so broke it by asking, 'Are you an actor then?'

'Well, some of my enemies accuse me of putting on an act and most people recognise me from my voice. But no, not an actor.'

'Ok, let me guess. A golf commentator?'

He shook his head.

'A Smooth Radio DJ?' He shook his head again, this time laughing.

'A preacher?'

'What?'

'One of your evangelical boys off the telly who pulls bits out of the Bible to show their genius as phone lines flash, demanding viewers send him cash or they'll burn in Hell.'

'No, definitely not. Maybe you don't know me because you're Irish. Belfast, I'm guessing?'

'Aye.'

'East or West?'

'You mean am I Catholic or Protestant?'

'Well, no. I mean are you a loyalist or a nationalist?'

'Well, my daddy's about as loyal to the Crown as they come, if that's any help.'

'Good man. I've a lot of time for people like him. Especially at a time like this.'

'Och, I don't really care about politics. I think most politicians are phoneys. What was that Billy Connolly said? Something about the desire to become a politician should bar you from ever being allowed to become one.'

'Well, I don't know about that. There are some fine politicians. And, as funny as Connolly is, I'd rather the country was run by politicians than comedians.'

A smirk danced across Sadie's lips and the words, 'if only you knew who had you by the bollocks,' crossed her mind. She lifted up Lance's testicles and penis as she moved the probe down to his perineum, turning the pulse up when it reached his most sensitive area, in honour of Mick.

Lance yelped and his thighs shuddered. Sadie apologised and toned down the intensity of the electric waves.

'It's fine. Just a bit of a shock,' said Lance. 'You turn that up as high as you want because, at the moment, it doesn't appear to be working. I'm still not performing.'

SICK MICK

Sadie told him that this was only his second of six visits and that miracles don't happen overnight. 'It's not a big dick competition, you know. I'm not holding a magic wand here that's going to make you suddenly start banging away like a twenty-one-year-old. And as for talking about performing, maybe that's at the root of your issues.'

'Sorry, I don't follow you.'

'Half the problem with men is they feel that they need to be putting on a performance, and the pressure to impress, I dunno, their wife or mistress or boyfriend...'

'My wife. Definitely, definitely my wife.'

'...can lead to psychological problems that affect their ability to sustain an erection.'

'Maybe you're right. My job is essentially that of a performer I suppose.'

'Hang on, you're not a rock star are you? Let me guess, you were in Genesis?'

'What? Definitely not.'

'UB40?'

'Perish the thought.'

Land of Hope and Glory rang out from his phone, but he didn't want to lift his mask to check the caller ID, so left it.

'You can answer it you know,' said Sadie, gently lifting his testicles to one side.

'No, somehow it doesn't feel like the right time to be holding a conversation.'

A message pinged through seconds after the 'Land of Hope and Glory' ringtone was cut dead. He held the phone up to his face, lifted his mask just enough so his eyes could decipher it, and as he did his mouth turned up at either side like the Joker's.

A video was attached. He pressed play and a comedy posh voice boomed, 'I've been Lord Hercules Spondooliks and you've been educated.' Lance's left hand dropped the mask back on to his eyes and punched low above his thigh as he muttered, 'get in,' through clenched teeth.

He lifted up the mask again and typed the reply: Great news. Get back to London ASAP. No-one else must know, then hesitated, deliberating how to sign off, and went for: Well done you x before glancing at Sadie to see if she had been looking at him then thrust the phone back in his trouser pocket.

Sadie had been busy concentrating on the toadstool when the video played but there was something familiar about that voice coming out of the phone. She couldn't pin it down, so let it go, then moved the probe from Lance's perineum to his shaft, allowing the lubrication to let it glide up and down. He leaned backwards and let out a long groan of pleasure which, this time, had nothing to do with Sadie's expert technique.

Two hundred miles away, as Panda Fitzroy-Price stared at the 'x' on the end of Lance's text message, her face flushed hot and her stomach did somersaults. The loving touch was such a rare sight at the end of a message from her married lover. Her moment of rapture was interrupted by Garlick waving the Avanti West Coast phone app in front of her eyes, which showed they had just missed the London train and the next one out of Lime Street was not for an hour. Obviously that was Garlick's fault and he duly received a severe bollocking, even though if it had not been for his thorough research they would be staring down the barrel of another night in Liverpool, chasing their own tails in a fruitless Mick hunt.

Garlick had asked a geeky tech guy to monitor every comedy club in the country which puts up feeds from their shows. It was merely a hunch, a wild stab in the dark, but it had paid off, when an hour after Hercules Spondoolicks had left the Antelope & Turnip stage, the second half of his act was uploaded to the comedy club's website.

Geeky tech guy, under instructions from Garlick to send him a link to any comedian who looked younger than forty and heftier than fifteen stone, had forwarded the Spondoolicks video, and despite the lack of facial or cranial hair, the shades and the Brando cap, Mick had been swiftly outed. The giveaway had not been his references to the duke's coma or the planned vigil, but his attempt to say "chicken" in the style of an Old Etonian. Or rather, his failure to disguise the Scouse tendency to sound like you are hacking out a gallon of phlegm over a late night takeaway with a two-star hygiene rating, in the middle of that word.

Panda recognised she had been too harsh on Garlick, hailed a waiter and ordered a bottle of champagne, which left her stringer stunned. It was not just the 'x' on her lover's text that had made Panda's spirits soar but the current surroundings. After that day's lunch, Garlick had suggested they meet a like-minded friend of his called William who ran a libertarian blog called Deus Nobis Haec Otia Fecit. The Latin phrase, which translates to 'God hath given us these days of leisure,' is the city of Liverpool's motto which adorns its coat of arms, and was much quoted by local wags with a knowledge of Virgil during the 1980s, when a quarter of the workforce was given compulsory leisure orders. Not by God but by Margaret Thatcher.

The prime aim of Deus Nobis Haec Otia Fecit was to challenge the established view that Liverpool was a one-dimensional, left-wing monoculture. Not the complex, multi-political city comprising all classes and diverse thinkers that it was, but one made up of an anti-Tory proletariat who had ditched the Deus Nobis Haec Otia Fecit motto in favour of 'Scouse Not English.'

William, his insistence on being called that name in full a defiant refusal to compromise with the local preference for Bill or Billy, had insisted they meet in his club, The Athenaeum, which was established in 1797, as a place where local gentlemen would meet to exchange ideas and knowledge of worldly affairs. Its stunning elliptical stairwell, indoor columns and handsome reading room, not to mention, as Panda put it, 'The woody smell of old books and leather wiping out the sweaty stench of the shopway dossers outside,' had wowed her. As she sipped on her champagne, she asked William to tell her more about this delightful club, which was his cue to launch into a rhapsody of civic pride. He described how the Athenaeum was founded during the Napoleonic Wars to keep the city's wealthy merchants updated with news of maritime events, how past members include the Roscoes and the Gladstones, how it housed such unique documents as a Virginia Woolf-amended copy of TS Eliot's *The Wasteland* and a second copy of the Declaration of American Independence, and on and on, Panda's will to live diminishing with every fresh bullet of local history that was being drilled into her wandering brain.

Seated in this provincial club alongside this raging bore, trapped in this alien city, was not where Pandora Fitzroy-Price was meant to be. Ever. But certainly not now. Not when she held the key to the type of scoop that would establish her as a serious investigative reporter and earn more from Lance than a mere x.

'Sorry to interrupt your fascinating story,' she told William, 'but this champagne is distinctly tepid.'

'Really?' said the horrified host who was drinking mineral water. 'It's usually fine. Let me tell the waiter to chill it.'

'Oh, it's too late now. The moment has passed,' she replied, standing and motioning to Garlick that it was time to leave.

'But I was just getting warmed up,' said William.

'Yes, dear, but sadly so was the champagne. Delighted to have met you. And thank you for inviting me to this quaint little gathering place, the, erm…'

'The Athenaeum,' replied William.

'Yes, it's a truly magnificent building,' Garlick butted in.

'Indeed. And so handy for the train station that will deliver us from all evil, amen,' said Panda, as she raced to the stairs.

21

FRIDAY LUNCHTIME

The blood oozed crimson and thick out of Mick's flesh causing his head to go woozy. He staggered towards the nearest wooden bench and dropped onto it. He pulled a clean McDonald's napkin out of his back pocket—clean because he had perfected a way of never wasting a particle of meat or a droplet of juice from a burger—and staunched the bleeding.

After a few seconds, he removed the makeshift bandage and sucked the blood from the cut, deep into his mouth. It tasted metallic and salty, altogether quite appealing, a bit like licking melted butter off a crumpet. Maybe Dracula was on to something, he thought, attempting a screengrab of his brain which was outlining a sketch about a vampire version of *Come Dine With Me* called *Come Suck With Me*.

As the red stream eased into a weak bubble on the tip of his finger he surveyed it with pride. Sure, he had been wounded in battle, but as he looked down at the spoils of war, the lesion had been worth it. A faint heart never won a fair lady, and the six pink roses had put up a decent fight with their thorny stems, but his mitts had won the day.

Floral displays weren't really Mick's scene but even

he had to admit that his view, from the bench in Queen Mary's Gardens, was quite spectacular. There were thousands of roses spreading as far as the eye could see. He could understand why Sadie lost herself most lunchtimes in this explosion of scent and colour whenever the weather was fair.

Today, with only the occasional fluffy ball of cotton wool in the otherwise clear, azure sky, to Mick's eyes, it was fairer than the hair in a Viking's arse-crack. Sadie was bound to turn up here with a sandwich and drown herself in nature. And when she did, what a surprise it would be to see her long-lost boyfriend waiting for her with a bouquet of roses.

He wondered if he'd picked a variety that would appeal to her. The white ones whose, display plaque told him were called Champagne Celebration, had caught his eye. They seemed apt for the off-the-cuff proposal he had in mind. But as he went to pluck them from the soil an old woman dressed in a tweed suit with a straw boater, who looked too much like Miss Marple for comfort, walked past slowly, throwing him an inquisitive glance that said, 'you better not be doing what I think you're doing.'

So he walked alongside the plentiful beds, whistling, and was drawn to the red Ingrid Bergmans and the pink blooms called Rock 'n' Roll. But in the end, when he was sure nobody was looking, he knelt down and nicked half-a-dozen pink stems called Lovely Lady. Can't go wrong with that name, he thought.

His phone rang. It was Ayesha. He picked it up after one ring and said, 'Tell me you've found him.'

She hadn't. The hunt for Vinny had intensified, with Ayesha adding a private detective to her SWAT team, but there was still no sign of him. No-one answering to his description had been seen approaching Lance Fleury and no-one answering to his name had been booked into a London hotel or, according to the private dick, left the country. Which had a lot to do with the old soldier knowing that when you are stalking the enemy on manoeuvres, you always cover your tracks.

Vinny had booked into the Premier Inn at Euston on Tuesday under the name of Eddie Hobson (his paternal grandfather's Christian name and maternal grandma's maiden name) and paid cash for a two-night stay. He feared he had compromised the operation by telling Fleury on Wednesday that his name was Eddie so, not needing to be in London until their Friday rendezvous at the Cenotaph, he pulled back from the front line, taking the short train ride to Watford where he paid cash for two nights at another Premier Inn. Those breakfast sausages were a loyalty masterstroke.

'Are you sure he's not still in Liverpool, staying with one of his mates to get away from my shitshow?' Mick asked, only to be told by Ayesha that Robbo had been asking around Vinny's favourite watering holes and nobody had seen him all week.

'Is there anywhere else apart from London he could have gone to? Any friends or relatives he's gone to stay with just to get away from all the fuss in his street?' Ayesha asked, deliberately failing to add that a brick had been thrown through the front window of his house, a note tied to it bearing a Smiley badge with a Hitler moustache-and-side part makeover, the warning: 'Get out before we burn you out' scrawled beneath.

A glazer friend of Robbo's had repaired the window and Ray Moon had summoned an emergency meeting of the Spirit Of Ebro in the Casa, telling his men the Hitler Smiley badge was the calling card of LAF, the Liverpool Aryan Front, and now was the time for 'our glorious band of brothers' to 'take the fight to the fascists on the streets of Liverpool the way our International Brigade forefathers had done on the streets of Madrid, Teruel, and Aragon.'

All five Spirit of Ebro members present agreed to go to war, although Lenny The Limper (so-called because he deliberately sacrificed three of his toes in a factory lathe accident to claim industrial compensation) asked if he could go home first to feed his cat.

'None outside Liverpool that I know of. Hang on, he used to have an ex-Army mate down here in London called Craig but I don't think he's seen him for years,' Mick replied.

'Oh genius. Now you tell me,' said Ayesha unable to disguise the anger in her voice. 'Why have you only just mentioned this?'

'I've told you. He hasn't seen him for years,' said Mick.

Ayesha pushed him for details about Craig but he didn't have any, other than he sounded like a proper Cockney Eastender and his name was Duggan or Dougan. She told him she would get the private detective to start digging as soon as this call ended.

'He's got to be down here,' said Mick. 'I showed you the text he sent me about his little faithful and how the fella who wants me hung for treason is getting it. I know exactly what that means. I'm telling you. He'll have done a recce and he'll be waiting for his moment to pounce.'

Mick told her that he should be in the centre of London looking for his dad because he could spot him a hundred yards away, but Alesha shot that down telling him he couldn't go anywhere near Fleury as he was still Public Enemy Number One.

That morning, the *Daily Mail* had done a

backgrounder on him under the headline JUST WHO IS SICK MICK? in which various anonymous people, who claimed to have been school classmates, described him as a 'playground bully' a 'psycho who placed worms on his model railway track' and an attention-seeker who was so desperate to make people laugh he once told a teacher he'd taken a day off school because 'my arse is so sore I have to stand up all day.' To be fair to the *Mail* reporter, only one of those things was made up.

'I spent some of your money on a cool hat by the way,' said Mick. 'The sun was battering my baldy head, making my dome look like someone had slapped half an Easter egg on it. Hang on...'

'What?'

'Bingo.'

'What? You're playing bingo?'

'No. Nothing. Got to run.'

On the opposite side of the circular rose bed, peaking out above the bushes, dwarfed by a couple of tall men in suits, he could make out the small figure of Sadie. She wore a thin, green, North Face fleece over her scrub top and black trousers, a small grey backpack hung loosely from one shoulder and she walked slowly, her 'sexy secretary' glasses trained on the floor, seemingly oblivious to everything around her.

SICK MICK

Sadie sat down on a bench, pulled the backpack onto her lap and took out a tupperware box containing a home-made Greek salad, delved deeper for a plastic fork and looked around her little slice of paradise.

She inhaled deeply through her nose, closed her eyes, and let the smell of the roses dance into her brain. This was the first release of tension in a truly shitty day. Before she had taken her coat off inside the Hardman Clinic she had been summoned to her boss's office where she was told that Lance Fleury had lodged a complaint about her behaviour. She had been too chatty and too probing throughout yesterday's session, apparently. The accusation left her gobsmacked. As she told Grace Fairfax, *he* was the one who started the conversation after showing her his face, the one who asked if she had recognised him, who wanted to know her religion and who slagged off the shockwave treatment for not giving him an instant, raging hard-on. She was the one who claimed not to know him and who reassured him that it was early days in his treatment. Had she known he was going to file a complaint she would have told him she recognised him as that Pound Shop Hitler off that Pound Shop Nazi TV channel and showed him what being probing' was all about by turning the machine's current to maximum, wiping off the lubricant and ramming the probe up him. A response which did so little to impress Grace she shook with anger before issuing Sadie with a verbal warning.

Still, Fleury was becoming impatient so had booked another session for first thing Sunday morning, asking if this time the nurse could keep her mind on the job in hand. And Sadie's would have to be that hand, despite her having Sunday off, and the appointment was scheduled for 8am.

What is it with men and their fragile little egos, she thought, sliding a fork of feta cheese and red onion into her mouth and picturing Mick in Moses Street, firing a gun into the air because his pride had been hurt by reporters who were only doing their job. As she lowered her head to look for a bottle of water, a bunch of pink roses held together by a blood-stained McDonald's napkin appeared below her face. She recoiled, 'what the—?' then looked up to see a grinning Mick and dropped the tupperware bowl into her lap.

When Mick launched into an impression of Cilla Black singing, 'Surprise, surprise,' she picked up a handful of Greek salad and threw it at his face.

'The unexpected hits you between the eyes,' he carried on singing with tomato seeds dripping down his nose and off his chin.

'What in the feckin' name of God are you doing here?' Sadie asked, her pale face turning as red as the bed of Nostalgia roses behind her.

'I'm missing my lovely lady, which is why I bought you some Lovely Lady roses to let you know I love you,' he replied.

Sadie stared down at the roses with disgust. 'You didn't buy them, did you? You stole them. You actually destroyed a beautiful part of nature and thought it would, what? Impress me? Are you out of what's left of your tiny feckin' mind?'

'Well this isn't panning out as I expected,' said Mick, sitting down on the bench, the stolen roses marking out No Man's Land between them.

'What. You. Expected?' Sadie spat back at him. 'What *did* you expect, Mick? Your agent has told you not to come anywhere near me because you're a wanted man with an actual feckin' price on your head.' She lifted up the brim of his cap, 'A head that's been shaved so the papers or the police can't recognise you, which is why you've got a hat on that makes you look like you're in the feckin' Village People. What if I've been followed here, eh? Do you ever, ever engage that pea-sized brain of yours?'

'I just missed you, love, that's all. Is that a crime?'

'No, but stealing flowers from a park is a crime. And thinking I wouldn't guess they were stolen and that I'd actually be impressed is a feckin' crime against my intelligence. And in case you've forgotten, back in

Liverpool, you actually committed a real crime and you're going to prison for it,' Sadie said, picking up the roses and throwing them at Mick, as tears welled up in her eyes.

'Come on, there's loads more flowers left for everyone to look at. Thousands of them.'

'Well why don't you go and pick them all then, big man? Get a load more cuts on your fingers.'

'Says the woman who gets about ten pricks on her fingers every day,' he joked, trying to make Sadie laugh but realising instantly that he had horribly misread the moment.

'Don't you dare go there. Thinking that if you make a joke out of it, everything will be alright. Because I'm sick to death of the whole Mick O'Shea act,' she shouted back at him through heaving sobs.

'Me too. That's why I'm thinking of changing my stage name to–' he adopts a posh voice, '–Lord Hercules Spondoolicks.'

Sadie's sobs stopped. She turned her head slowly to Mick, her eyes blazing. 'Say that name again.'

'What?'

'Say that name again. In that same voice.'

'Erm, okay. Lord Hercules Spondoolicks.'

Sadie slapped him hard across the face, picked her bag up, and walked away shouting 'That's it, you waste of feckin' space. We're done.'

22

EARLY FRIDAY AFTERNOON

Had Bob Woodward and Carl Bernstein known the monstrosity they were about to inflict on the English language, they might not have reported on the 1972 burglary at the Democratic National Committee headquarters in Washington.

Sure, their dogged journalism brought down Tricky Dicky Nixon, but Watergate, named after the office building where the break-in by Republican stooges took place, spawned a thousand bastard children as the suffix 'gate' became accepted shorthand for every ensuing scandal in the English-speaking world. In American politics, Bill Clinton alone sparked a dozen separate gates linked to the wider Monicagate, and Donald Trump was almost brought down by Pussygate and Shitholegate—the latter being when he asked government officials why it's always people from not very pretty countries who emigrate to America.

The British Royal Family had had its fair share of gates over the years. There was Tampongate (the tape of Charles telling Camilla he wanted to be reincarnated as one of her menstrual pads that Mick referenced in The Laughter Bucket), Squidgygate (a tape of Diana speaking very intimately to a male friend), Toegate (The Duchess of York being photographed having her feet sucked by a lover on a sunbed) and following Queen Elizabeth II's death, Queuegate (when TV celebrities jumped the line to see her coffin).

Now, the annals of history had another gate to document—Easelgate—following the theft of the gold-trimmed, wooden tripod that stood inside railings at the Palace of Westminster, holding the framed note which gave updates on the comatose duke's health. The sacred easel had vanished between the hours of 8pm Thursday and 8am Friday, when police moved it out of public view and stored it in a room inside the St Stephen's Entrance. The right-wing media was apoplectic, calling for a heavy jail sentence for the thief and the head of the Metropolitan Police chief. 'Is this the surest sign that modern Britain has lost every ounce of respect and decency?' asked a *Daily Telegraph* editorial. The front page of that morning's *Daily Star* demanded to know, 'Who is the WEASEL with the EASEL?' It would follow up the next day with: '*Star* readers demand – Douse the WEASEL with the EASEL in DIESEL.'

Sophie Atkins had told her *Voice of Britain* viewers that, when the thief is found, they should be dragged through the streets of the capital by a distemper-suffering horse, hung outside the Tower of London's Traitors Gate, then decapitated and their head put on a spike outside the entrance to Westminster. To persuade anyone contemplating stealing a royal easel to have a rapid rethink.

Not to be outdone, Lance Fleury went on to *Brit Talk* to describe it as 'the most despicable and humiliating theft in London since the World Cup was stolen in 1966,' before referencing how the trophy was eventually found, by asking: 'Who will be our modern-day Pickles the dog?' He had thought of offering a reward for information leading to the easel's discovery, but remembered he was already ten grand into a pledge to find Sick Mick so kept schtum.

In what the *Daily Mail* described as 'a show of British defiance reminiscent of the Blitz Spirit that dear old Blinky exhibited in spades,' a substitute easel (minus the gold trim) had been found in a Westminster cupboard and placed outside St Stephen's Entrance that morning, bearing news that the duke's condition was 'unchanged' and asking all who gazed upon it to pray for him.

Six days on from the Great Chelsea Flower Show Pergola Disaster, pleading with the Almighty for an intercession was very much the theme of the day. A twelve-hour, televised Vigil for the Duke had been arranged in Hyde Park, starting at 11am, with a two-minute silence to be observed across the nation at 1.17 pm. The exact moment the wayward pergola beam struck the royal crown.

Police estimated more than 150,000 people had crammed into the section of the park that runs south of Marble Arch alongside Park Lane, where the annual British Summer Time concerts are held. The focal point was a huge black stage, wrapped in screens, showing images of the Duke of Dorset and King Charles, with Diana skilfully edited out of all of them at the behest of Queen Camilla.

The main point of the quasi-religious event was to remind the world that the man who was a mentor for Supreme Governor of the Church of England was fighting for his life and if God could spare a few seconds, any time soon, Britain would appreciate it if he could flick the switch back on in the duke's brain.

In between appearances from half-a-dozen South London gospel choirs, a few famous acts from the Christian rock world took to the stage. American pop sensation Jaidon Deaver, wearing a reverse baseball cap bearing a message in Hebrew that translated as 'dying sucks' was met with a cacophony of screams from thousands of young women. He told the crowd that, thanks to his presence, he knew everything was going to be okay with the duke because if Jesus walked the earth today he, too, would be a 'Deaver

Disciple.' Then sang his new single *Girl Get Yummy with my Dummy.*

Well-known faces from the showbiz world, most of whom had been knighted, took the mic to say a few words in support of the royal family, with virtually every actor weeping on cue. Darren Merton's PR team had managed to swing a slot next to the showbiz knights and he read out a prepared speech.

'I played my heart out for Queen and country, now it's time for the country to pray their hearts out for the Queen's favourite cousin,' before looking pleadingly at the TV cameras as if to say, 'if this grovelling doesn't finally land me a bleeding knighthood I don't know what will.'

The vigil was not exclusively about Christianity though. In a nod to multi-faith Britain, the five celebrities who were still left in ITV's The Masked Singer (two former soap stars, one ex-footballer, a woman from a sister band that had one hit back in the 1970s, and a fake-smiley man commonly known as 'that smug prick who's in everything') appeared in garish costumes and masks representing the Tibetan guru Padmasambhava, and performed a Buddhist cham dance.

Topping the bill was eighty-five-year-old British pop legend Sir Clive Roberts, a veteran of Christian events and Royal swoonathons. Sir Clive sang two songs he had written especially for the vigil, called The Duke in Heaven Loves all the Dukes on Earth and The Pergola Prayer which he was releasing as a single, with all proceeds going to Green Relief, a charity that supports victims of garden accidents. He urged the nation to buy the single as an even greater cause than Green Relief would be served: allowing him get heard on the radio once again.

On the left of the stage, towards the eastern edge of the Serpentine Lake, stood the media zone where TV presenters from around the world did their pieces to camera and reporters chased VIPs, who were mostly very keen, for PR purposes, to deliver lachrymose quotes. As with most media zones at live events, the scene bordered on anarchic, as anchor men and women had heated slanging matches with their producers back in the studio, runners wrestled interviewees away from rival channels and sound engineers threatened noisy by-passers with painful deaths if they would not shut up. One argument in particular stood out for its ferocity, a few yards to the right of where Jane Goodwin was guiding *Brit Talk* viewers through the historic event.

'What do you mean he's walked off and left you?' barked Lance Fleury at Panda Fitzroy-Price, his eyes bulging like a rat's just as it is about to be mashed by an oncoming beer truck.

'It's over. Garlick's walked,' she replied.

'So who in God's name is going to find O'Shea for me now that Mulder and fucking Scully have split up?'

Panda shrugged her shoulders and went to touch him, but he pushed her away. Lance was already raging at Jane Goodwin's masterly commentary and the praise that fawning *Brit Talk* producers were lavishing on her. And now it looked like his plan to undermine her by swinging the spotlight back onto him was in ruins.

Thirty minutes earlier there had been an ugly falling-out between Panda and Jason Garlick which left their relationship, like the Nation's Great Grandfather, on life-support.

The pair had arrived back from Liverpool yesterday tea-time, having worked out their modus operandi on the London-bound train. Mick's Hercules Spondoolicks act in Camden had been, to quote Panda, a game-changer. Why would he bring up the Hyde Park vigil and tell the audience he was thinking of attending if he had no plans to? Surely this was the point of his whole trip to London, ran Panda's logic. Surely this was the moment he would try to pull off another anti-royal publicity stunt, possibly by sneaking on stage and spewing his bile before the world's cameras? She had to find him, identify him, have him arrested, claim she had thwarted another Sick Mick act of treason and chalk up a celebrated scoop.

Garlick and Panda had arrived at Hyde Park at 10am, an hour before the gates opened, to study the gathering crowds through their sunglasses. May had turned to June and the hottest day of the year was coming to the boil. As the mercury climbed towards the 30s, the vigil-observers were already stripping off coats and sweaters to tie around their waists. It was not going to be one of those scorching London days when an egg could be fried on a well-polished leather brogue as it was too early in the summer, but still a muggy one that would see the trees used for a rare function: providing shade. Although, as the vigil progressed and the ash, oak and beech found themselves being hugged and talked to by stoned grievers, they performed an even rarer function: bearing messages to the cosmic spirits to forgive the Duke of Dorset for taking the dreaded Covid vaccine, which some conspiracy-theorists believed was the real reason he was in a coma.

As the scent of freshly-cut grass mingled with the tangy smell of burnt flesh from the burger and kebab stands that were firing up around the vigil area, this was unmistakably Hyde Park in summer.

Mulder and Scully, as Lance called them, had

combed every inch of the vigil site in search of Mick, with no success. They had a still of him from the pub video, wearing shades and Brando's *Wild One* cap, and clothes that suggested he was modelling for a new range of gear called Geography Teacher Goes to Matalan, but they were conscious he may have swapped disguise again.

Two hours in, they thought they had struck gold when they spotted a tall, bulky man standing at the back of a queue for the Portaloo, dressed in a white tee-shirt, turned-up jeans, sunglasses and a black woollen skull cap on his bald head. Garlick joined the queue, as Panda followed close behind with her camera phone trained on the skull-capped head. She motioned to Garlick to confront him, which he reluctantly did by tapping him on the shoulder. Skull Cap guy turned his head around. Garlick stared at him. His wide face was vaguely similar to O'Shea's and he could just about pass for being in his early thirties but the large SunGod Renegades shades made it hard to know for sure. He was stumped.

'What do ya want?' the man asked in a gruff, non-specific northern voice, similar to the mongrel one you hear in Carlisle: part Geordie, Lancashire and Scots. Exactly the kind of voice a Scouse performer might land on if he was trying to hide his own accent.

'I was just wondering if your name was Mick by

any chance?'

'Mick? Why? Who's asking?'

'Well, is it?'

'I don't like your tone or your questions, pal. You'd best do one, yeah?' he said, turning back around, to see Panda pointing her camera into his face.

'What the fuck's going on?' he asked, turning back to Garlick, who had switched his phone to record and was moving it towards the man's mouth.

The last thing Garlick saw before the large forehead came crashing onto his nose were these words on the stranger's tee-shirt: Bikers 4 Britain. The last thing he heard before plunging backwards onto the grass was the crunch of bone and cartilage in his nose, followed by a hissing sound as blood spurted out in an arc like black gold from a Texan oil well. As the back of his head hit the ground, the blood spattered down onto his face and hair, then streamed from each nostril past the top of his mouth to his neck, below which was a light blue shirt that was beginning to resemble a butcher's apron.

Panda let out a wild yelp, pulled a hankie from her bag, knelt down and held it over Garlick's nose, screaming, 'you animal' at the Biker 4 Britain, followed by 'someone get a policeman' and 'don't just stand there, do something,' at the gaping onlookers, none of whom appeared to want to lose their place in the Portaloo queue.

A woman with a sleeve of serpent tattoos on her left arm and a can of strong cider in her right hand ran over shouting, 'Ryan, what have you done?'

To which the biker replied, 'Sorted out some nosy bastard,' before grabbing the cider, swigging it, and heading calmly back towards the stage.

'Stop him, stop him,' yelled Panda to widespread indifference, as Garlick grabbed the hankie from her, sat up and told her to find a police officer.

'Are you sure?' she asked.

'Course I'm sure,' he replied, staring at her in disbelief. 'I've been physically assaulted.'

'Yes, but won't it take up too much time finding one and then having to give a statement and all of that palaver? We need to catch O'Shea.'

'He's broken my fucking nose,' Garlick shouted, pulling away the hankie to reveal a nasty red gash across the bridge of his swollen, bloodied snout.

'You'll be okay once you get over the shock,' Panda replied, wincing at the ugly, battered face turning black around the eyes that was staring back at her.

That was the final straw for Garlick. He stood up and unburdened months of pent-up resentment, leaving her in no doubt about what he thought of her with a clinical deconstruction of her many faults that climaxed with 'you self-obsessed, talentless, tight-fisted, horrendous, over-Botoxed, Daddy's girl, public school, semi-aristocratic, She-devil wanker.'

The story did little to impress Lance Fleury, who shrugged and told her to hire some more 'goons' then find O'Shea. She bit her lip as she contemplated the least combustible way of asking Lance if he could possibly join her in the search, but swiftly concluded that one did not exist, so just blurted out the request which triggered a similar outburst to Garlick's, albeit peppered with far more expletives preceding and following the word 'incompetent.'

His main objection was that he, Lance Fleury, was so well-known he would become a magnet for attention which was not a good look for an undercover job whereas she, Pandora Fitzroy-Price, was such a nonentity that she could ride through the crowds naked, on horseback, like 'Lady Go-fucking-diva' and nobody would bat an eyelid. Jane Goodwin motioned to Lance to come into camera shot and he scurried towards her like a miniature lapdog chasing a gravy bone treat. Panda trudged out of the media zone back towards the masses and reached into her bag for her iPhone to beg a friend to come to her aid, but she could not find it. Just as she could not locate her Dior purse or her Gucci make-up case. The realisation dawned that her Mulberry bag had been rifled while she was attending to Jason Garlick, leaving her feeling utterly hopeless.

As she fell to her knees screaming at the circling police helicopters whose juddering blades helped drown out the sound of her rage, two St. John Ambulance volunteers ran towards her to administer the first emergency grief aid of the vigil.

SICK MICK

23

FRIDAY AFTERNOON

Mick strolled aimlessly across Regents Park, shoulders heavy, eyes locked on the yellowing sunburnt grass, wondering what else could go wrong with his life. Sadie's words had cut deep. She had never kicked off like that before. She had never broken down in tears over something he'd done and she had never given him a smack that was so hard he could still feel his skin stinging fifteen minutes later. He replayed her most ferocious barbs, using them to further beat himself up by acknowledging their accuracy. What had made him think, without a gram of weed in his system, that proposing to her today was an inspired idea? With stolen flowers. When he's on the run from the law and under orders to stay away from her. Not to mention having a head like Kojak. What woman, apart from one who had been certified insane, would think of marrying that? 'I'm sick to death of the whole Mick O'Shea act,' she'd said. Her and most of the country, he thought. Including himself. Because his act must be parked in the knackers' yard if it makes the only woman he's ever loved cry her heart out and the only parent he's ever loved believe he needs to protect his son so much that he's picked up his old gun and headed off on some crazy vengeance mission.

A white plastic football landed at his feet. He looked up to see a young boy playing with his dad and kicked it back to him, thinking that would be something he would never do in his life now, as a father or a son. Time to call time on this comedy lark, he thought. It was causing too much pain.

He found himself standing in front of a busy Euston Road and, instead of heading left down Albany Street to where he'd parked his cab he crossed over by Great Portland Street tube station and walked into the Green Man pub, thinking he may as well spend what was left of Ayesha's advance on a couple of pints before handing himself in to the cops.

The pub seemed strangely mute for a sunny Friday afternoon, although as he ordered a pint of Greene King bitter, he noticed that was mainly due to most of the punters staring up at the big screens in silence. The BBC and Sky had thrown over their schedules to the Hyde Park vigil and as Mick sipped on his pint and looked up he could make out that ancient national treasure, Sir Clive Roberts, holding centre stage, eyes closed, hands in a praying pose, chanting something about a falling pergola being a message from the Lord for us all to look up to heaven and see his glory. Mick snorted into his beer and looked around to catch a fellow cynical eye, but saw only a few concerned ones glued to the TV screens and many disinterested ones on their phones.

The TV cameras panned to what looked like a cordoned-off VIP section to the right of the stage where dignitaries, including most of the Government and Shadow Cabinet, jostled to grab the grieving money shot. Tory and Labour leading lights, all trying to show the electorate that no party humps the flag quite as hard as they do.

Mick's eyes drifted away from the TV screen to the bar landing on the snacks that were tempting his stomach like seductive mermaids with brightly-packaged tails. He fought off the desire to pig-out on dry roasted peanuts by contemplating whether it was the rise of vegetarianism, or the amount of teeth they broke, that saw off pork scratchings. You just didn't see them around anymore. Or those pickled eggs floating in jars in old men's pubs, like body parts in a laboratory. Just then, he noticed a TV screen to the left of the counter that wasn't showing the vigil but a middle-aged woman talking in animated fashion. Believing it was *Loose Women*, he picked up his pint and headed to a table underneath the TV, hoping the Scottish MILF with the dyed-blonde bob cut and sexy turn in her eye, whom he had the hots for, was on today's panel to take his mind off things.

It wasn't *Loose Women* but *Brit Talk*, and the middle-aged bottle blonde was Edina McLeod, the newly-appointed Common Sense Tsar, praising the vigil, arguing that monarchy, family and religion are the historic bonds that tie us all together and make Britain the great country that it is and rebuking the many young people expressing apathy towards the duke's fight to reach one hundred. When this great national treasure wins his battle to live, she said in her patronising, posh South Liverpool accent, the country must win the fight against the politically-motivated voices who seek to impose their woke ideology on us. This was her cue to lambast the liberal elite for creating a 'take everything, give nothing' generation, which despises 'who we are, what we were and everything our forefathers created.'

She attacked teachers for filling children's heads with gender politics when they should be teaching them the dates of famous British military victories, laid into the tent cities that had sprung up on high streets calling homelessness 'a lifestyle choice,' claimed there had only been an explosion in foodbanks because scroungers had discovered a way to get mugs to buy their meals while they spent their benefits on booze and cigarettes and ended by booming 'and don't get me started on the male menopause.' Then patted herself on the back for being, in her words, 'one of the few high-profile politicians with the guts to say what the majority are thinking.'

A smile spread across Mick's face as he imagined the expletives flying out of his dad's mouth if he was hearing this. How, whenever McLeod appeared on TV, he would turn to a disinterested Mick and spit out the names of all of the celebrity Tories who emerged from Liverpool such as Ken Dodd, Cilla Black, Kenny Everett, Jimmy Tarbuck and even, in his words, the 'up their own rich arses' Beatles for whining about how much they were paying the taxman on the *Revolver* album, calling them all treacherous bastards who should be thrown off trains at Runcorn Bridge if they ever tried to come back home.

He finished his pint and was walking to the bar for a refill when a man in his forties walked into the pub in an agitated state, his backpack almost knocking Mick's empty glass out of his hand.

'Miss the train?' asked the pub manager.

'Cops have shut Euston,' he replied in a Mancunian accent.

'Bomb scare?'

'A load of crusties holding a mass sit-in for that gobby comedian who wants the royals shot. Give us a pint of Moretti, will you?'

Mick stopped in his tracks three feet from the bar as his brain froze. Did he hear that right or was he participating in some weird out-of-body experiment?

He sought the truth.

'Sorry mate,' he spluttered in his normal accent before realising he was not Mick O'Shea but a fake posh boy dressed like he was auditioning for a Village People tribute band, and switched persona to Hercules Spondoolicks. 'Did you say Euston was closed, only I'm planning to take a train to Milton Keynes.'

'Yeah.'

'Why?'

'Hundreds of layabouts with fuck all else to do but sit on their arses holding placards blocking actual fucking taxpayers trying to get to their trains.'

'What kind of placards?'

'A copper told us it was for that fat Scouse twat who everyone's calling sick.'

'Poor show, poor show,' Mick replied, uncoiling his fist and resisting the temptation to show him how sick he could be, before planting his glass on the bar, walking slowly to the door then darting across Great Portland Street in front of an oncoming taxi and a Deliveroo driver who hit the brakes on his e-bike and was nearly thrown over the handlebars, then weaving across Euston Road amid a cacophony of shrieking car horns, narrowly missing being turned into roadkill by a petrol tanker.

As the hefty, sweating figure in the leather cap, shades and eccentric line of clothing attempted to sprint the third of a mile down the pavement of the dual carriageway to Euston station, forcing tourists with wheeled suitcases to dive towards shop windows, he looked to the world like the star of a comedy chase movie. Indeed, some bystanders peered around for the film crew they were convinced must have been following him.

At Gower Street, with the lights against him, he tore in front of oncoming traffic holding one arm aloft, the other pointing straight ahead, shouting 'armed police, stop that man,' nearly causing a three-car pile-up.

And then he reached that soul-sapping monument to the ugly nihilism of 1960s town planning, Euston station, where hundreds of people, most weighed down with bags, were stuck outside staring at the police who blocked the entrances.

Mick hobbled around for thirty seconds attempting to get oxygen back into his lungs, then strolled up to the thin blue line planning to bullshit his way through but his adlib genius deserted him and he blurted out to a policewoman, 'I need to get to Milton Keynes, can I please pass.' She looked the sweaty hulk up and down, then past his shoulder, and replied with disdain that the station was closed for public safety reasons and he needed to wait with the rest of the passengers for further information.

He was about to move to the other end of the line

and tell a copper with less of an attitude problem that he had a sick aunt who had locked herself in the toilets and it was imperative he be allowed to liberate her when a deep, guttural roar thundered up and out of the London Underground entrance followed by a fifty-strong mob dressed in balaclavas and black hoods who ran towards the police swinging fists and backpacks, hoping to force their way into the station.

As the police line moved to face down the surging horde, Mick was pushed through an open automatic sliding door, landed on the hard floor, rolled over three times like a prima donna footballer appealing for a penalty, then stood up and jogged towards the station concourse. The scene that met his astonished eyes almost blew him back out of the station. There were hundreds of people sitting cross-legged by the information screens and dozens behind who had literally glued themselves to the floor, blocking the platform entrances. Yellow-jacketed police looked on, some kneeling down to talk to the protestors trying to coax them to see sense, occasionally dragging an abusive figure towards the exit, while other officers roared through megaphones that this was an illegal protest and they would be arrested if the station was not cleared. But nobody was moving. Instead the crowd, made up of mostly young people, some holding up Socialist Worker flags or wearing anarchist bandanas, chanted, 'What do we want? Free speech. When do we want it? Now.'

Rigged across the upstairs balcony in front of the cafes was a two by thirty foot banner which read: ALL WE ARE SAYING IS GIVE MICK A CHANCE. Next to it a smaller one said: REPUBLICANS FOR MICK O'SHEA.

He spied placards with his face on, bearing the words 'Je Suis Mick; 'This is the REAL vigil;' 'NOT MY DUKE - NOT MY COMA:' 'You can stick your fucking easel up your arse;' 'WHO ARE THE REAL SNOWFLAKES?' and one that made him cackle out loud and clap his hands, 'STERILISE ALL ROYAL COCKS AND FANDANGOS.'

Outside WH Smith's the crowd referenced Mick's Moses Street theatrical tour de force by shouting 'Attica, Attica' as police formed two regimental lines readying themselves to walk the length of the concourse to sweep the protestors up and out.

The sit-in had been organised on the dark web as an antidote to the royal vigil by an umbrella of left-wing political groups, republican sympathisers, environmentalists, anarchists, trans lobbyists, anti-fascists and students. The *Independent* newspaper would sum it up in the next day's editorial as 'Britain's disenfranchised youth unleashing a spontaneous howl of support for their new anti-hero.'

Mick looked on in awe, allowing the enormity of the scene to wash over him. How did a few minutes of spontaneous piss-taking lead to this, he thought? How had a lad from the Dingle gone from being a nobody, to the despised Sick Mick, to the voice of a generation. He thought of his dad who was out there somewhere, maybe close by, trying to gain vengeance for him. He wanted to grab him and hug him and tell him that he didn't need to avenge anything. That if it hadn't been for him, and all the things that they had both been through together, he wouldn't be who he is. There wouldn't be any of this. It was Vinny whose love, devotion, politics and principles had forged the man Mick had become and unknowingly inspired him to do something that he will always be proud of. His dad had made him a someone. He needed to find him and tell him that. He also needed Sadie to see what was happening in front of him. To see that there were hundreds of people, millions maybe, who weren't sick of the whole Mick O'Shea act.

As he turned away from the overpowering scene to draw breath he could see two policemen staring at him suspiciously and conferring, then talking into their phones and looking around as though seeking assistance. Before panic could set in, he was pushed aside by a dozen-strong gang who had pierced the cordon and were heading towards the platforms, drawing the attention of the two policemen who Mick believed had rumbled him. Mick righted himself, looked to the exits, saw chaos in the police line and darted back into the sunlight.

24

FRIDAY EVENING

Ayesha was winding down a very long, boozy lunch with a potential new client in a Covent Garden restaurant. Joe Allen's had once been a legendary hangout for cravat-wearing, air-kissing thespians, its vintage posters of obscure shows on bare brick walls, dim lighting and dirt brown floorboards giving it the feel of a cool Manhattan supper club. Until it moved around the corner to Burleigh Street where, despite the owner's best attempts to preserve the original boho vibe, it morphed into a themed burger bar. A kind of Hard Luvvie Cafe. From being a place where agents and talent wanted to be seen in, it became one where those who guarded their reputations would choose not be seen dead in. Which was why Ayesha had deliberately booked a table there for her initial meeting with Aussie comedian, Mark Moran. A meeting she had never wanted to happen. She had told her boss, Miles, that Moron (her pronunciation) was an egotistical, semi-neanderthal racist who openly mocked everything this black, lesbian leftie stood for, so they were probably not a good match. Miles had agreed with the ego and the cavemen accusations but drew a line on Moran being racist. He told her that if the agency was to grow it needed to be across both camps in the culture wars and she was the most adroit agent on the books. The one who told the ego-monsters what they needed to hear.

'So why don't you just go and get drunk with him and see what you think? You never know, you might find you click,' Miles had told her.

She did. They didn't.

The afternoon started frostily but warmed up with a couple of gin and tonics. The warmth lasted as long as a blast from a flickering match flame. It completely vanished three bottles of a half-decent Malbec in, when Moran referred to two of Ayesha's clients as being 'up their own arse with their leftie shit.'

She asked, through teeth grinding so hard her front crown almost came off, 'how do you mean?' and Moran replied, pouting his lips and rubbing his eyes with finger and thumb in a mock-crying manner, 'all this, I'd do anything for the working-class, crap. Yeah, except actually fucking mix with them.'

When he followed up with 'come on love, wokeness is like anal sex. It's far better in your mind than going there,' she told him she found him offensive. He apologised for calling her 'love.' When she told him that didn't bother her, he shot her a quizzical frown and asked, 'sorry, are you into anal?' She came back with 'no, I'm into comedians who write their own lines, not ones who rip shit ones off second-rate American comics.' Then asked for the bill.

It was 5.30pm when she walked unsteadily down Burleigh Street towards The Strand, cursing Miles for setting her up with Moran. A big, yolk-yellow sun was still high in the sky above the city rooftops, its beams hitting her flushed face, reviving her gin and wine buzz and making her float above the hot pavement. Yes, she was in for a bollocking but she had a full weekend before that and, besides, as her job description was to know about comedy, she had been right to tell Mark Moron that he was recycling Dennis Miller to impress her.

She carried on along The Strand, dodging the rush-hour traffic as she crossed at Catherine Street and followed the semi-circular bend past the Novello Theatre which, depressingly, was still staging *Mamma Mia!*, when a taxi with its bright yellow light on roared past and pulled up outside the Waldorf Hotel. As she walked towards it, a middle-aged man in a suit, followed by two young men and a woman carrying heavy bags, darted past the uniformed hotel concierge who held open the cab door, allowing them to climb into the back seats.

'Oh my holy God,' she muttered, looking behind her, seeing another free taxi, which she hailed. As it pulled up and the passenger window came down she pointed at the Hackney that was doing a U-turn to join the westbound traffic heading back down The Strand and said to the driver, 'Follow that cab.' Then fell into the back seat laughing and immediately apologised for her 'wanky instruction.' When the cabbie replied, straight-faced, 'as long as it ain't goin' south of the river,' she said, 'I take my apology back. I didn't realise we were playing cliche top trumps,' but it went over his head.

The taxi reached Trafalgar Square and made a left onto Whitehall, causing Ayesha to mutter, 'come on girl, get your shit together,' then nervously dig her phone out of her handbag and punch in Mick's name. He answered on the first ring.

'Where are you?' she asked.

'Driving around Harley Street stalking Sadie and committing so many traffic offences I think I've just invented three new ones,' he replied.

'Well commit a few more by driving as fast as you can towards Westminster.'

'Never mind Westminster, have you heard what's been going on at Euston? I'm a cause now. An actual friggin' cause. There were hundreds of—'

'Shut up and listen,' she yelled at him. 'Fleury is in a cab in front of me with what looks like a film crew and…oh, shit…hang on…yes, just here is fine,' she told the driver, holding her credit card up to the black card machine and leaping out before the receipt was printed.

'Are you still there?" she asked as she landed on the pavement.

'What do you reckon?'

'Well put Whitehall into your satnav and get here as quick as you can. I've got a bad feeling.'

Ayesha stood opposite the bronze Women of World War II memorial looking down towards Westminster. It felt like a normal Friday evening, as civil servants weaved through rush-hour traffic, heading home or to nearby beer gardens to enjoy the last few hours of the sun. She crossed the road in between two stationary red buses and walked past the gated entrance to Downing Street, where tourists were taking photos of the large number of armed police officers and groups of mild-mannered protesters from half-a-dozen different causes held up placards and handed out leaflets. She took one for Justice for Grenfell from a middle-aged woman in an orange saree and gave her a clenched fist and a blown kiss in solidarity.

Ten yards ahead of her, at the front of the Cenotaph, in a central reservation that divided the Whitehall traffic, under the words 'THE GLORIOUS DEAD' that were carved into the white Portland stone, a cameraman and sound engineer were setting up, with a *Brit Talk* producer crouching as she attempted to establish the most photogenic position.

Along the side of the Cenotaph, standing next to the Royal Air Force Ensign, Union Flag and Red Ensign, Ayesha could see an animated Lance Fleury talking to three men, two of whom appeared old and stooped. As she walked along the pavement to get a closer look she noticed medals on the men's chests with one of them wearing a beret. Fleury had their undivided attention as he drew them into a blokeish yarn, the punchline of which saw the two older men roar with laughter, and the one with the beret belatedly join in, almost politely, then remove his hat and scratch his grey head as he looked around, frowning and surveying the scene.

Ayesha knew straight away it was Vinny. A mixture of relief and fear shot through her system as she fumbled in her bag for her phone and hit it.

'He's here,' she told Mick.

'Where's here?'

'The Cenotaph.'

'Is that the war thingy?'

'It's that big monument where they lay wreaths every year.'

'What's he—out the fuckin' way will ya,' he screamed at another taxi driver who was cutting him up.

'He's wearing a beret and medals and he's standing

with two other veterans and they're talking to Fleury. How far away are you?'

'Five, maybe ten—oi dozy bollocks, just go through the light will ya—minutes. But the traffic is shite.'

'They're walking to the front of the Cenotaph now where there's a camera. I think they're about to go live.' Mick could sense the escalating panic in Ayesha's voice.

'Oh God. What's the stupid bastard going to do? Can you see a gun?'

'No, but I'm about ten yards away. I can't tell. Look, there's loads of armed police here. Shall I warn them.'

'No, no. That'll freak everyone out,' Mick screamed back at her. 'Right, I'm jumping these lights. Be there in five.'

At the front of the Cenotaph, Lance Fleury was being counted in by the producer as Big Ben's bells could be heard booming six times, adding to the poignancy of the moment.

'A warm welcome to a very special programme,' Lance said in a slow, sombre voice. 'As our gracious duke lies in a coma a few miles from here, surrounded by his nearest and dearest, we're coming live from the Cenotaph, a London landmark which we know is very close to Blinky's heart.

'This is a place he has visited on many November mornings, to lay a wreath to people he never knew who were, as it proclaims in the stone behind me, our glorious dead. Countless British and Commonwealth men and women who, in their early years of adulthood, laid down their lives for their king or their queen.

'Well now, as one of the most beloved royal family members fights for his life, I've gathered three men who all saw comrades fall on foreign battlefields, to show their solidarity with a legend who ventured out on cold winter nights of 1940 to defy Hitler's Luftwaffe by guiding the men, women and children of London to the safety of air raid shelters.'

Fleury left a dignified silence as the camera panned out to the three veterans, the eldest propped up by a walking-stick, the youngest wearing a beret, all with medals on their blazer chests.

'Let me introduce you to my very special guests. Desmond Halsall was one of sixty thousand British troops who fought valiantly and sustained more than a thousand losses, in the Korean War. Barry Ross was a fearless Para who helped take back Goose Green from the Argies, a pivotal battle in winning the Falklands War. And Eddie Hobson was a Desert Rat who defeated Saddam Hussein's elite republican guard in the First Gulf War, where he lost his left leg from below the knee fighting for all our freedoms.

'These heroes, and all who fought with them, did

you, your country and the world a great service. Desmond helped prevent communism from spreading right across Asia, Barry helped overthrow a fascist coup on British overseas soil and Eddie helped drive an evil dictator out of a peaceful, neighbouring country.

'And yet the lefties, the bleeding-heart pacifists and the history revisionists would have you believe that all we British have done on the world stage down the ages is murder, pillage and exploit. Shame on them."

His narrowed eyes looked deep into the camera and shook his head so hard his earpiece wobbled.

'Gentlemen, I am honoured to be in your presence. Our country owes you a tremendous debt, and I, personally, owe Eddie a debt of gratitude after he literally leapt to my defence two nights ago when I came off-air outside Westminster and was abused and threatened by a thug.

'Eddie, thank you. You, and the two men beside you, are the best of us. Now on Wednesday, when you so bravely took down the deluded lunatic who was ranting at me, you had been queueing for hours, despite having a prosthetic leg, to see the Westminster easel. The real easel I may add, before it was stolen by some despicable excuse for a human being.

'When I asked if you were there for love of your country, I think I am right in saying that you answered; There is no finer love.'

'I did,' replied Vinny.

Ten yards to their left, across from the slow, passing traffic, Ayesha looked on impotently, the weight of fear cementing her legs to the pavement, leaving her unable to move.

'And it's that love of king and country, that patriotism, which cuts to the very heart of what it means to be British, isn't it?'

Vinny hesitated with his answer and hardened his glaze. 'It depends how you're defining patriotism, to be honest.'

'Sorry, Eddie?'

'Well, what I love most about this country is the idea that everyone has the right to express their own opinions.'

'Sure, but—' Lance cut in.

'That we don't live in a dictatorship.'

'Which is why you were so right to fight Saddam Hussein.'

'Forget Saddam Hussein. He's dead,' Vinny answered in a calm tone.

'And that's no small thanks to brave men like you.'

'I'm talking about this country. Now. I'm talking about stopping the Saddam Husseins at the top telling British citizens what they can and can't say.'

'Exactly. I'm with you on that one hundred percent.

SICK MICK

There are people out there who want to close down our words and thoughts if they don't like what they are hearing. Like the trans lobby and—'

'You.'

'Sorry?' said Lance followed by a fake, nervous laugh.

'People like you who are hounding a comedian who was just doing his job.'

'Well hang on, Eddie,' said Lance, his eyes darting sideways to his producer.

'I'm not Eddie. I'm Vinny. Vinny O'Shea. Mick O'Shea's father. I'm the one you said didn't know the price in blood that servicemen have paid, the one you think is not a patriot because he didn't turn his son in.'

'Let's move on to Barry Ross—' said Lance, his voice quaking, his eyes shifting towards Downing Street where Ayesha was gesticulating wildly in front of a policeman.

'Eh, phoney, look at me when I'm talking to you,' Vinny continued. 'Look me in the eye while I show you what patriotism means.' As Vinny slowly opened his jacket and went to reach for the inside pocket, Fleury instinctively crouched and shielded his face with his arms.

Two yards away a policeman pointed his Heckler & Glock G36 carbine at Vinny's chest and shouted, 'get down on your knees now and put both hands in the air.'

Vinny grinned and said, 'I'm done with being on my knees' before reaching inside the jacket.

A single shot rang out from the semi-automatic assault rifle which tore through Vinny's shoulder forcing him backwards and down onto the ground. Ayesha and the *Brit Talk* producer screamed, Fleury fled towards the Downing Street gates, the police gunman moved forward keeping his rifle trained on Vinny and a shaven-headed, seventeen-stone man pushed past the gobsmacked war veterans and fell to his knees next to the man lying face up in a pool of thick, red blood.

'Dad...Dad!' yelled Mick, slamming his hand on the shoulder wound trying to stop the blood from gushing out, and screaming, 'Why did you shoot him?' at the policeman as four of his colleagues reached the Cenotaph and pointed their rifles at the O'Sheas.

One of them grabbed Mick and pulled him up while another removed Mick's jacket and clamped it over Vinny's shoulder.

'Get off me you bastards. He's my Dad,' Mick yelled, as Vinny's fingers moved slowly, motioning his son towards him.

'Get down here and keep him talking,' said the policeman, who was pressing hard on Vinny's shoulder.

SICK MICK

Mick knelt and gently cradled his dad's head. 'You stupid old get,' he stuttered in a low, quaking voice. 'What's all this about?'

'It's in my jacket?'

'What?'

'My inside jacket pocket.'

The policeman pressing down on the wound knocked Mick's hand away as he went for Vinny's jacket, motioning to a colleague to search the pocket. He fumbled inside the jacket, pulled out a crumpled glossy photo and handed it to Mick.

It was a photo of Mick, as a twelve-year-old, dressed in his Army Cadet Force uniform, standing to attention, his face steeled with defiance, offering a salute. Taking the salute was Vinny, beaming proudly down at his son. As Mick stared at it tears fell from his eyes.

'Why have you got this?'

'I wanted to show them you're a good lad.'

'What?'

'And that I'm proud of you.'

'I'm proud of you, Dad,' Mick whispered. 'You always did me proud. You still do, ya daft bastard.'

'I just wanted to stand up for you, son,' said Vinny, the words coming out slower as he struggled to breathe.

'You're gonna be okay…you're gonna be okay,' said

Mick, pushing his face onto Vinny's and letting his tears mingle with the blood which had congealed into a brownish hue.

'I never deserted you,' said Vinny, the words coming out slower and more indistinct.

'You didn't, Dad. Never. You, you made me who I am. I'm no-one without you.'

"I'd never be…a deserter, son."

'Never mate, never,' said Mick now cradling his dad's head to his chest.

'I just…wanted everyone…to know that…' Vinny took a big gasp of air and slowly squeezed out the words '…that I love you.'

'I love you too, Dad, and we're going to sort this. You'll soon be knocking them back in The Irish House. It's all going to be okay,' said Mick, picking up the beret with the Desert Rat insignia, brushing back his dad's blood-matted hair and placing the cap gently on his head.

A blaring ambulance siren grew louder as Vinny's breathing started to fade, its flashing lights making the medals on his chest glint. A policeman pulled Mick off his dad to let the paramedics in.

Lying still and silent on the scarlet-stained concrete beneath chiselled words that honoured The Glorious Dead, Vinny's eyes closed.

25

SATURDAY AFTERNOON

A black prosthetic leg lay forlornly on the eggshell-coloured IKEA sofa couch in Sadie's Marylebone flat. The early afternoon sun flooded through the ivory-shaded wooden blinds, bouncing off the alabaster walls and champagne carpet, transforming the whitewashed lounge into a studio set for Heaven's waiting room.

This was not great news for Mick's bloodshot eyes as he plodded in from the kitchen with a liver-shredding hangover, clutching a pint mug of black coffee and a packet of paracetamol, cursing the sun and slamming shut the blinds before slumping down next to Vinny's leg. He stared at it for two minutes, indulged himself in a lifetime of memories, then gently picked it up, kissed it, hugged it to his tee-shirted chest and gave off a mournful sigh. Then re-lived last night, which had been the longest and toughest of his life.

He had sat next to his stretchered dad in the ambulance throughout the three-minute drive down Whitehall and across Westminster Bridge to St Thomas's Hospital, watching helplessly as the paramedics fought frantically to keep him alive.

On arrival, Vinny had been rushed into theatre leaving Mick with Ayesha and two armed policemen sitting silently in a nearby waiting room. At 10pm a sombre-looking surgeon sat down next to Mick and said: 'The bullet ripped through your father's subclavian artery in his shoulder causing major blood loss. But we've managed to stabilise him and although he's not out of the woods completely he's got a good chance of pulling through.' Mick fell into Ayesha's chest and wept like a baby.

Ayesha had come into her own, despite being a few sheets to the wind after drinking like a merchant sailor on shore leave. After police led her away from the shooting, she spotted the Beatles taxi parked in Whitehall on the opposite side from Downing Street, back towards Trafalgar Square. The Cenotaph mayhem had saved it from being clamped and the keys were still in the ignition so, guessing Vinny would be taken to St Thomas's, she drove it the short distance, praying she would not be stopped and breathalysed, and found a space in the hospital car park. She then texted an assistant, telling him to get to the hospital and drive the cab to the nearest car park to Sadie's flat in Weymouth Mews. She then rang the company lawyer, Nick Burridge, who had been on extremely lucrative standby all week awaiting the moment Mick surfaced, telling him his services would be required that night.

As she walked towards St Thomas's, the private detective she had hired messaged to say he had tracked down Craig Duggan and passed on his mobile number. Minutes after the surgeon had given Mick the update on Vinny one of the policemen told him he was under arrest and they were taking him to Scotland Yard to be charged. He agreed to go with them once the hospital had given him Vinny's prosthetic leg so he could keep a piece of his dad close by.

Ayesha alerted Burridge, then Sadie, then Craig and accompanied Mick to the Yard where he was questioned and, after explaining he had chosen not to hand himself in until he had tracked down his clearly unhinged father, he was charged with possession of an imitation firearm and released on bail to appear in court at a future date.

Half-an-hour later, as Sadie opened the door of her flat to Mick giving him a silent, wet-faced bear-hug, he could see, over her shoulder, a stranger sitting on the couch.

'This is Vinny's friend Craig,' said Sadie.

The old soldier stood up, walked towards Mick, clinched him tightly, asked him to sit down and poured him a large whisky from one of the bottles he had brought after Ayesha had rung to tell him he would probably find Mick at Sadie's flat.

'Look, there's no easy way of saying this but your dad's dying of cancer. They didn't get it all out from his prostate, it spread to his bones, he refused treatment and he only has months left to live,' he told a gobsmacked Mick who sunk silently onto the couch, grappling with the prospect, for the second time in a matter of hours, of losing his dad.

'He told me all about it a few nights ago when he asked me to help him humiliate that Fleury wanker,' said Craig as Mick stared forlornly at the floor. 'He told me that you were the only reason he kept going but he found it so hard to let you know that. As he talked me through his plan to get back at Fleury for the shit he's caused you I'd never seen his eyes so alive. He felt like he was on a mission.'

'Did he want to get shot?' asked Mick.

'He never said that to me. He just said he wanted to get on camera with him and see the fear in his eyes. You know, watch the big man with the big words crumble before his viewers like the shithouse he is. But, your old fella was, sorry is, a clever man. He'd have known the place would be crawling with armed Bill and as soon as they saw him reach for his pocket there was a chance they'd take him out.'

'But why go out like that? If he knew he was dying and he wanted to end it all, why didn't he just take an overdose or throw himself in the Mersey?'

SICK MICK

'He was doing it for you.'

'How does that work?'

'By standing up for you. He loved you more than anything, son, but because he was so messed up in the head with all he'd gone through he never thought he'd shown you that love.

'He wanted to use his final act to prove you meant the world to him. And being the old soldier he was, when it came to kissing his arse goodbye, he wanted to do it on his terms. I know you're ripped apart, Mick, but I'm telling you, your old man will see this as a result.'

'What? lying in a pool of your own blood in the middle of the road is a good result?'

'Yeah, because he's going out with a bang. Not taken out by the enemy on a battlefield. Not topping himself like a coward or putting up a losing fight against cancer with chemo, which would have made everyone pity him. He'd well had his fill of pity, son. When he took a bullet tonight he thought he was doing the best thing a good soldier and a good father could do. He was defending his own flesh and blood.'

There was a long silence before Mick grabbed Craig, hugged him hard and said, 'How much booze have you brought?'

Guessing that with Vinny's son the grape hadn't fallen too far from the vine, he had brought enough for the pair to get hammered until dawn: two bottles of Famous Grouse whisky, a bottle of Bombay Sapphire gin, two bottles of 19 Crimes red wine and a dozen cans of Stella.

And hammered they both got, until the Tube restarted and Craig could ride one back home to Bermondsey. Sadie had a couple of Stellas and a few gin and tonics before turning in at 1am, leaving Mick and Craig to laugh and cry as they relived tales about the man who was usually attached to the prosthetic leg that sat on the coffee table in between them.

'He always was a jammy bastard, your old man,' said Craig, pointing at the leg. 'How many people will have a part of them present at their own wake when they go?'

Mick grinned as he thought back to that conversation with Craig ten hours earlier, put his dad's leg back on the couch, popped two paracetamol out of their plastic casing and swallowed them with a long glug of coffee.

He heard keys in the front door followed by Sadie bursting into the lounge carrying two shopping bags and gasping for breath.

'Have you heard?' she asked Mick, grabbing the remote from the coffee table and switching on the small television which sat discreetly on a shelf in a white, ceiling-to-floor bookcase to dissuade visitors

SICK MICK

from thinking that Connie, the trust fund flat owner, was more interested in *Emmerdale* than *Emma*.

'Your man's on the mend,' she continued, tuning into Sky News where veteran anchor Alice Carney was standing opposite the entrance to the National Hospital for Neurology and Neurosurgery.

The world's media had descended on the hospital in London's Queen Square after news had leaked that the duke was coming out of his week-long coma. Carney had once again grabbed centre stage, fending away any reporter who threatened her prime location by transmitting the ferocious body language of a Tasmanian Devil protecting her young, and killing hours of air time with prime cuts of absolute horse shit.

Details were sketchy, and the Palace had yet to issue a statement, but it was refusing to deny the picture emerging from within the hospital that earlier that day there had been a blinking of Blinky's eyes and a movement of his head when he had heard Princess Anne scream, 'Tell Andrew he's got more chance of getting a naffing job as a naffing lifeguard at an all-girls' swimming gala than he has of speaking at our uncle's funeral.'

Carney, a brunette sixty-something who had stayed at the top of her game thanks to a pin-sharp journalistic brain and an even sharper surgeon's scalpel, was doing her best to establish the facts. With little success.

A procession of self-styled 'royal experts' comprising sacked regal hacks, former editors of *Tatler* and *OK!* magazines and retired Buckingham Palace press secretaries, paraded themselves before the assembled cameras (at £200 a time) regurgitating the same long, hollow soundbite: 'We cannot know for certain what is going on inside those hospital walls but what we can be sure of is that the inner circle of the family, what we like to call the Working Firm, will be urging His Grace to pull through, and devising a strategy in conjunction with the medical teams, who are, by the way, among the finest in their field in the world, focussing on how and when to let the people know he is out of danger and on the mend. Providing that he is, of course, actually on the mend.'

Such circumspection, however, was not being shared among the wider public. The major TV channels replaced all scheduled programmes with running broadcasts on the duke's nascent recovery and social media exploded with joy and a large dose of counter-cynicism.

As devout Catholic and Old Etonian Tory MP Jasper Reith-Hogg posted on X: Let us give thanks to the Almighty for once again lavishing his mercy on the English, the people he has shown down the centuries to clutch the closest to his eternal bosom.

To which @Alfie57blink replied: Even if your vile arselickin brings him out of his coma wart-hogg he aint gonna blow ya.

Sadie put her arm around Mick and asked, 'How are you feeling today, love?'

'Ah, you know,' he replied with a shrug and a forced laugh. 'Head that's sicker than a plane flying to Lourdes and a mouth like a hanged man's undies.'

'That's allowed,' she replied, rubbing his stubbly head.

'Thanks for letting me stay here and being nice and…'

'Houl yer wheesht,' she said, putting her finger to his mouth. 'That photograph of you dressed up like an Action Man that Vinny kept. I never had you down as a wannabe Tommy.'

'That was my auntie Helen's idea. She thought it would help my dad get over his PTSD. Might stop him hating what happened to him by remembering how he felt when he was young and wanted to be a soldier.'

'Okay, so seeing your son in an Army uniform is a way of getting over having your leg blown off in an Army uniform, right?'

'Right.'

'Weird.'

'I only lasted a month. Hated every minute of it.'

'Well you looked all pumped up with patriotism on that picture.'

'Nah, I was trying to hold a fart in,' said Mick, causing the pair of them to giggle in unison.

'That's more like it. The old Mick O'Shea's coming back. Listen, things are looking up. You're no longer Britain's Most Wanted, your dad's still alive and the blessed duke's coming round.'

'Why are you so bothered about old Blinky's health all of a sudden? Are you going to stick on your dad's sash and get your flute out now?'

'Wise up. If he pulls through it'll work in your favour.'

'Oh yeah?'

'Yeah. If he'd died you'd have looked a right mean wanker and there would be loads agreeing with Fleury that you should be up for treason. If he recovers everyone will forget what you did. It'll just seem like a stupid fuss over nothing. Which will be better for you when you go to trial.'

'Thanks for reminding me,' he said, throwing back the last mouthful of coffee. 'I need a proper drink.'

'Mick, come on, you've just got up. It's only two o'clock.'

'I'm on the floor here, Sade. I need a lift. Now that Craig's not here will you join me?'

Every instinct in her body told her to say no,

especially as she would have to get up early for that 8am job at the clinic tomorrow morning. Instincts she discarded after looking into Mick's lost eyes. 'Aye go on. Give us a glass of Whispering Angel from the fridge,' she answered as he kissed her on the head saying, 'that's my girl.'

The following five hours descended into a bacchanalian orgy minus the roasted hogs and the sex, with Sadie knocking back far more than she was used to. At one point she rang Booze2U for an express delivery of vodka, tequila and rosé and was so smashed she failed to focus on the driver's card machine instructions and gave him a £50 tip.

Her mood was lifted with the early evening confirmation from Buckingham Palace that the Duke of Dorset was, indeed, out of his coma and on the road to recovery. Which led Sadie to say, 'Right, let's get some music on,' grab the remote and fail, due to her pissedness, to locate the MTV 80s channel, landing instead on *Brit Talk*. And a familiar face.

Seated in the conservatory of his detached home in Kent on a grey rattan sofa, clutching his bemused Danish wife's hand, sat Lance Fleury, opening his heart to the nation about his traumatic live TV ordeal with a mad man.

With the duke on the mend, the news agenda was moving on and Lance was doing his best to ensure the limelight fell on him and his courageous attempts to defend the royals who had been viciously defamed by a comedian, which almost resulted in what he termed a 'live TV assassination.' That's despite Vinny carrying no gun.

'God I despise that man,' said Sadie.

'Do you think I should ring him up and claim the ten grand reward for turning myself in?' said Mick.

'I'll bet it's not his wife's hole he can't get his feckin' toadstool up either,' she muttered.

'I mean, technically, I handed myself…what was that you just said?'

'What? Me? Nothing. Just how I hate him for what he's done to Vinny.'

'No, hang on. Rewind,' he makes the sound of a tape recorder playing backwards. 'How do you know he can't get his toadstool up?'

'Just a guess is all. Another drink?' she asked, getting up in a hurry, her pale complexion turning blood red.

'I know you, Sadie West. You can't hide nothing from me. How do you know he…? Wait…no...no…no way…yes way…you're joking me.'

Sadie put her blushing face into her hands and sat back down on the couch.

'You've worked on him, haven't you?'

'I still am,' she replied, without lifting her head

from her hands. 'But you can't tell a soul, Mick, or I'll be sacked. Promise me.'

'Wow. While all this shit with me and Fleury was going on, you were playing pat-a-cake, pat-a-cake with his limp dick?'

'Mick, I didn't have a say in it. It's my feckin' job. And I was sworn to secrecy. I couldn't break my word.'

'I'd have broken more than my word if I'd had that knob in my hands. You said you are still working on him?'

She nodded. Then blurted out everything.

26

SUNDAY MORNING

The cunning plan began to germinate in Mick's head around 7.30pm, roughly halfway through the brutal probing of Sadie which forced her to cough up every fine detail of her Hardman Clinic job. The tantalising potential unleashed by his partner's soul-baring diluted the alcohol in his veins, allowing his sobering brain to retain every tiny fact he was squeezing out of her. And with Sadie having complimented the demolition of two bottles of Whispering Angel with half-a-dozen tequila shots, and being consumed with the terrible guilt of caressing the penis of the devil who had cast his evil spell over her lover's family, the details were not hard to draw out. Especially when Mick insisted they move on to gin and tonics, handing her large tumblers of Bombay Sapphire while he sipped tap water. He coaxed out the full picture of her planned Sunday morning encounter with Fleury like a veteran CIA interrogator.

When she passed out at 10pm, Mick carried her to bed and picked up the keys to his taxi, left the flat and walked around the corner to the NCP car park. He opened the taxi's front passenger seat door, hit the release knob on the glove compartment, grabbed the yellow and black object he referred to in a whisper as 'you beauty,' then returned to the flat and joined Sadie in bed, gently leaning over to kiss her goodnight and unplug her radio alarm clock.

Mick barely slept. He was not tired due to his mid-afternoon lie-in and it was a warm night, but the possible repercussions of what he was about to unleash had his brain doing mental acrobatics and his body whirling like a dervish underneath the duvet until he crawled out from underneath it at 6.30am.

He knocked back two cups of strong coffee as he ran through final Google checks on Sadie's computer. At 7.15am he put on his black bubble coat, black cashmere scarf and thin woollen gloves that he had left in the flat from his trip in April, grabbed the keys attached to a fob saying 'clinic' which lay on the kitchen table and placed the beauty from Robbo's cab in his inside pocket. He checked on Sadie, whose rabid snores reminded him of a copulating pig he had once heard at Croxteth Park petting farm, then slipped out of the front door.

The cool air hit him like an iced flannel and sharpened his focus. The metal grey sky that threatened rain allowed him to zip-up his coat, lift the hood over his head and pull the scarf up over his mouth without any passer-by suspecting he was a man en route to carrying out a nefarious deed. Not that there were many passers-by on his five-minute, early Sunday morning canter along Weymouth Street for Devonshire Mews West, a quiet cul-de-sac full of pretty, pastel-coloured townhouses that ran directly along the back of Harley Street.

He casually strolled along the cobbled road, which looked like it had been used by film producers to recreate the Swinging Sixties since Carnaby Street became too trendy, and counted the properties. He passed a light green door, a purple garage, a house with a creamy-minted frontage and a pale yellow mews with an iron staircase running up to the first floor door, until his target was located.

As Google Maps had shown him, it was the fifth one along, a pink door with the letters 'HC' on a small brass plaque next to the bell. The cul-de-sac was deadly still with just the occasional hum of an electric car on a nearby street intruding on his thoughts. His eyes darted around for reasons to abort. He noticed a bedroom light on in the house directly behind him, but a scan of the street detected no human activity. He fumbled for the keys in his pocket and singled out two that looked like they would open the mortice lock near the door handle by his midriff. The lock was freed on the second attempt.

He opened the door to reveal a hallway illuminated by fanlight. He walked in, shut the door, fell back against it, heaved a sigh of relief and wiped the sweat from his brow. He dropped the scarf from his mouth and began to take his gloves off, then quickly remembered why he was wearing both and pulled the scarf back up so that only his eyes and forehead were on show. Not that he had spotted a CCTV camera inside or outside the clinic.

At the end of the small, narrow hall was a white, wooden door with the words VIP attached in black-lettering. He turned the handle, switched on the light and saw before him a leather treatment table with a paper sheet laid on top and a small table with kitchen roll next to it, a large machine, a metal sink, cupboards filled with medical supplies and, in the corner, a comfy leather chair and a trouser press. As he inhaled in triumph, he was pleasantly surprised to catch fragrances of jasmine and lavender instead of the usual nostril-burning disinfectant he associated with medical rooms like this, which warned you that you were one infected cut away from death.

'So this is where she works her magic,' he thought as he walked towards the Duolith SD1 Ultra Shockwave machine. He turned it on and held it against his crotch until he gauged what frequency was far too much.

There was a loud thump on the door to his right, directly opposite the one he had entered through. He crouched down behind the shockwave machine, pulled his scarf up to the bridge of his nose and stared over it at the door handle, waiting for it to be opened and searching for a pretext for being there that did not exist. But there was no handle-turning, no second thump, no voice asking if everything was okay.

He looked at his phone. It was 7.36am. If everything Sadie had told him last night about the timing of this procedure was true he needed to be out of this treatment room soon. He gave it two minutes before he stood up, walked to the door where the thump had come from and opened it expecting an ugly confrontation that would end in his arrest. But there was nothing to see. Just a small garden with a path that led to the main Hardman Clinic building which had no lights on.

It was deathly still and he was alone. Apart from a small burnished red fox staring back at him from the garden wall, the menace behind its dark, vertically-pupiled eyes saying, 'I had you there big time with that bang, didn't I?' No wonder they call them sly, Mick thought. He checked the time again. It was 7.39am.

At least the street-fighting Basil Brush had allowed Mick to establish for certain that he was the only person on the Hardman Clinic premises. As Sadie had told him, they were opening especially for Fleury, and she was responsible for locking up after he had gone.

He walked confidently back into the treatment room, re-attached the probe to the shockwave machine and looked around, racking his brain to think if anything else needed doing. No point in worrying now, he thought. No room for doubts. He'd either set everything up correctly or the plan was doomed.

He exited back through the door to the garden, closed it, moved a Lafuma recliner out of the main clinic's line of vision, relaxed into it and gathered his thoughts for what lay ahead.

He thought of Vinny and how many times he must have felt the adrenaline pumping through his body and his guts rocking with fear on a hushed, peaceful dawn before charging into a scene of barbaric anarchy and possible death.

Was he doing this for his dad, he asked himself? Or was he only doing it for himself? Maybe he was doing it for his country, as his dad had done many times, without question? Maybe there was a different kind of war from the type his dad used to fight going on. A fight for the country's soul, maybe?

His overriding fear was Sadie's fate. If Fleury discovered his new nurse was Mick, she would almost certainly be sacked, but the way she had been slagging off the clinic and her snooty boss who had put her on a warning for no reason, she wanted out anyway. At least that is what he needed to tell himself before he could do what he was about to do.

The sound of a door slamming inside the treatment room brought the shutters down on his soul-searching. He leapt from the recliner, put his ear to the door and made out shuffling noises and a faint whistle. Mick tried to visualise exactly what was happening in the room through all the details he had gleaned from last night's interrogation.

Fleury would be taking off his shoes, his socks and trousers, and placing his kecks over the press. He would recline on the treatment table, put a piece of kitchen roll over his cock, check his phone, then put the face mask on and—a loud buzz sounded; Fleury was ready for the nurse to enter.

'Laddies unt gendermersh,' he whispered, 'put your hands together for the Laughter Bucket's very own Mick O'Shea.'

He pulled his scarf up past his nose and pushed open the door. Lance Fleury was reclined on the leather treatment table, face mask in place, decked out in his Sunday country squire outfit from the waist up. Below that lay kitchen roll covering his manhood and legs whiter than the hood of a Ku Klux Klansman. Mick moved towards the machine and fiddled with a few buttons, trying to appear in professional preparation mode, praying he wasn't making an alien sound that would give the game away. If there was a single lifting of the mask by Fleury, he was done for.

'Listen, I'm sorry about filing that complaint against you. I was not in a great place. I do apologise if I landed you in any trouble,' said Lance. Mick said nothing as he reached into his coat pocket.

'I get it. You've been told not to engage with me. I'll shut up,' Fleury added.

Mick froze. He stared at the tazer Robbo kept in his cab to incapacitate dodgy customers that he was clutching in his right hand and thought about aborting the mission. What if this all goes tits-up? How many years am I looking at inside? What about Sadie's job? What would Vinny want him to do?

Sod it, thought Mick. In for a penny and all that. He lifted the kitchen roll from Lance's penis, pointed Robbo's defence mechanism at the bare groin that lay before him on the treatment table, closed his eyes and pulled the trigger.

There was a loud crackle followed by a savage, ear-splitting roar from Lance as 50,000 volts shot through his nether regions like a bolt of lightning, stunning him with the force of a metal cricket bat landing on his solar plexus, freezing every muscle in his body and turning him stiffer than a cast iron poker. Which, to be fair, was the whole point of visiting the Hardman Clinic.

SICK MICK

Mick wiped the taser down with his gloved hands to erase any fingerprints, dropped it, walked to the door, turned round to observe his screaming, pole-axed persecutor, smiled and said:

'Now that's what you call sick.'

EPILOGUE

To the delight of the British nation (well, those who do not harbour a desire to see the Windsors meet the same end as the Romanovs) the Duke of Dorset recovered from the Great Pergola Disaster and made it to his 100th birthday when, by unspoken royal decree, every newspaper in the land had to run the headline: AMAZING GRACE.

There was a slight complication, though. Due to suffering from Foreign Accent Syndrome (a rare speech disorder that causes a change in accent after a stroke or traumatic brain injury) the duke came around speaking and gesticulating like Adolf Hitler addressing the Reichstag in 1936. Consequently, His Amazing Grace was never again seen in public.

Lance Fleury refused the Hardman Clinic's offer to report the Great Taser Incident to the police, demanding they destroy all CCTV footage and computer records which showed he had ever been on their premises seeking treatment for erectile dysfunction. The experience scarred him though. Six months later, when taking part in ITV's *I'm A Celebrity (Get Me Out Of Here)* he threw what medical experts described as a delayed epileptic fit in the Australian jungle, when he was forced to chew a koala bear's forked penis.

Panda Fitzroy-Price broke off her relationship with Lance Fleury and became the face of The Institute of Rightful Thinking, guaranteeing her extensive exposure on TV dissing all things woke. She sold her Pandora's Box website to Rupert Murdoch's News Corp, who changed the title to *Take a Peek at Pandora's Box* and the logo to a micro-skirt and a pair of tanned thighs with the hemline sitting just below crotch level.

Robbo's Ticket to Ride tours became so popular after word spread that Mick O'Shea was one of the drivers that he bought a third taxi. And three more tasers.

Vinny O'Shea recovered from his gunshot wound but died three months later from cancer and was cremated in Liverpool's Springwood Crematorium with dozens of neighbours and old comrades turning up. At his wake in his old local opposite Central Station, £470 was placed in notes in Big Carla's bra as she sang Simply the Best in his honour. Which was enough for forty-three fish and chip suppers from The Lobster Pot.

Craig Duggan adopted a three-legged labrador cross from Battersea Dogs Home and called in Vinny. He doted on it.

Ray Moon led an assault by The Spirit of Ebro on what his intelligence reports had told him were the headquarters of the Liverpool Aryan Front (LAF) in Garston High Street. But his intelligence was wrong, it was Tiffany's Massage Parlour, and Tiffany (real name Janice Kelly) hospitalised three of them with a claw-hammer she kept by the till to attack the knees of non-paying punters. Lenny the Limper was expelled from the group for not joining the LAF operation after feeding his cat.

The royal easel turned up a year later on the BBC's *Cash in The Attic*. It had been stolen by a Palace of Westminster cleaner who thought the gold trim was real. When questioned by police, she claimed the easel was an heirloom that had been passed down through her family. She was convicted of theft and given community service, not the hanging, drawing and quartering being demanded by Fleet Street legend, Sue Nolan.

Keith 'The Griff' Griffin had a fatal heart attack live on air breaking the news that the actors union Equity had insisted that 50% of all actors in an Bristol Old Vic production about the 1666 Great Fire of London had to be black or Asian. On his gravestone someone had daubed the graffiti 'Gone to Hell in a handcart.'

Audrey Woodington became a broadcasting leper after walking off another TV set. During an epic rant on *Question Time* about the disgrace of an all-girls secondary school in Worcester banning teachers from referring to girls as 'girls,' a Yorkshire comedian said 'calm down, old girl,' and then refused to apologise.

Sophie Atkins was taken off air by Ofcom after she incited a right-wing mob to storm a barge housing asylum-seekers in the Humber Estuary and make all 200 inmates walk the plank.

Jason Garlick is now manager of the outdoor plants section at a garden centre in Runcorn's Bridge Retail Park.

Mick O'Shea pleaded not guilty to possessing an imitation firearm with intent to cause fear or violence when he appeared in Liverpool Crown Court. His lawyer, Nick Burridge, offered the defence that his client was performing street theatre for the benefit of the local community. Two hoodies appeared as witnesses (not wearing hoods but the new Hugo Boss suits they had demanded the Grin talent agency paid for) stating Mick often put on impromptu plays in Moses Street, with one of them claiming he had been so inspired by the excerpt from *Dog Day Afternoon* that he had joined the Unity Youth Theatre and given up petty crime. Three women in the Scouse jury wept and all twelve of them took ten minutes to unanimously clear him.

So high did Mick's fame soar in his home city there was a petition signed by 76,250 people to replace Cilla Black's statue in Mathew Street with his. It's still running.

Ayesha Ritter was promoted to Grin's board of directors after booking Mick on to a regular slot on NBC's *Saturday Night Live*, which he does via Zoom from the company's Manchester offices. His stateside success saw him inducted into the British Comedy Hall of Fame with this citation: From being deplatformed to the biggest comedy platform in the world. Take a bow.

Sadie West was sacked by the Hardman Clinic for not turning up for Sunday duty, which they claimed had led to a VIP client taking his custom away from the company. Her redundancy settlement included a secrecy clause banning her from revealing the identity of any of her clients on pain of a £250,000 fine. She moved back to Liverpool to resume her old job in Broadgreen Hospital's prostate clinic.

And one afternoon, while sitting, lost in her thoughts on a bench in Calderstones Park's Japanese garden, six pink roses were thrust under her nose by a man with mad hair that grew in four directions and a beard, who was down on his knees.

When she turned, he asked her, 'Will you marry me?'

And she replied, 'Only if you've got the feckin' receipt for those flowers.'

Mick lied that he had.

ABOUT THE AUTHOR

Brian Reade is an award-winning journalist who writes for the Daily Mirror and former British Press Awards Columnist, Sports Columnist and Feature Writer of the Year and winner of the Cudlipp Award for Journalistic Excellence for his campaigning on behalf of the Hillsborough families. Brian's non-fiction books include: *44 Years With The Same Bird*, documenting his life spent following Liverpool FC, the bestseller *An Epic Swindle: 44 Months with a Pair of Cowboys*, which charted the doomed ownership of Liverpool FC by Hicks and Gillett, and *Diamonds in the Mud*, which tells the stories of working-class heroes Brian has met through life and journalism. *Sick Mick* is Brian's debut fiction novel.

WRITING ON THE WALL

Writing on the Wall (WoW) is an award-winning Liverpool-based community organisation, renowned for its celebration of writing in all its diverse forms. Hosting two dynamic festivals and a variety of year-round projects, WoW embraces literature, creative writing, journalism, poetry, songwriting, and storytelling.

With a commitment to inclusivity, WoW collaborates with local, national, and international writers, providing invaluable opportunities for individuals to nurture their creativity and share their unique stories. Beyond its festivals and projects, WoW's creative writing initiatives serve as a catalyst for personal growth and community development, promoting health, wellbeing, and fostering connections across diverse communities.

Whether you're an experienced writer or embarking on your creative journey, WoW welcomes all who have a story to tell or a desire to explore the power of words.

Mike Morris and Madeline Heneghan
Co-Directors
www.writingonthewall.org.uk